Nicole Abrams

Edited by: Scarlett @ Scarlett's Proofread Services

Cover Designer: Nicole Abrams

Synopsis

McKenzie Knight.
My enemy's daughter. I had planned on using her, corrupting her completely. She was to be my revenge.
Until she became my obsession. One I didn't want.
Finally, my chance to rid myself of this hunger and get my revenge arrived. I bought her. Forced her hand in marriage; all to make her mine.
My obsession only intensified before she was kidnapped. I vowed to kill anyone involved; everyone who dared touch what's mine. After months of looking for her, she's found. The only problem is she has no memories of what I did. Of how I deceived her.
No, instead she falls in love with the man I wish I had been. The one she deserved from the start.
When we finally begin our happy ending, my newest deceits unravel. As her memories return, it leads me to uncertainty. Will her hate from before tear us apart or is the love she has for the man she fell for strong enough to hold us together?

Dedication

To the one's who survived the trauma.

Author Note

***I Will Find Her* is the second book of *The Society* duet. Read *He Will Come For Me* first.**

This is a mature spicy contemporary romance (18+) and contains some situations that may trigger readers.

Trigger Warnings Include:

Public Sexual Encounters

Human Trafficking

Discussion of Asphyxiation

Amnesia

Kidnapping

Panic Attacks

Mention of Sexual Assault

Gun Violence

Unaliving of People

Playlist

Every Breath You Take – Chase Holfelder

Work Song – Hozier

Always Remember Us This Way – Noelle Johnson

Where's My Love – SYML

All I Want – Kodaline

No Time To Die – Billie Eilish

I Wanna Be Your Slave – Måneskin

Fire and the Flood – Vance Joy

Is There Somewhere – Halsey

Him & I – G-Eazy & Halsey

Devil's Backbone – The Civil Wars

How Villains Are Made – Madalen Duke

Take Me to Church – Hozier

Endgame – Klergy

Make It Rain – Ed Sheeran

Can't Help Falling In Love – DARK – Tommee Profitt & brooke

Silence – Marshmello & Khalid

High For This – The Weeknd

Mastermind – Taylor Swift

Chapter 1

Phoenix

Seven Years Ago

Senior year. One hundred eighty more days of this godforsaken place and I can finally get out of here. Walking across the courtyard of Brighton Academy, I stop in my tracks. My eyes narrow at the sight of McKenzie Knight sitting on the brick wall with Caleb Johnson standing between her legs. *This fucker.* I glare as his hand caresses her knee. Balling my hands into fists, I imagine smashing his face into the brick wall.

He must have not received the memo. McKenzie is off limits. He's about to be educated. Changing directions, I turn toward them, my steps determined. McKenzie pushes a piece of her silver hair behind her ear, smiling at something Caleb says. Gritting my teeth, I lengthen my strides until I'm standing behind Caleb. Mckenzie's eyes catch mine and they widen slightly.

"Phoenix," she greets me. Her cheeks turn a pretty shade of pink.

Caleb pivots around, taking a step away from McKenzie. His face pales as he crosses his arms in front of him. He did receive the memo: he just chose to ignore it. That's the only mistake he'll ever make.

"McKenzie. How was your summer?" I don't take my eyes off Caleb, enjoying the way his eye twitches.

"Uneventful," she replies. The sound of her feet hitting the ground pulls my attention to her. She looks sexy as hell in her school uniform. My gaze takes in her big brown eyes, her slender throat, and her shirt that's buttoned up all the way like the good girl she is. One day I plan on corrupting her. Just like her daddy corrupted my mom. "How was your summer?" she asks.

I turn, giving her my full attention, and put myself between her and Caleb. "Uneventful." I repeat her answer and her lips tip up slightly. My summer was anything but uneventful, but I won't tell her what I was doing. The same thing I've been doing for the past four summers. Looking for my mom.

I'm not old enough to go to the auctions yet, but that will change in a few months when I turn eighteen. I plan on attending my first during winter break. If I see her dad there, she may never see him again. How he raised a daughter as sweet and innocent as McKenzie is beyond me.

"Uh...McKenzie I need to go. I'll see you later, okay?" Caleb says, trying to duck out from his punishment. I hide my smirk as I rub my hand up my jaw. Her eyes fly over my shoulder as she squints at him. She pulls her bottom lip between her teeth and shakes her head slightly. She forgot he was there.

"Oh, okay. I need to go anyway. I'm being someone's guide today." She waves at Caleb, but her eyes linger on me.

I lick my lips and her eyes follow my tongue, just like I wanted. *I'm going to fuck her one day. And she's going to love it.* She walks away and her skirt sways along the back of her thighs. My mouth waters at the thought of putting my mark on her soon.

Turning, I'm not surprised to see Caleb's back to me as he tries to make his getaway. But I wrap my hand around the back of his neck, squeezing until he grimaces. "What do you think you're doing with McKenzie?" I ask him in a low voice as I walk us toward the side of a building where there aren't a lot of witnesses.

His eyes flit around as I push his back against the wall until they finally land on me. "We..." He swallows convulsively as I wait.

What many don't know is that my great grandfather founded this school. My mother, Alice Brighton, is an alum and was to be the next dean. But I don't flaunt my lineage for all to see. I'm a quiet force to be reckoned with. People don't see me coming until they're left picking up the pieces.

"I don't have all day." I stand in front of him, waiting patiently. To any bystander, it looks like we're having a conversation.

"We did a work-study program together over the summer and became friends." He pauses. "Then more than friends."

I chuckle as I rock back on the heels of my feet. "Yet, she said her summer was uneventful. How unfortunate for you."

A flash of anger and embarrassment shows in his eyes, but he conceals it quickly. He tries to explain it away. "You make her nervous." I tilt my head at him and sigh.

"Why do you think that is? I have made it abundantly clear she belongs to me."

"Yet she doesn't know that," he interrupts. I take a step forward until my chest is almost touching his. He swallows loudly and looks back toward the courtyard, but I get in his field of vision, forcing him to look at me.

"She knows it. She just doesn't know she knows it."

He sucks in a breath and tries to break eye contact with me, but I refuse to let him. "So, what? Do I break up with her?"

I step back as I think this through. McKenzie is gorgeous, but she doesn't realize it. I also know she gets shit from the girls on the cheerleading squad. All of them except Anna. Caleb has a decent reputation and it might help keep the girls off her back.

"No, don't break up with her. But you are not to touch her. Ever. Understand?"

His mouth opens and closes. "What? How do you expect me to do that? She's going to wonder, eventually."

I roll my eyes at him and take another step back. "No, she won't. She'll think you're being a gentleman and you're going to let her believe you are. And you won't touch anyone else either."

Caleb glares at me when he realizes what I'm saying. He has to spend his senior year being a monk. That's his punishment for going against the decree I put out freshman year. He knew the consequences, yet he did it anyway. He's lucky I'm not cutting off the fucking hand that touched her. It's in his best interest to keep his mouth shut and he knows it, so he doesn't say anything else.

Turning, I begin my trek back across the courtyard toward the front office. Opening the schedule I stole from McKenzie, I notice there are a few classes she's in that I'm not. That needs to be fixed before classes begin tomorrow. I told the Executive Director of Administration I'm to be in all of her classes, but this year it's not like that. Seems like more than one person wants to test me this year.

They'll learn. They always do.

I stare at the new dean as he tries to give me shit for wanting to change my schedule. "It's extremely last minute. We need more notice."

"I'm not explaining myself to you again." I lean back and look at the plaque on his desk. "Dick. Can I call you Dick?"

He scowls at me. "My name is Richard. And you may call me Mr. Reynolds or Headmaster."

I stand from my chair, circle around his desk, and lean against it, staring down at him. I try to hold my amusement back at the look of shock on his face. "Well, Dick, my name is Phoenix Stone. My great grandfather was Alexander Brighton." His eyes widen at the realization. "I know you're new, but you will change my schedule and you will not question me again."

He nods slowly, then presses the intercom on his desk. "Ms. Kole, please update Phoenix's schedule. He'll be out there to see you in a moment."

I push off his desk and walk to the door. "I'm pleased you decided to see things my way." Exiting his office, it takes all my self control not to slam his door. *Who the fuck does he think he is?*

After I get my schedule fixed with Ms. Kole, I call my dad.

"Hey, son," he greets me as a car door slams in the background.

"Did you know there's a new dean?" I ask him. Walking toward the locker room to get ready for practice, I grit my teeth when I see Kelly and her plastic friends heading toward me.

"I found out this morning, but I've been busy, so I haven't had a chance to call and warn you." I duck between two buildings, trying to avoid Kelly, but I know she'll find me soon enough.

"Why are you just now finding out?"

He huffs. "They haven't been as forthcoming with information since your mother went missing. I reminded them of the funding we provided and that I would pull it if it happened again." There's some talking in the background. "I have to go. Send me your lacrosse schedule. I'll make sure to come to a few games." He hangs up before I can respond.

I inhale slowly as I put my phone in my pocket. My father is hiding something from me and I haven't been able to figure out what it is yet. I never wanted to follow in his footsteps. The only person I've voiced that to is McKenzie. It was the one and only deep conversation we had. But even if I don't want to, I know I will. I've already started.

I made it my mission that I would destroy Marcus Knight. That includes making his daughter mine.

Chapter 2

Phoenix

Three Months Later

Standing in line waiting to be greeted by the host, I watch everyone, as I search for McKenzie's father. Everyone's identity is hidden by the masks we are required to wear. Each color mask means something different. The white ones mean they're selling, the black ones mean they're buying. The red ones mean they're for sale, the black and red ones mean they're taken, but willing to share. Silver means they've been purchased and not up to share. Gold means they are an owner and aren't buying.

I'm wearing a black one. I don't intend to purchase anyone today, but there isn't a mask available for those who want to observe. If you attend an auction, you are expected to participate in some way. So, when I put in my application to receive an invitation for an auction, I put down the type of woman I'd be interested in buying.

A woman with silver hair, big brown eyes, legs that go on for days, and full red lips. One of the things I've learned from my father is when a person is purchased, because women and men are sold at these auctions, they are required to have sex in front of anyone who wishes to watch.

My eyes narrow at a man who is balding. He's short and stocky. Like our new dean. He has a black mask on as well. I know Brighton Academy has questionable attendees and staff, but this? It pisses me off thinking of him eyeing the girls he wants to buy one day. I have a lot of questions about this society and the auction they host on a quarterly basis.

How did it get started? Who founded it? And how do I become a member of the council? My father, who hasn't shown up yet, is how I found out you have to receive an invitation before attending an auction. I filled out my application, he turned it in, and my invitation arrived three weeks later. He isn't part of the council and has never tried to become part of it, which irritates me because I'm sure the answer lies in being a part of it. But I get it. He misses my mom and he won't have sex with anyone who isn't her.

I step up in the line as it moves and my eyes are drawn back to the man I'm sure is the dean. I stop in my tracks when I recognize he's speaking to none other than Marcus Knight. I'd recognize that man anywhere, with or without a mask. Someone behind me runs into my back.

"I'm so sorry," a high-pitched voice says.

I turn. "My apologies," I reply. I quickly school my features when I recognize Karla. She was the cheerleading captain last year. Her eyes widen when she recognizes me. Turning to face her escort, I know immediately it's her father. He's wearing a white mask, and she's wearing a red one. *He's selling his own daughter. What. The. Fuck.*

❧

My father never showed up. Something is up with him and I will figure it out. Putting that out of my mind, I pay close attention to how the auction is run. Every bid begins at half a million dollars. Men and women are sold. Some want to be sold and others are terrified. It's almost as if those who are terrified had no idea they were being sold. This doesn't surprise me considering what happened to my mother. However, I assumed the girls being sold were kidnapped. I didn't realize their own fathers sold them.

It doesn't surprise me though. I've recognized a few of the girls, all of them graduated from Brighton within the last year or so. I also keep an eye out for my mom. But I already know she won't be one of the women. I'm sure if she were going to be sold, it would have already happened.

Sitting in the back row, I watch how everyone bids. There are more black masks here than there are people to buy. *Will they stay and watch those who were bought have sex with those who purchased them?* I've been asking myself the same question. *Should I stay to see how it operates? Or should I wait?*

"You're selling your daughter?" a woman asks Karla's father. I keep my eyes on the auction, but eavesdrop on their conversation.

"Yes," he says curtly.

"Did you tell her?"

"We're not supposed to tell them," he says, like she should already know this.

She huffs. "I'll never understand why it's a requirement the council has to sell their first daughter, but not their first son."

Karla's father grabs the woman's bicep, causing her to squeak. "Shut your mouth, Angie, or you won't be allowed to attend again."

"Fine."

My mind whirls. One of the requirements to be in the council is you have to sell your first daughter.

So, can you join the council before you have a child? Or is it a contract that's signed? What if they never have a daughter? Is something else promised instead? I'm going to have to immerse myself completely in this world in order to find out.

Walking off the field after our first game and first win of the season, I wipe my hand across my forehead. We're going to the playoffs this year. I'm determined to end this season as champions. Glancing up at the stands, I smirk at the sight of McKenzie, her face buried in a book. She hasn't even noticed the game is over.

Changing my direction, I walk to the stands, staring up at her for a few moments. First to take in her expressions as she reads. She's always been expressive when she reads. *I wonder what she'll look like when I finally have her under me.* Second, to see how long it takes for her to notice someone is watching her.

When she's mine, I'm going to have to teach her to be aware of her surroundings. I've been standing here for a few minutes and she hasn't looked up yet. Clearing my throat, her head pops up and her eyes connect with mine.

"Phoenix." The sound of my name on her lips makes me hard quicker than I'd care to admit. *Fuck. This girl.*

"McKenzie," I reply. "What world are you living in today?" Her cheeks pinken and I smirk. She glances from me to the field, then back to me.

"Did you win?" she asks.

"We did."

She smiles and stands descending the bleachers until she's in front of me. She's still in her school uniform looking sexy as hell. Every other female in this school tries to make their uniform sexier. Some leave buttons undone, others fold their skirts making it shorter. Not McKenzie, but she's still the sexiest woman in this school.

One day I plan on living out my fantasies. She'll wear this uniform while I bend her over a table in the library and fuck her until her voice is hoarse from screaming my name. Jesus Christ. When I first met her, my plan was to break her. But as I've gotten to know her, I've realized she's a victim.

She doesn't talk about her father much. From the little she's told me and the one deep conversation we had when she found out some of what her father does, I've gathered that he sent her here to get rid of her. He hasn't been to one parent's weekend and each time it makes me look forward to the day I get to destroy him.

"Congratulations." She holds her book close to her chest. "I'm sure Timothy will be happy." She looks toward the locker rooms like she's trying to find him. He's another close friend of hers and he's on the lacrosse team. He's probably the reason she comes to the games, but I secretly hope it's to see me as well.

"Thanks." I push away from the bleachers and begin my walk toward the locker room. She falls into step next to me.

"Do you think you'll go to the playoffs this year?"

"Yes."

She chuckles, so I give her a sideways glance. "You're very confident."

I shrug. "I'm captain this year. Last year's captain was an idiot." She laughs and shakes her head. "Where's your boyfriend?"

She squints as she stares down at the ground. "I don't know." I don't like the sound of her voice; she sounds sad. "I don't think he likes me that much, but he hasn't broken up with me." She shrugs.

I'm the reason he hasn't broken up with her. The fucker better not be walking out on her. I'll kill him.

"Anyway, I'll see you later. I'm going to the library." She does a little wave with her fingers and she walks away.

"I'll see you there later," I call out to her. She smiles at me over her shoulder. *Damn. This girl is going to break me.*

Chapter 3

Phoenix

One Month Later

"Hey Phoenix." Kelly sidles up next to me as I watch McKenzie. It's parents' weekend, and it looks like her father didn't show up. Again. Anna walks up to her with a frown and hands her an envelope. She leans down and hugs her, whispering something in her ear. McKenzie offers her a fake smile and nods.

"Are you ignoring me?" Kelly asks.

I scoff. "What was your first clue?" I swear this girl gets on my last nerve. She's so desperate for it. She giggles like I'm joking and I roll my eyes.

"Who are you looking at?" She turns her head and when she sees I'm watching McKenzie, she huffs. "Even her own family doesn't like her. They never show up."

I ball my hands into fists and remind myself I shouldn't hit a girl. Even a bitch like Kelly. My father already came and left. I still think he's hiding something because he was very evasive the entire time he was here, but I did find out how to get into the council.

You have to be a member for at least a year before they'll consider it. If you don't have a daughter to put up for sale you have to buy someone else's daughter, you have to pay a membership fee, and you have to have sex with the person you bought twice. Once in front of everyone and the second time in front of the council. I don't quite understand that, but it's their twisted way to have some semblance of control, I guess.

I know McKenzie's father is on the council, so he's agreed to sell his daughter. And I'm going to buy her. Then I'm going to get him removed from the council. The daughters have to be sold between the ages of nineteen and twenty-three. So, I will make sure I'm at every auction so I can buy her when her father finally does it.

"Do you plan on going to prom?" Kelly asks, interrupting my thoughts.

"No." Prom is the same night as the next auction. If I plan on getting in the council, I will be at every single auction they have.

"What? Why?" Kelly whines.

I grind my teeth and stand. *Never hit a woman. Never hit a woman.* "Because I don't want to." She doesn't know how to take a hint. I regret the day I stuck my dick in her.

McKenzie is still staring at the envelope Anna handed her. I wonder if she's going to open it. I walk toward her slowly just in case she does open it she'll have time to read it before I reach her. But she never does. She just stares at it.

When my shadow falls over her, she looks up, startled. "Phoenix?" The lines between her eyebrows show as she squints up at me. Her eyes are glossy and I know she's trying her damnedest not to cry. *I'm going to make Marcus Knight pay.*

I climb up on the picnic table and sit next to her. "Your father didn't show." It's a statement, not a question.

She sniffs. "No. I'm sure he had something important to do."

"You are important." She inhales sharply, but doesn't reply. I imagine wrapping my hands around Marcus Knight's throat and watching the life drain out of his eyes. She has no idea. No idea one day her father is going to sell her and one day I'm going to buy her.

She probably has this plan for her life that doesn't involve me. What she doesn't know is I am her future. I'm going to make sure she has a good life if it's the last thing I do. The heat from her gaze is penetrating my skin, so I turn and look at her.

She offers me a small smile. "Thank you. I really needed to hear that."

I have this overwhelming urge to lean the few inches between us and kiss her. Take her full plump lip in my mouth and suck it. Then I would mark her so everyone knows she's mine. My fingers tingle with the need to wrap them around her neck, pull her to me, and show her how good we would be together.

Instead, I stand, tap her on the nose with my index finger and walk away. It's the hardest thing I've ever had to do.

"I've been keeping an eye on her and she's doing okay. You don't have to worry," Dick is saying as I walk into his office without knocking. His eyes widen when he sees me, making me wonder who he's talking to. "I have to go." He hangs up without saying bye, and I arch an eyebrow at him.

"You didn't have to end the call so abruptly on my account." I sit down in the chair in front of his desk and place my foot on my knee.

He narrows his eyes at me. "I don't know who you think you are walking in my office without knocking."

I wave his comment away. "What were you doing at the auction?"

He stops breathing, and his face turns bright red. If he passes out because of lack of oxygen, I will not be resuscitating him. He takes a deep breath, like he's coming up out of water.

"What are you talking about?"

I laugh and his face begins to turn red again. "You really need to work on your poker face." His mouth opens and closes several times like a fish. I lean forward and place my hands on his desk. "What were you doing at the auction?"

I want to ask him why he was talking to Marcus Knight at the auction as well, but that will be showing my hand and I'm not doing that. Not with this sleaze. It's been a month since the auction, but I've noticed how he looks at some of the girls and it makes me wonder what his ulterior motive is for being the dean here.

"How do you know about the auctions? And what were you doing there?" He tries to sound haughty, but the questions come out panicked. I'm beginning to lose my patience.

"I was there because I was invited. Who invited you?"

He swallows and glances over my shoulder, probably hoping someone will come save him. "I was invited as well. You can't go unless you've been invited."

"Who invited you?" I ask.

"None of your business."

I stand so abruptly he jumps. I snort. This man is our dean and he can't stand up to an eighteen-year-old. "Listen, Dick, if you don't start answering my questions, I'm going to go to the board and tell them their newly hired dean was at an auction selling girls that graduated from this very school last year. Who invited you?"

He inhales sharply, his eyes darting around the room. "A friend of mine. Marcus Knight." Just like that, the floodgates open and he tells me more than I asked for. "He helped me get this job. He said he needed someone here to watch out for his daughter because she was in danger."

I narrow my eyes at him.

So, he must have been talking to Marcus when I walked in. He was telling him she's doing okay. He can't show up for parent's weekend, but he's doing this. Does he think she's in danger because of me? Or is something else going on?

"Why is she in danger?" I ask.

"I...uh...I don't know." I tilt my head. "I swear I don't. He didn't tell me. He just said he needed me here to watch out for her."

I sit back down and lean back in the chair, mulling this over in my mind. "He thinks she's in danger." It's not a question, but Dick nods anyway.

"I don't know why he thinks that. He didn't tell me, but he calls me every day to make sure she's doing okay."

I want to ask why he didn't come to parents' weekend since he seems so worried, but again I don't want to show my hand. I don't want him reporting back to Marcus that his enemy's son was asking questions about him or his daughter.

"How did he help you get this job?" I ask. The last dean was told to resign when news came out that he was sleeping with a senior. I think the two wound up getting married over the summer. It was all very hush hush. A lot of influential people send their children here to go to school. Some of them are influential in illegal ways and others influential in other sectors of society.

Marcus controls the drug trafficking from Florida to South Carolina. Anna's father plans on running for president one day. My father has a number of businesses he uses to launder money. Mainly strip clubs and he's started a few underground fight clubs, but lately he's shown interest in taking Marcus' territory.

I don't care either way. If we can destroy him in more ways than one, I'm on board. I stand again and stare down at Dick. He sinks back in his chair and clutches the arms, his knuckles turning white.

"You need to remember your place here and how easily you can be replaced. This is my school, so if any of its students are in danger, you need to notify me. Understand?"

He nods in agreement. "Of course. Yes."

"Seems like you get to keep your job for one more day." I walk out of his office, leaving the door wide open. Heading toward the library, I have to see for myself McKenzie is okay. I just saw her during the last period of the day, but the fact she might be in danger I need to see for myself. This girl has no idea the control she has over me.

I wonder if she'll figure it out one day and use it against me.

Chapter 4

Phoenix

Two Months Later

"Where the hell are you?" I want to snatch this fucking mask off my face. Instead, I grip my phone so hard it groans under the pressure.

"I'm not going to make it," Dad responds. I take a step forward as the line moves up.

"Why? I thought we were doing this together, but you're hardly around anymore. What is going on?" I keep my voice low as I glance around to see if I can spot Marcus or the dean. I'm pretty sure I recognize Anna's father. She's probably going to be sold, too.

The auction isn't a terrible idea if people are doing it willingly. From what I can tell, there are some people that do. But not all members are vetted, so there's no guarantee if they're bought they'll be treated well. I've set my sights further than just trying to find my mom.

I want to take these sons of bitches down and turn this into something people want to participate in. Not something they're forced to do.

"I think I've found a lead on your mother."

My jaw aches from how hard I'm clenching my teeth. "What do you mean? And why am I just now hearing about it?" My voice is deadly and if I was talking to anyone else, they'd be back tracking right now, but not my dad.

"Because I'm still not sure. I'm going to follow it and I'll let you know." He hangs up. I want to punch something. I glance around again; maybe I can find Marcus and punch him. I'll be going to one of the fights tonight after the auction to blow off some of this built up tension. Something is not adding up, and it's pissing me off.

I inhale slowly as I stop in front of the host and hostess. I tip my lips up in a small smile and they both return it. "Thank you for coming," the man says. The woman doesn't speak, and she doesn't look at me; she keeps her eyes downcast. She doesn't look afraid like the last hostess. Maybe she wants to be a part of this.

When I turn to walk away, I hear him praise her. "Such a good girl, pet."

"Thank you, Sir," she responds.

The interaction does something to me. Opens up a world of possibilities. The thought of having that type of relationship with McKenzie flashes through my mind. The girl lives for praise. Or maybe it's approval because of the asshat she grew up with.

I turn that part of my brain off so I can focus and see if I can gather any more information about these auctions. I find my seat at the back of the room again. I like to be able to see everyone. The auctioneer steps forward in a black tuxedo and blue mask.

"Good evening everyone. Tonight we have nine up for bid." There's some grumbling. Last time there were thirteen. Even then, there were more buyers than people for sale. He motions for everyone to quiet down. "There is another graduation happening soon, so hopefully there will be more at the next one."

Fuck. Will Marcus try to sell his daughter at that one? Or will he let her have a life for a little while?

I still have six more months before they'll consider allowing me to join the council. I'll find a way if that happens.

Marcus and Dick sit in front of me, not realizing it, and I want to punch the air at my luck. They're deep in conversation, so I'm sure that's why they haven't noticed. I shake my head. *Marcus should be more aware than that. Unless he doesn't realize I'm here.* I've been wearing masks that cover my entire face. I know my eyes give me away, though, so I've tried not to look at anyone directly.

"Will she be in the next auction?" Dick asks Marcus.

Marcus shakes his head before he finishes. "I'm waiting until the last possible moment." Before they can continue, the auction begins.

I sit back in my seat and watch while I think over Marcus' words. He almost sounds like he doesn't want to sell her. After the auction is over, we're told where to go. If you want to watch, it's on the other side of the house. Those who want a room to themselves know where to go. They escort those who are sharing to a larger room upstairs. And those who want to mingle can go to the dining area.

I walk that way so I can listen some more and see if I can begin networking. I didn't stay last time. I couldn't stomach the thought of everything going on. This time I told myself not to be an asshole and suck it up.

When I enter the area where the food and drinks are, I'm greeted by more people than I expected to see. I assumed the majority would be ready to go watch or participate in whatever activities they had planned for the evening. I didn't expect to see Marcus or Dick in here, either.

I grab a drink and find a corner to stand in as I observe and try my best not to be noticed. It's been a while since Marcus has seen me, so he may not recognize me, but Dick would probably recognize me.

"You didn't buy anyone?" A woman stops next to me. She has cropped black hair. She's wearing a black mask and a black dress.

I take a sip from my drink. "I didn't see anyone that interested me."

She hums as she takes a drink from her wineglass. "It's disappointing more men aren't for sale at these things." She sighs. "Would you be interested in going to a room?"

I chuckle and eye her. "No, thank you."

She sighs again and gulps down her wine. "I figured as much, but thought I'd ask anyhow." She taps her empty glass against mine. "Maybe I'll see you at the next one." She disappears in the crowd and I shake my head in amusement.

At least she wasn't another Kelly that gets offended at everything. The girl would not drop the fact that I wasn't going to prom tonight.

She even had the nerve to text me earlier today and say she'd save a dance for me.

Dick passes in front of me, filling his plate with finger foods. Marcus is walking with him, but he's not eating anything. "You should have stayed at the school tonight. With prom going on, someone needs to be there to watch her."

This man confuses me. He never shows up to parents' weekend. He's going to sell her at an auction. But he seems concerned about her.

"She's not going to prom," Dick says around a mouthful of food. Marcus grimaces as do I. *Caleb didn't ask her to prom?*

"I thought you said she had a boyfriend," Marcus says.

Dick shrugs. "I think they're more friends than anything else. He did ask her, but she said she doesn't dance and told him to go with his friends."

I scowl. I assumed she was going to prom with Caleb. I already had a discussion with him after he left her at the lacrosse game. He swears he hasn't touched another girl, but I don't know if I believe him.

"Will you be coming to graduation?" Dick asks.

Marcus runs his hand through his hair. "Yes. I'm not missing that. I'll have security with me when I come." Dick nods and begins eating again.

I push off the wall and leave. I can't give them an opportunity to spot me, so it's best I leave now. Marcus seems concerned about McKenzie's safety. It doesn't make sense. The man who took my mom. *Is he nervous that my dad and I will take her in retaliation?*

That was the plan when my dad first told me she was at the school. Even the first time I saw her, I was determined I would break her. But the more I got to know her and the more I realized she was a victim, I realized I couldn't do it. She's unlike anyone I've ever met. So, I decided instead of breaking her, I was going to make her mine. She is mine. She just doesn't know it yet.

Chapter 5

Phoenix

Graduation

I search for McKenzie. This will probably be the last time I see her for a while. I've learned that her father is going to let her go to college before he sells her. I've also learned that Dick is going to buy her. He promises Marcus he'll protect her, but since I found out, I've been keeping an eye and ear on him and he's lying. He's not going to follow through with their plan.

Marcus thinks Dick will buy her, then bring her to him. But Dick is not going to follow through. He's going to have sex with her and he's going to keep her. Why Marcus puts his trust in this man, I'll never know. But it's obvious he's not a man of his word.

McKenzie walks into the courtyard with Anna. She's gorgeous. Her silver hair swaying behind her as she walks. She glances around and I know she's looking for her father. I know he'll be here today and even though I hate the man, I'm glad he's going to show up for her.

Her red lips lift in a smile at something Anna says. I wonder what those lips would look like wrapped around my cock. I suck in a breath and force myself to think of something else. One of the perks of wearing my graduation gown is it hides the evidence of how attracted to her I am.

Her eyes land on me, and I smirk. Anna says something and pushes her toward me. I take that as my cue to head their way.

"Hey Phoenix," Anna greets me.

I nod in her direction. "Anna."

I turn toward McKenzie, and her eyes widen slightly. "McKenzie, can you go for a walk?"

Her mouth opens in surprise as she looks between me and Anna. She acts like I'm not around her all the time. The amount of times I've walked with her to class, walked with her to the library, sat with her at the library, and just sought her out because I wanted to hear her raspy, sexy voice.

"Sure... sure," she replies. I take her arm and lead her toward the lacrosse field. She fidgets with her gown and looks around. She has no idea of the power she holds over me.

"Are your parents here?" she asks. I grind my teeth. She has no idea about my mother. Who she is or who I am. And I'll keep it that way. She doesn't need to know.

"My father is," I reply, hoping she'll let it go.

"What about siblings?" she asks. According to my father, I was a miracle. They had a hard time getting pregnant, so after I came, they stopped trying and were grateful they had me.

"No."

I stop when we get to the bleachers. She glances from me to the bleachers. I have a reputation for taking girls under the bleachers. But usually I just used them to get off. I'd push them to their knees and fantasize it was McKenzie.

"So, did you want to talk about something?" She's nervous. I wonder what she would do if I took her under the bleachers. Actually, I'd never take her under the bleachers. The things I want to do to her are better done somewhere more private.

"Your father doesn't like me," I tell her, forcing my mind to focus on the conversation at hand.

"No. He doesn't like your father either." She's blunt, which surprises me. I like it though. He finally came to one parents' weekend and he and my father made a scene that I had to break up.

"Do you know why?" I ask her.

She looks away and shifts. "I've learned some things in the years since I've been here. It seems your father is encroaching on my father's business."

I snort and put my hands in my pockets. My father *is* doing that. "Not in the way you think, though." I know I'm being vague, but how do you tell someone that their father took your mother?

My father is encroaching on her father's business as payback, but also as a way to find out more information. At least that's the story he's telling me. I don't care about getting into the drug business. I've focused more on the fights.

"What do you mean?" Her eyebrows dip as she narrows her eyes at me.

I run my hand through my hair to keep myself from rubbing my thumb over the worry lines between her eyebrows. I want to comfort her, but now isn't the time. I have to keep my distance.

"I mean, when you realize what an awful man your father is. I'll be there to rescue you. I promise."

It's the closest I'll ever come to warning her. I want to tell her that her father is going to sell her. He's going to try to sell her to the dean of this school. But I know she won't believe me. She still holds onto the hope that her father is a good man. I can see it in her eyes.

She sucks in a breath and glances around again. "I should probably go. My father should be here soon."

I don't want to let her go, but I nod anyway. She walks away and I know this is the last day I'll see her until the day her father sells her at an auction. But I will find her again one day. I will always find her.

Five Years Later

"Dad, please stop talking to me." McKenzie's voice comes from behind me and it takes everything within me not to turn around. She's here, which means she's going to be sold tonight. I have been waiting for this night for five years, but I still feel unprepared.

I was accepted as an initiate into the council almost one year ago. They said I had to make a purchase within three years to become a member. I've paid more than my share of fees and dues trying to get in their good graces, and it's worked. Once I buy McKenzie, then we'll have to have sex tonight, we'll have to have sex one more time in front of just the council. Hopefully, she'll forgive me one day.

I greet the host and hostess and make my way into the area they're having the auction. I sit in the middle and force myself not to look around. Marcus avoids me at all costs at these things when he attends. He doesn't come to all of them, but I do. Mainly because I never knew when he'd show up with McKenzie.

Dick sits a few rows in front of me. I want to strangle him. He has no idea I'm going to outbid him tonight. All bids start at half a million dollars, sometimes they're more. Usually, that's for virgins.

Marcus shows up and sits next to Dick. "You ready?" he asks. Dick nods enthusiastically. I ball my hands into fists to stop myself from strangling them both. *Marcus is an idiot to trust this man.*

Dick comes to every auction as well. He's bought two other girls. Where he gets the money, I don't know. And I haven't cared to look into it. When Anna was sold a few months ago, he tried to buy her, but a senator who most likely will be our next Vice President outbid him. If I had known Rex at that time, I would have bought her.

The auctioneer comes up and tells how many are up for auction tonight. There's more than usual. Part of me hopes McKenzie is one of the first, so she doesn't have to wait, but the other part hopes she's toward the end to give me time to come up with an explanation for her.

Five people have been bought so far, but I stay focused. After tonight, she's going to be mine.

"The next person up for auction is McKenzie Knight. She's twenty-three years old, recently graduated from NYU, and is an excellent baker." Someone escorts McKenzie onto the stage. The fear in her eyes makes my stomach clench.

How the hell am I going to have sex with her in front of a group of people when she's terrified? I grind my teeth and force myself not to focus on that right now.

"The starting bid is seven hundred fifty thousand dollars." Dick raises his hand. "We've got seven hundred fifty thousand."

"One million," someone says from the back.

"One and a quarter million," Dick says quickly. Too quickly.

"One and a half," the person from the back says. I want to turn and look, but I keep my eyes focused on McKenzie. She keeps wiping her hands down her dress.

I know she has to feel uncomfortable in that. It doesn't look like something she'd wear willingly. At least not the girl I remember from high school. The one that always made sure her skirt was long enough and her buttons were all done up. I'm sure her father made her wear it. The majority of those who are being sold wear revealing clothing to make them more appealing.

The bid gets up to four million. A third person has joined in on the bidding. I stay quiet and wait them out. Every auction I've been to, no one has been bought for more than four and a half, so it's almost time for me to throw in my hand.

"Four and a quarter," Dick says. It's silent after that.

"Going once, twice."

"Four and a half," I call out. Dick begins to turn around, but Marcus puts a hand on his shoulder to stop him.

"What do you say to that, sir?" the auctioneer asks.

Dick looks from him to Marcus. "Four and three quarters," he says, but it's strained. The auctioneer looks at me.

"Five." I sound bored, but I'm anything but. I have been preparing for this for over five years. *She will be mine.*

"Five and one hundred thousand." Dick replies, sounding strained.

I snort. "Five and a half."

Dick shifts in his seat, and Marcus runs his hand through his hair. They were expecting the bidding to stop around four and a half. If my suspicions are right, I'm sure they were counting on it. *I'm going to win.*

"Five and six hundred thousand." Dick's voice is so low the auctioneer has to strain to hear him. The auctioneer looks between the two of us. I stay quiet.

"Going once, twice." Dick squirms in his seat. I shake my head. *He thinks he's going to win.* "So—"

"Six million," I say calmly. Dick squeaks, and the auctioneer looks from me to him. He shakes his head slightly, finally giving in.

"Sold, for six million." I stand and allow one of the ushers to escort me toward the front so I can claim my prize. As I pass the row with Dick and Marcus, I smirk at them and give them a small salute.

Chapter 6

Phoenix

Present Day

All the canvases I had removed from our wedding day are now in their rightful place. Pinching my lips, I stare at the one above the mantle in our living room.

Did she remember I forced her to marry me? Did she remember the second time we had to have sex in front of the council? Does she know the plan was to rescue other girls that were being sold against their will? And the only way to get out of having sex with them was to be married.

I don't know if she got all her memories back or just a few.

It had to be the night she woke up and said she wasn't feeling well. I knew something was off with her. I clench the glass in my hand, causing it to groan. Squeezing harder, I don't react when it shatters in my hand. Blood slowly drips from the gash. I swallow as I watch it drip onto the carpet.

Kenz isn't going to be happy I'm getting blood on her carpet. *I'll call her McFeisty. She'll be pissed. We'll have amazing sex.* Squeezing my eyes shut, I replay every moment over the past six months. It's everything I've ever wanted with her. We were in our own little bubble until I had to take her to that last auction.

If she got her memories back, that's probably what did it. I wanted to forget about The Society, my mom, and her father. But I made a promise when I found her in that godforsaken place, chained up, freezing, and starving. I would make her father pay and whoever else was involved.

Selling his daughter, then kidnapping her and chaining her without nourishment or any other common courtesies. How could he do that? That's why McKenzie got an IUD when we realized no matter how hard we tried to stay away from each other, we couldn't. I sure as hell am not selling my first daughter and she was more than willing to agree. She'll never have a child with me anyway.

"Sir!" Rex's voice brings me back to the present. Opening my eyes, I watch as he runs to the kitchen and comes back with a towel. He wraps it around my hand, the coppery scent surrounding us. "I'll call Dr. Chamberland. You might need stitches." I don't reply. *She left me. She wasn't taken.*

"She wouldn't have left her bag on the dock," Anna says from the doorway. She rarely leaves her room, but if Rex is home, she tries. I frown as I wait for her to expand further. She steps further into the living room. "I think she was planning it. She was being unnaturally quiet when we had our girls' day. I could tell something was bothering her, but I didn't ask her about it."

She sighs and sits on the chair closest to me. "We've been through a lot and with her having amnesia, I know she was trying so hard to remember things. I thought maybe it had something to do with that." She rubs the fabric of her T-shirt between her fingers. "I wish I had asked her."

Rex takes a step toward her. "You've been through a lot too, Banana."

She lifts one shoulder. "It doesn't matter. She's my best friend. Instead, I fell asleep." She clears her throat and lifts her eyes to look at me. "I think you should go look again. Is there someone who lives close by? Maybe they saw her?"

I stand abruptly and share a look with Rex. "Old man Larry," we both say at the same time.

"Who?" Anna asks.

"He lives down the lake," Rex explains.

"He wouldn't hurt her, would he?" Anna asks, rubbing her palms down her thighs.

"No. He's just a grumpy old man." Rex tells her. I walk to my downstairs office, grab the gun and extra magazine I keep in my drawer. Right next to it is a picture of McKenzie. I run my finger down it.

"I'll always find you, love. Always."

Larry opens the door, but I look over his shoulder looking for McKenzie. I know she's here. I can smell the pineapple and coconut. "Where is she?"

"Listen here, son. I know you're used to getting your way, but that won't work with me," Larry responds. I arch an eyebrow at him, but he only stares back at me. I sigh.

"Larry, where is my wife?"

He grunts. "You know I'm offended I wasn't invited to the wedding."

I roll my eyes. "We got married before I met you," I tell him. "Not too long after we got married is when we moved across the lake."

"On a property I sold to you. Don't you forget it." I share a look with Rex.

"Yes, that made you rich. Now, where's my wife?"

Larry looks over his shoulder. Instead of inviting me in, he pushes his way out and closes the door. I narrow my eyes at him, three seconds from moving him and going in without an invitation. He holds his hands up in a placating way, knowing what I'm thinking.

"She's taking a nap."

I tilt my head at him and place my hands in my pocket. "Is she ill?" I school my features, but the rapid beating of my heart is proof of my anxiousness. After the scares we've had, having her out of my sight for any length of time is not something I care to repeat.

"No, but we were watching Jeopardy, and she fell asleep on the couch." He explains before sighing. "Look, whatever happened, she's hurting." I ball my hands into fists inside my pockets. *I'm the reason she's hurting. I know it.*

I finally take a step back and run a hand through my hair. "I don't know what happened. She seemed fine, then she left."

Larry scoffs, obviously not believing my lie. "She didn't mean to leave." That catches my attention and I motion to him to continue. "She said she was thinking about it, but she came to the conclusion that she was going to stay. She got in the rowboat to think, got lost in her thoughts, then when she decided to get out of the boat, she realized she had floated downstream and ended up at my house."

I share another look with Rex. *Anna was right.* "Okay. And?" He has a point he's getting to and I need him to get there quicker than he is.

"I think you need to give her some space. Let her have a bit of freedom. I'll check in with you every day to let you know she's safe, but let her come to you when she's ready. And she will be, eventually."

I walk off his porch, pondering what he said. She's never had any freedom. The most freedom she's ever had was at Brighton; even then I watched her every move or I had her every move watched. That won't change if I allow her to stay here. I'll send security here to watch her every move. But every part of our relationship has been forced on her.

The only time I ever asked her anything was the day I gave her wedding rings back to her. I asked her to be my wife, and she said yes. I think back to our wedding day. She told me then if I had asked her she would have said yes and I'd never know. But I do know now. She was telling the truth.

I have lied to her so much. I inhale deeply and turn to Larry. "I'll let her stay." His eyes widen in obvious surprise. "But you will text me three times a day letting me know she's okay." He gives me a *really* look. "That is not up for discussion. I have to know and see she's okay. I'm also going to have one of my security guys watch her."

Larry shakes his head. "It doesn't seem like your security does a very good job. How did she wind up getting away without being noticed?"

I look at Rex, but don't respond to Larry's question. It's a good question. Every one of the guys that was on the premises was fired. Rex has hired two new guys that he's been talking about for a while now. I should have listened to him sooner. He's been saying for a while that we missed something with McKenzie's last kidnapping.

"We took care of that," I finally say. "Will you text me?"

He nods. "Yes, I'll text you. Do you have specific times?"

"Yes, nine in the morning, one in the afternoon, and six at night. You still have my number?" I want him to give me his phone so I can check myself, but when he nods, I take him at his word. Larry is grumpy, but he's harmless. I wouldn't have bought his property or moved so close to him if he wasn't.

"Alright, one of Rex's guys will be here at night keeping watch. If you miss one check in, I'll be back to get her."

He waves his hand at me and starts back toward his front door. "Yeah. Yeah. The only reason I'm allowing this is because I understand what it feels like to be in love." I don't respond as he walks back into his house and closes the door.

There's a part of me that wants to barge through the door, throw McKenzie over my shoulder, and make her go home. But I need her to choose me this time. And I know she will. She loves me. Almost as much as I love her.

Chapter 7

Phoenix

Two Months Later

Sitting at my desk in my downstairs office, I glance at the time again as I count down the minutes to the text I'll receive in about six minutes. I finish the sentence in the email I'm writing and hit send. Gil and I are working on the plans for the upcoming auction and making as many changes as possible. I've been working on making these changes since I became a member of the council, and Gil has supported me along the way. Glancing at the time again, I push my chair back and reach for my belt. Three minutes.

My fingers play with the buckle, the steel cold between my fingers as my cock stirs with anticipation. The number of times I've fucked my hand to the pictures I receive should be alarming, but the obsession I have for McKenzie is borderline psychotic. She's under my skin, in my blood, in every single thought and decision I make. I will never get enough of her, even if it is just a picture.

One minute. I pull on my belt, ready to undo it when there's a knock on my door. I scowl, but don't look up from my phone.

Everyone in this house knows not to disturb me during the check-in time. *This better be important.*

"Come in," I say without looking up. My phone dings with a notification just as the door opens. I still don't look up to see who it is. I open the text from Larry and pause at the selfie of McKenzie, my eyes narrowing. Larry's never sent me a selfie before. She has a small smile on her lips. Her eyes are bright with a bit of mischief. Her silver hair hangs in waves around her shoulders. She's standing in front of...

My eyes snap up and I'm face to face with a mirage. A fantasy. A figment of my imagination. She takes a step forward, the same mischievous smile on her face. She's wearing a red silk dress. It's low cut with two slits that stop at her hips. I wonder if she's wearing any panties. I narrow my eyes. I know that dress came out of our closet upstairs.

If she got on this property and my security guys didn't see, there will be more than a firing this time. Heads will roll.

"Relax. Rex met me. He knows I'm here."

Fuck. Her raspy voice washes over me first, then her pineapple and coconut scent. The constant uneasiness I've felt for the past two months settles and I'm finally able to take a deep breath. I don't know whether to be relieved or pissed. Relieved she finally came to me or pissed that Rex didn't warn me.

Her gaze wanders over me. She looks at the tattoos peeking out of my shirt, the sliver of my chest that's showing from where I unbuttoned my shirt, down to my arms where my sleeves are rolled up, and stops on my unbuckled belt.

Walking forward, she rounds my desk and leans against it. Her legs are on display. Her petite feet are in a gorgeous pair of black fuck me heels. Her left ankle is wrapped with an anklet I bought her for our first anniversary. *Does she remember that day? I have to find out what all she remembers.*

My eyes continue up her calf, to her knee, her thighs, her cleavage, her slender neck, her plump red lips, and her big brown eyes that show she loves how I look at her body.

"Hello, love." The small exhale she releases tickles my ear. Unable to keep my hands off her, I rub my knuckles up her arm, my lips tipping up when goosebumps break out along her skin.

"Hi, Nix," she whispers.

I don't break eye contact with her as I intertwine our fingers. "Are you home?"

She sighs and takes her hand out of mine. I want to grab her and pull her down in my lap, hold her hands behind her back, and mark her. "Depends," she answers.

I lean back in my chair and cross my arms over my chest. Her eyes flicker to my biceps, making me smirk. "On what?"

She shifts on her feet, breaking eye contact with me. "If you're going to be honest with me."

Unease settles in my stomach. I know I need to be honest with her, but if it leads to her leaving me, then she really will be my prisoner because I'm not letting her go. Not again.

"I'll be honest with you." She drops her shoulders as the tension leaves her body. "But I need you to understand I may not answer every question. If I promise to be honest with you, you have to take into consideration that there are some things I can't tell you for your safety."

Her eyes narrow as she processes that. She twists her lips to the side and inhales slowly. "I think I'll be safer if you don't keep anything from me."

I force myself not to show any emotions as I stare at her. "Why do you think that?"

She scoffs. "I was kidnapped twice. It doesn't seem like keeping things from me helped."

"What do you remember?" I ask her.

She swallows and looks out the window. "I remember everything until the first time I got kidnapped."

I watch her profile as I think back to when I first bought her until she got kidnapped the first time. I did not treat her the way she deserved. It makes sense why she didn't want to come back. She turns back toward me, her eyes connecting with mine.

I nod in agreement. "I'll try." It's all I can promise right now because I've kept so many things from her. *What if she hates me when she finds out all of my secrets?*

She twirls a piece of her hair around her finger as she thinks. "Okay," she whispers.

I tilt my head at her. "Does that mean you're coming home?" I ask, needing her to say it.

"I'll come home, but I want to stay in the room I was in right after you rescued me."

I stand so quickly my chair rolls back and bangs into the bookshelf behind my desk. Stepping in front of McKenzie, her eyes widen and her breathing quickens. I place my hand around her throat and her mouth opens slightly. I don't even think she realizes it. She practically pants every time my hand is around her throat.

And, fuck, does it look good around her neck. My tattooed hands against her sun-kissed skin. I place one leg between hers. She clutches the desk, trying to force herself to be still. But just as I anticipated, she bucks against me. "I see McFeisty is back," I murmur as I lean my forehead against hers.

"What?" she moans as I rub my thigh against her hot pussy.

I don't answer her question as I grab her hip and pull her even closer. My hand slides over her ass. "You will stay in our room," I demand.

Her eyes fly open and she sees this is not a compromise I'm willing to bend on. She takes a deep breath. "Okay, but no sex."

I run my hand from her ass to the curve of her waist, and cup her breast, running my thumb over her nipple. "Are you sure?" My breath ghosts over her lips.

She whimpers, places her hands on my chest, and pushes me away. I could easily stay where I'm at, but I step back until my back hits the bookshelf. She stares at me, pleading with her eyes.

"You went without a long time after the first time at the auction. In fact, you didn't have sex with me again until our wedding day, then months later at the next auction. Then, as far as I know, we didn't have sex again, even at the next auction." Her voice cracks and I suck in a sharp breath. I wait for her to continue, but she doesn't say anything else.

"It's not because I didn't want you." She scoffs and I know she's remembering how I forced her, how I promised her I'd make it good for her. I did anything but that, at least in the beginning.

Realization dawns on me. "You don't remember anything after the third auction."

She shrugs. "So. I'm sure I'll remember, eventually."

"You remember being taken?" She crosses her arms under her tits, pushing them up and giving me a glimpse of more skin.

"Yes. I told you that."

"By who?"

She hugs herself tighter as she looks from my eyes to my shoulder and back to my eyes. I tilt my head slightly, waiting for her answer.

"I don't know. They put something over my head." *She's lying. Why would she lie to me?* She told me that before, so it should seem true, but I can always tell when she's lying. And she did the same thing the last time she told me that.

She wants me to be honest with her, but she's not doing the same. I'll leave that for now. At this moment, I need her to trust me. Maybe if she trusts me, she'll tell me things she didn't tell me before. "So, you don't remember what happened after we got you and brought you home?"

She sighs and shakes her head. "I remember going to the auction, then going to the bathroom, then being taken, and that's it." She squeezes her eyes shut like she's trying to force herself to remember more.

She pushes away from my desk and begins to pace in front of the windows. "And I remember the first auction. At least parts of it. I thought you saved me from someone else buying me." A sob escapes her, and she places the palms of her hands against her eyes. "But you were using me. For this vendetta you have against my father."

I want to grab her and pull her into my arms, but I know she won't welcome it right now. She stops pacing and faces me, tears brimming in her eyes. I know she won't let them fall though, not if she remembers those months after I bought her.

"Do you really love me?"

I stare at her for a moment before I finally give in, grab her hand, and pull her into my chest. I wrap my arm around her waist, cup the back of her head, and place my forehead against hers.

"What I feel for you is more than love." I brush my lips against hers, but only briefly. "These past two months without you have been something I never want to experience again. When you were kidnapped and I had no idea where you were, that was torture. Not knowing if I'd ever see you again. I had already determined I wouldn't live without you." She gasps and grips my biceps.

"Life isn't worth living without you. Yes, when I first met you, I wanted to use you to get to your father. But I quickly realized you owned me. Even before we graduated, I knew I would do absolutely anything to have you and keep you."

I kiss her and she responds like she always does. She wraps her arms around me as I lick into her mouth and suck on her tongue. She's a drug that I'll never not be addicted to. She feeds my black soul. Even though I know I should give her up, I won't. Because I'm that selfish. She will always be mine. Always.

Chapter 8

McKenzie

I've missed this. I've missed him. I know I need to tell him about who took me the first time. Who I'm almost certain took me the second time. But he has his mom on this pedestal, and I'm not sure he'll be willing to take her down. Not even for me.

He kisses me like his life depends on it. Like I'm the very essence of his life. When he pulls back, I suck in a breath. *Maybe he would take her down for me.*

"So, you do love me," I murmur.

He chuckles and pulls me over to his chair. He sits and pulls me into his lap. "I do." He has no idea how much I needed to hear him say that. "I hate the first time I said that to you was when you couldn't remember everything else we've been through together."

I lean back and stare at him, letting his words sink in. "So, we never said that to each other before?"

He shakes his head as he runs his hand through my hair, his eyes tracing the movement. "No. I regretted it every single day. When you came back after the first time you were taken, you were..." He pauses as he thinks back to days I still don't remember. "Different."

I tilt my head at him as he continues to run his fingers through my hair. "Different how?"

His hands pause as he looks over my shoulder like he's remembering. "You were sick of my shit and you called me out on it."

I chuckle, imagining what he means. I realized it was his mom and his whole reasoning behind buying me was bullshit. But if he's saying now, he wanted me in spite of that. That he loves me. Maybe he will choose me. I wouldn't have known that then.

Pushing those thoughts out of my mind, my eyes land on the spot just below his ear. I frown that there isn't a mark there. *Why would there be? I've been gone for two months.* He smirks and tilts his head. "Go on, love."

I want to deny him. Deny what I was just thinking. But this isn't sex. It's foreplay. Foreplay can last for minutes, hours, weeks, maybe even months. After I've justified it in my head, I lean forward and lick his neck.

"I remember the first time I gave you a hickey," I murmur as I suck his skin between my lips. The sharp intake of breath has me humming.

"Do you?" he asks as his hand grabs the back of my head to keep me in place.

I don't answer him, instead I suck harder. He gets hard against my thigh and everything within me wants to ride him. But I've put up boundaries and I'm keeping them up until I can trust him again. My hand travels down his chest to his unbuckled belt. I grip him over his slacks and he moans. His head tilts back further. "Fuck, Kenz."

I pop off his neck and inspect my work. My lips tip into a smile and I sit back, removing my hand from his hard dick.

His eyes are dark with desire, but he doesn't try to take it any further. "When did you get your tattoo?" I ask.

"The day after you gave it to me. I wanted to make sure it was in the exact same spot."

I narrow my eyes at him. "I hope a man gave it to you."

He laughs and nods. "No other woman will ever touch me except you." The satisfaction that settles in the pit of my stomach is hard to hide.

"Why didn't you tell me?" I ask.

He sighs. "I was an asshole."

"I'm not going to argue about that." He smirks and leans up, kissing me on the forehead.

"I was trying to stay away from you. The amount of times I fucked my hand while you were sleeping…" My mouth pops open in surprise. "Anyway, one morning a few weeks after I got you back, you came down for breakfast." He licks his lips and smirks.

"We were eating in silence and you said, 'I wonder if I had married Caleb if he would have kept me satisfied.' So I made everyone leave, and I fucked you right there. From that point on, I refused to stay away."

I stare at him in disbelief. "I can't believe I said that," I admit.

One side of his mouth lifts in a half smile. "Like I said, you were sick of dealing with my shit and you knew exactly what to say to get a response." He runs his fingers through my hair again. "So, needless to say, you will be staying in our bedroom. And I'll give you space, but we will be having sex again soon."

My heart beats heavy in my chest. *Maybe this was a bad idea.* Maybe I should have stayed with Larry. Maybe I should have followed through with selling my rings and going somewhere he wouldn't be able to find me. But I couldn't. Every time I'd even think about it, I knew it wasn't a wise decision and I knew I'd be back.

I can't live without him. I don't want to live without him. I nod slowly, accepting his terms. "Okay, but you're going to tell me something I don't know every single day."

He nods. "I'll do whatever it takes to keep you with me."

I want to tell him it was his mom that kidnapped me. But I'm missing some key bits of information with my memory loss, so I'm going to wait until I can put those pieces together myself or my memory comes back completely. Whichever comes first.

"How about we go out and celebrate tonight? Then we'll start having hard conversations tomorrow," he suggests. A flash of a piano bar enters my mind from the dream I had the other night.

I tilt my head at him. "Do you own a piano bar?" I ask.

The lines next to his eyes crinkle slightly as he returns my look. "Yes."

"I had a dream about it the other night. I don't remember anything concrete, but I remember the feeling I had when I was there. I knew I was with you and we had fun. Can we go?"

He smiles and nods. "Of course. It was one of our favorite spots." He pushes me off his lap and buckles his belt.

I arch an eyebrow. "What were you about to do before I walked in?" I ask him.

He chuckles as he stands. "I was going to look at your pictures and imagine it was your hand and not mine." I shake my head and laugh as my neck and cheeks heat up. "By the way, you're wearing that dress tonight and you're not going upstairs to put panties on. You'll go just as you are."

My mouth pops open. "How did you know?"

He arches an eyebrow at me. "That dress leaves little to the imagination." His hand trails from my shoulder, down my waist, and over my ass.

"And you don't mind that?" I ask.

He smirks as he pulls me back into his arms. "I don't mind people looking as long as they don't touch." I wrap my arms around his neck as I gaze up at him, unable to stop from smiling back at him. He places his forehead against mine, his hand sliding up to cup the back of my head. "You're mine. I'm the only one allowed to touch you. I don't share."

He's said that before and I remember it. "Neither do I," I whisper as his lips land on mine again. He has no idea how much I've longed for him these past two months. I know we have a long road ahead of us, but we'll come out on the other side. There isn't another choice.

Chapter 9

Phoenix

McKenzie is leaning against the door as Rex drives us to the piano bar, trying her best to stay as far away from me as possible in the confined space. From the time she was in my office until now, she's gone deep in her thoughts and is now pulling away from me. I want to force her to talk to me, but I don't want to be anything like her father. From the things she's told me about growing up, I know her father was a hard man.

He didn't allow her to speak her mind. He didn't give her the comfort she craved. And after her mother died, he shipped her off instead of dealing with her emotions. I stare at her profile as she looks out the window. Then he sold her. In spite of all that, she still has this hope that he's a good man.

No matter how many times I've told her he's the one that took her, she refuses to give up. I know she remembers who took her the first time. If she doesn't tell me soon, I'm going to have to get it out of her by telling her I know she's lying. I exhale slowly. *Why would she lie about that?*

She shifts slightly, the soft glow of the moonlight reflecting off her hair. *She is gorgeous, and she has no idea.* I have missed being able to stare at her whenever I want over the past couple of months. Unable to stop myself, I lean over slightly and rub her jaw with my knuckles and push her hair behind her ear.

She startles slightly, like she's deep in thought, but she doesn't push me away. She turns toward me, her lips tipping in a slight smile. *The days and weeks when I first got her back, when she'd flinch anytime I'd try to touch her...* Things were different after I got her back the first time, but not like these past months after she lost her memory.

I wanted to fulfill my promise that I would make it good for her. I did anything but that in the beginning. So, in my own way, I fulfilled that promise during those months when she realized we were married. I stopped trying to stay away from her after that day she called me out on my bullshit, but it wasn't anything like it has been.

We experimented. A lot. We used the auctions as a way to delve deeper into the Master and pet role playing, but there was always something missing. She remained at arm's length and nothing I did helped.

When she gets the rest of her memories back, will it be like that again? Did something happen when she was taken the first time to put me at arm's length?

I inhale slowly and focus on her.

"What are you thinking?" I ask her. Her tongue darts out, wetting her lips as she looks down at her hands clasped tightly in her lap.

"Are you sure you want to know?" she whispers. Rex and I share a look in the rearview mirror. I grip her chin lightly with my forefinger and thumb, lifting her face until she looks at me. I want her to see the truth in my eyes. She swallows as she returns my stare.

"Yes, love. I want to know. I may not like it, but I have always encouraged you to speak your mind. I never want you to water down anything for me." She pulls her bottom lip between her teeth as she gathers her courage and I drop my hand, giving her time to collect her thoughts.

"The night of the auction," she begins. "My father stopped us as we were leaving and said he had someone else that was going to buy me." Her voice cracks and my heart aches. "And you knew."

I stare at her, contemplating what to tell her. I finally decide she needs to know the truth. If this is going to work between us. I have to be honest with her. "I started going to the auctions when I turned eighteen. It was a plan my father and I had come up with. Try to infiltrate The Society and its council, but I learned your father was on the council and part of the bylaws to become part of the council was to sell your first-born daughter."

Her mouth drops as her nails dig into her jean clad thighs. "Aren't you on the council?" she asks.

I nod. "Yes. You can sell your first-born daughter or buy someone else's daughter to be on the council. I chose to buy you."

She closes her eyes and inhales slowly. "So, you weren't trying to save me at all. You were using me."

"No," I reply right away.

Her eyes pop open. "What?"

"I wasn't using you. I knew your father was going to sell you. He had planned on selling you to the dean."

Her hand comes up to her throat as she processes what I'm saying. "The dean of Brighton?"

"Yes. But your father didn't go to every auction. So, he didn't see the two other girls the dean bought and had sex with in front of everyone. I don't know what he did with those girls after, but I knew he wasn't going to abide by his agreement with your father. I knew you'd wind up in horrid circumstances. So, yes, I bought you to save you. But I also bought you because I wanted you. I've wanted you since the first moment I laid eyes on you."

She doesn't respond, instead she stares at me wide eyed, probably trying to decide if she believes me or not. "Why didn't you tell me that? Instead, you made me believe..."

"I told you I bought you because I wanted you. That was the truth."

Rex pulls up in front of the club before she replies. "We're here, sir." Kenz stares at me before inhaling deeply. When she turns to get out of the car, I put my hand on her thigh.

"I'll come around." I share another look with Rex, and he gives me a *good luck* look. "You can pick us up in a few hours." He nods as I get out. I know he'll park the SUV and stand outside with our other security, but Kenz doesn't know that, and I want to make this as much of a normal outing as possible for her.

Glancing around the street, I see one of the new security guys waiting a ways down the street. He blends in nicely, like he's waiting for someone. Rex has been trying to talk me into hiring these guys for a while now. Ever since we got McKenzie back, he's been convinced there's a leak within.

I've tried to pinpoint who it can be, but after McKenzie left this last time and no one stopped her, everyone was fired. And Rex hired all new men. Rex still feels responsible for her leaving, even though he wasn't on the premises when it happened. Getting to Kenz's door, I push those thoughts aside. Looking around one more time before opening her door, I extend my hand to her and she takes it as she climbs out of the SUV.

My eyes roam over her full red lips and the red dress I told her she had to wear. Her nipples pebble against the cold and goosebumps break out along her arms, but she doesn't say anything. Every nerve in my body wants to rub my thumb, then my tongue over her nipples, but I force myself to take a step back.

She looks up at me under her eyelashes. Her brown eyes tell me she knows what I'm thinking. She raises one eyebrow at me and smirks. As much as I have enjoyed the past few months with her, I missed this McKenzie. When I got her back, it was like she had reverted back to her shy high school persona. I know it's because she couldn't remember the relationship we had, but I missed the flirting. The texts that said she needed my dick now because of some smutty book she was reading.

I was hoping after the auction maybe that part of her would be awakened. I didn't realize the auction would help her remember and push her further away. I close the door and wrap my arm around her shoulders. As we enter the bar, I give the bouncer a slight nod. The show hasn't started yet, but there is music playing as people order their food and drinks.

I lean down, my lips brushing her earlobe. "There will be people here who know you. If someone speaks to you, just be friendly. You don't have to have long conversations. If you get uncomfortable, tap your wrist. You remember that?" She swallows and inhales sharply. She taps her wrist, showing me she remembers. I kiss her just below her ear. "Such a good girl," I murmur.

This time when her nipples pebble and goosebumps breakout along her skin, I know it's a reaction to me and not the cold. My cock twitches at the sight. I wonder briefly how much time she'll need before she'll let me touch her again.

I lead us to a booth that is secluded yet has a good view of the stage. McKenzie slides in first and I slide in next to her. The booth is round and has walls high enough that the people at the next booth can't see us. I've lost count of the amount of times I've made her come in this booth and she doesn't remember any of them.

"What's wrong?" McKenzie asks as I settle next to her.

"I was thinking about how you can't remember the times we've been here together." I could easily tell her exactly what I was thinking, but I don't think constantly making sexual innuendos to her will get her to trust me any faster.

She sighs and rubs her hand up my arm. "I didn't think about how my amnesia affected you," she admits.

"How it affects me isn't the priority. You knew me as the guy you went to Brighton with and nothing more. My first priority was making sure you felt safe with me." I run a hand through my hair, looking away from her and toward the stage. "I don't think I did the best job with that."

"That's not true." She begins to trace the tattoos on my forearms. "You let me be myself. Allowed me to bake and read. I felt more like myself than I ever did with my father or even at Brighton." Her eyes flick to mine for a brief moment before she returns to tracing my tattoo. "I think part of feeling safe is being able to express yourself without fear of being judged. You never judged me even when we were at Brighton. You never made fun of me that I'd read during lacrosse games, or I spent more time in the library than I did going to parties. You accepted me for who I was and never tried to change me. To me, that's feeling safe."

I open my mouth to respond, but I'm at a loss for words. Our server arrives, dropping off two glasses of water. "I assumed you two would want your usuals, so I went ahead and brought you drinks." He set a glass in front of McKenzie. "Rum and Diet Coke." Then a glass in front of me. "Bourbon."

I nod at him in thanks. "Very good, Clay." He sets two menus in front of us.

"I'll come back in a moment to get your orders."

McKenzie lifts the cup to her nose and sniffs. "Rum and Diet Coke?" she asks, taking a tentative sip and hums. "I didn't realize I liked this."

I chuckle and wrap my arm around her, pulling her in close to my side. "You discovered that at an auction. It soon became your favorite drink."

She takes another sip and chuckles. I raise an eyebrow at her in question. "I was just wondering if rum does to me what tequila did to the woman in that country song."

I try to think about what she's referring to. "Which song?" I ask as I take a sip from my glass.

"The one that says tequila makes her clothes fall off." I cough as I swallow the bourbon the wrong way. She laughs and I tickle her side, making her squirm.

I lift the cup back to her lips. "Drink up and let's find out."

Chapter 10

Phoenix

I open the door to the SUV and walk around to McKenzie's side. When I open her door, she jumps into my arms, wrapping her arms around my neck. I put my arms under her legs and cradle her against my chest. She lays her head against my shoulder and runs her finger along my jaw.

"I had so much fun tonight," she whispers.

I smile down at her as she gazes at me. She seemed more at ease tonight. Like me opening up to her about the night I bought her chiseled a little at the wall she has up. In the past, I didn't play fair when she'd put that wall up. I knew one look, touch, or word from me and it would dissolve. This time I want to do it the right way. I want her to trust me and, oddly enough, I want to earn her trust. I lean forward and kiss her on the forehead.

"I had fun too, love."

When we walk into the house Anna is laying on the couch snuggled under the blanket. She sits up when she sees us. McKenzie turns toward her and gives her a small wave. "Anna! I came to see you earlier, but you were taking a nap." I slowly lower McKenzie to the ground and she walks over to Anna as Rex steps in behind me.

"Yeah, sorry. That's why I was out here on the couch. I didn't want to miss you again," Anna replies. McKenzie sits next to her and they hug. "Don't do that again, Kenz," Anna whispers into her hair.

Kenz runs her hands down Anna's hair. "I'm sorry. I didn't mean to. I swear." Kenz leans back and smiles at Anna. "How about you and I hang out in the library tomorrow?"

Anna smiles. "That sounds great."

McKenzie stands swaying a little. Anna arches an eyebrow at her and Kenz giggles. "I drank a little too much. I found out tonight I like rum and Diet Coke." She puts her hand next to her mouth like she's being secretive. "A lot," she whispers loudly.

I put my hands in my pockets and chuckle as Anna grins at her, then glances up at me and Rex. "Could I maybe go out with you the next time..." She trails off and I realize she's been stuck in this house for months. She and Rex go on walks and she likes to paint. But she hasn't left these grounds since we found her.

"Of course," I answer right away. "The four of us will go out to eat at my restaurant in a few days." Anna's eyes light up and she and Kenz share an excited laugh.

Anna stands, giving Kenz another hug. "I'll see you tomorrow." Kenz smiles at her and walks back to me, wrapping her arms around my neck.

"Take me to our room, husband. Because there's no way I'm going to make it up those stairs without breaking my neck."

I laugh and lift her in my arms again. Her calling me husband makes my heart beat heavy in my chest. I imagine all the things I'd like to do to her in our room, but I respect her wishes and keep those thoughts in my head.

McKenzie

The next morning I wake up, my head is pounding and my mouth is as dry as the Sahara desert. I roll over, patting Phoenix's side of the bed, but he's not there. Cracking my eyes, I notice a note on his pillow.

Had to go into the city. Drink the glass of water on your nightstand and take the Tylenol. I'll be home in time for dinner. Love you always, Phoenix

I roll over and grab the glass of water he left for me on my nightstand and take the Tylenol. I didn't drink so much I don't remember last night, but I know I had at least four or five glasses while Phoenix only had one. He gave me the chance to let loose in a safe environment. I lean against the headboard and pull my knees to my chest.

He's not the same man that he was in the memories I had. Or he is the same man and the man in my memories was a show. Right before the auction, he got me a cell phone I never used. There wasn't a need for it, but now I want to hear his voice and I don't want to have to wait until dinnertime.

Walking to the closet he says I designed myself, I head to the vanity and open the drawer. It's still plugged in, so it's fully charged. Unhooking it, I swipe the screen and it does the face recognition thing and I'm in. I pull up the contacts and click on Nix's picture.

"Hello?" Nix answers on the first ring and I smile at the sound of his voice.

"Thank you for the water and Tylenol." I grimace at the reflection in the mirror as I sit in front of the vanity. My hair is like a bird's nest. Grabbing the brush, I begin to pull it through the strands.

"You're welcome, love," he replies with a smile in his voice. "I believe this is the first time you've used your phone."

I yank the brush through a stubborn knot and snort. "No, I called my boyfriend before I called you."

He chuckles. "Well, guess I'll have to add him to my kill list for the week."

I laugh and sit the brush down. Things feel different after last night. Him opening up to me and telling me about the dean at Brighton made things a little different. "I don't particularly like him, so good riddance."

He laughs, and my face heats up in pleasure. I take a deep breath as I grab some clothes to change into after my shower. "Are you going to tell me something I don't know today?" I ask him.

He's quiet for several moments and I almost regret saying anything because the conversation was flowing so easily, but I need him to know I'm not giving in easily. I want the truth and eventually I'll tell him the truth about his mom. I know he knows I was lying. I want to tell him, but I want to trust him first. I want to know he'll choose me.

"Yes, think of a question by dinner and I'll tell you something you don't know." I exhale in relief.

"Thank you," I murmur. There's someone in the background talking.

"I have to go now, love. I'll see you tonight." I tell him bye and hang up. Holding the phone to my heart, I send up a silent plea. *Please let him choose me.*

Phoenix

Walking into the house, I grit my teeth at the silence. My father showed up an hour late today, which made me late for dinner. I tried to call McKenzie to let her know, but she never answered, so I called Phillip to relay the message. I'm going to have to talk to her about keeping her phone on her. Heading to my downstairs office, I stop at the light shining out of the cracked door to the library.

Stepping up to the door, I listen to see if Anna and Kenz are still in here. When I called Phillip earlier, he said the two spent all day together watching movies and hanging out in the library. I don't hear voices, so I peek my head in and my mouth tips up at the sight of McKenzie in her favorite wicker swing. She's still awake, her nose buried in a book.

I watch her expressions as she covers her mouth with her hand and shakes her head. The only other time she's this expressive is when I'm wringing pleasure after pleasure from her. The day I bought her, she told me to make her feel good. I was determined to follow through with that. Watching her give into that pleasure, forgetting what her father did to her, and forgetting we were surrounded by men and women she didn't know; it was a high like I had never experienced before.

I had been a fool back then trying to stay away. I knew my actions only hurt her more, but there was a part of me that was trying so hard to protect her from my world. I didn't want to corrupt her, even if that had been my original goal when I first met her. She helped me see you could come from something bad and still be good. She sighs and her lips tip up into a small smile.

"You are absolutely beautiful, you know that?" I say as I walk the distance between us. Her head snaps up, and she greets me with a smile I don't deserve. All the hell I put her through, and she still looks at me like that. I don't deserve it, but I'll take it as long as she's willing to give it.

"Nix."

My name is like a prayer on her lips and I want to prove I am worthy of her. She puts her book down and climbs out of the chair. She extends her arms and I step into them as I return her embrace.

Kissing her forehead, her cheek, and her jaw, I lean my forehead against hers, silently asking if I can kiss her. I'm forcing myself to respect these boundaries she's put up, even though I'd love to tear them down.

She tips her head slightly, giving me permission, and I don't wait for her to change her mind. Leaning down, I run my tongue along her lower lip, enjoying how her body melts into me. She opens up to me and my tongue meets hers. As much as I want to turn this dirty, I keep it short and sweet before pulling away. I smirk at the small pout that forms on her lips. Good, she wants me too.

She smiles and pulls back slightly. "Are you hungry? I haven't eaten yet. I was waiting for you." I don't know why it surprises me, but it does. Kenz has always been kind and thought of others before herself, but she's so different from what I grew up with. As much as I love my mother, she wasn't the selfless person like Kenz is.

"You didn't eat?" I ask as I guide her back to the kitchen. She walks to the oven, grabs an oven mitt, and pulls out two plates that were left to warm. She turns the oven off and brings the plates to where we normally sit at the island. I grab some glasses and pour us some sweet tea.

"I ate an apple to tie me over, but I wanted to eat with you." I bring the glasses over and stare at her as she waits for me.

"Because you wanted to ask your question." She has her fork halfway to her mouth when she pauses. She tilts her head at me and places her fork back on her plate. Something like hurt and maybe disappointment flashes in her eyes.

“No. Because I haven’t seen you in two months and I wanted to see you.” She pushes her plate away. “I’m not so hungry anymore,” she says softly. Standing, she walks out of the kitchen and I listen as her feet pad up the stairs. I scowl at her plate, then mine.

“I’m such an asshole.”

Chapter 11

Phoenix

I open my eyes and wait for them to get used to the darkness, listening intently to my surroundings. Every muscle in my body is drawn tight as I try to figure out what woke me up. A screech erupts from Kenz, making me suck in a breath and roll over to see if she's hurt. Her knees and arms are bent with her hands in front of her face.

"Don't," she rasps.

My stomach hollows out at the tears streaming down her face. Cautiously, I place my hand in one of hers, flinching with how cold it is. I lower it slowly, then take my other hand and run it through her hair. She jerks her head away and tries to curl into herself. I inhale deeply and swallow.

"Kenz, wake up, love." I scoot closer to her, offering my body heat. She's shaking and I'm not sure if it's from the fear of her dream or how cold she is. She's kicked the blankets off, but since both my hands are occupied, I can't pull them over her. "Kenz," I say more firmly. Her eyes are moving behind her eyelids with whatever nightmare she's experiencing. Or maybe it's a memory.

She flinches as I shake her slightly, trying to get her to wake up. "Come on, love. Wake up." I'm desperate, but I keep my voice even. Her eyes blink open and she stops breathing. It's like she's trying to be invisible. "Kenz, it's me. You're safe." My voice is soft, barely above a whisper.

She blinks and sucks in a breath, slowly turning her head to look at me. Her lips tremble as she stares up at me. "You." Her voice cracks and she squeezes her eyes shut as tears continue to flow. My heart stutters remembering when I rescued her all those months ago, and she looked up at me with fear, whispering that same word.

Was she having a nightmare about that night? Was she remembering what happened to her in that hellhole?

That's the one thing I hope she never remembers. The one thing she'll never have to relive.

I run my thumb below her eye, wiping her tears. She's clutching my hand so tight it aches, but I'll let her break my hand if it brings her any semblance of comfort.

"You're not going to lick my tears?" she whispers.

I frown as a heaviness settles in my stomach, and my chest grows tight at her words. "Not tonight," I answer, wishing I could go back and change everything about those first few months. I want to pull her into my arms and offer her comfort, but I hesitate, not sure if she would accept it right now. I run my fingers through her hair and she doesn't flinch, so I pull her more firmly against me, trying to offer her as much body heat as possible. Removing my fingers from her hair, I reach down and pull the blanket over her. She grabs it and pulls it up to her chin, her lips trembling slightly. Her eyes wander, taking in the room, making sure she's really in bed with me. She takes a deep breath and rolls over onto her side facing me. I resume running my fingers through her hair as we stare at each other.

"Did you have a bad dream? Or was it a memory?" I ask. Her hand snakes out from under the blanket and she grips my forearm, her fingers still as cold as ice.

"They kept me in panties and a tank top all the time." Her voice cracks. I force my face to remain neutral and I don't speak because if I do, I might lose it. "I was always freezing. They'd remember I was there every week or so and take me outside, hose me down, and chain me back up."

I grit my teeth so hard I'm sure they'll break as I begin to plan the torture of whoever these people are. I will draw out their death for so long they'll be begging me to end it. She closes her eyes again and shakes her head.

"Why did I have to remember that?" Her voice is so low I have to piece together what she said.

I push her hair behind her ear. "I don't know, love. If I could take it all away, I would."

Her mouth tips up into a sad smile. "I know you would. That's why I love you." Her eyes close for a few seconds.

"I love you too," I reply, thankful she still feels that way about me after the past two months. She runs her hand from my shoulder, down my bicep, to my forearm, leaving goosebumps along the way. She opens her eyes slowly, like she's having a hard time keeping them open, her breathing already growing heavy.

"You always make me feel safe," she murmurs.

I lean forward and kiss her on the forehead. "Go back to sleep, love. I'll keep the nightmares away." I pull her close to me, wrapping my arms around her. Her breathing evens out as she drifts off.

"You always come for me," she whispers against my chest as she settles deeper into my embrace, finally falling back to sleep.

"And I will always find you, love," I whisper against her hair. Remembering my promise to her all those years ago when I found her the first time.

"You and McKenzie will be expected to come earlier in the day to see everything," Gil says. I take a deep breath, keeping my irritation at bay. I wonder if Kenz knows the next auction is coming up. It's still a couple of weeks out, but preparations are already being made. "I know this probably isn't the best time for you, but we have to keep up appearances, and you're next on the roster."

"We'll be there," I respond. Almost every council member that was there when I first started attending auctions all those years ago is out. I've slowly pushed them out. There are a few left, including Gil. I knew when I first met him he was different. I found out he joined because his wife's sister had been sold against her will. Unfortunately, they weren't able to rescue her. But they have bought several girls throughout the years to help them get out of an impossible situation.

He supports my idea of having the auction being something that's voluntary. Those who want to auction themselves off can fill out an application and put in their wants for a buyer. They can choose what kind of relationship they have with the person they buy. Whether it's sexual, dating only, or friendship. The choice is theirs.

Having the first daughter sold as some ritual to become a council member is barbaric. Unless she wants to be sold. My first goal was to remove Marcus from the council. I was able to do that within the first year after I bought Kenz. He still comes to auctions, but he doesn't have any power to make decisions. My second goal was removing the senator that bought Anna.

It proved difficult when he did become the vice president, but he had a heart attack and died while he was in office. Sometimes I wonder if Rex somehow found a way to cause that. He was on a long vacation when it happened. I know he was going to look for Anna because he found out who bought her. He didn't find her, but the man wound up dead. Not too long after that, his wife was in a fatal car accident. I haven't asked any questions and Rex hasn't offered any details.

Gil gives me some more details that I barely listen to as I think back to last night. I barely slept after Kenz woke up with that nightmare. I watched her sleep the rest of the night, making sure she was safe. Even in her dreams.

"There's been some murmuring about not having masks anymore," Gil says, bringing my attention back to the conversation.

"By who?" I ask. When I first started attending auctions, I wasn't fond of the masks, but now I like the anonymity of it. It adds to the fun Kenz and I have during the auction. It's like our own brand of foreplay.

"No one in particular, but apparently it's been talked about a few times and some have overheard."

I hum. "We can discuss it in our next council meeting." He agrees and we hang up.

Standing, I leave my office and walk to the library. I decided to work from home today so I can keep an eye on McKenzie after the memory she had last night. I reminded her at lunch that it would be a good idea to schedule an appointment with Dr. Pearl. They didn't get a chance to meet before she left.

She didn't disagree, but she didn't agree either. She was quiet and withdrawn. Understandably. Pushing the door open, my gaze immediately goes to her swing, but she's not there. Walking deeper into the library, I stop at the end of a bookshelf in the middle of the room and lean against it as I watch her.

She's sitting at the window seat, her knees pulled up to her chest and her forehead resting against the window. A book lays open at her feet. She takes a deep breath and leans back slightly to stare down at her book.

"Kenz?" I call out to her, trying not to startle her. She turns slightly and looks at me over her shoulder. "You hungry? I was going to eat lunch."

She nods and stands, walking to me. She doesn't speak, just looks up at me, waiting for me to lead the way. I keep my face a neutral mask even though I'm worried about her. She's acting like she did when I got her back. Well, not exactly like that. At least this time she's not flinching when I try to touch her.

I wrap my arm around her shoulders as we walk to the kitchen. Phillip is there plating the food he made for us. He gives us both a smile in greeting, his eyes crinkling slightly as he studies McKenzie. He looks at me, then back to her before turning back around.

Normally McKenzie greets Phillip and Clara. She loves them both, but today she hasn't spoken much. Anna walks into the kitchen with a plate. It looks like she's already eaten. Over the past several months, I've noticed Anna prefers to be alone. She's a lot different from the Anna I knew in high school.

Dr. Chamberland and Dr. Pearl both said that's normal after the trauma she experienced. But it's been a while, and I was hoping she'd feel more comfortable around us. The only people she's comfortable with are Rex and Kenz. She's polite to Phillip and Clara, but they haven't formed friendships like Kenz has with them.

Once she was fully recovered, she also asked if she could stop seeing Dr. Chamberland. I didn't question it even though I wanted to ask her why, because she still sees Dr. Pearl occasionally.

"Kenz?" Anna says. Kenz looks up and smiles slightly at Anna, but the smile doesn't reach her eyes. Anna crosses the kitchen and stops in front of Kenz as I go to the island and sit down. I watch them to see if maybe Kenz will brighten up slightly, but she doesn't. "Are you okay?" Anna asks.

Kenz blinks her eyes rapidly and I can tell from the glossy look in them she's trying her best not to cry. I wonder if it's because she remembered all those years ago when I licked her tears away and told her if I lick it, it's mine. She rarely cried in front of me for that reason, and I hated myself every day because of it.

McKenzie nods and does her best to give a decent smile, but anyone who knows her can tell it's fake.

"You're not okay," Anna says.

"I don't want to talk about it," McKenzie finally says.

Anna stares at her a moment longer before nodding. "I'm here if you need me." She hugs her quickly like she knows if she holds on for too long, it will be the straw that breaks Kenz.

Kenz doesn't reply as Anna turns and walks back to the hallway that leads to her room. She sits next to me and rubs her hands down her thighs as she waits for her food. Phillip places plates in front of us with turkey club sandwiches and some sweet potato fries, then leaves the kitchen. I take a bite from my sandwich and chew, thinking about what I can say or do to help bring Kenz out of this fog she's in.

"I think I owe you an answer to a question," I say as she picks at her sandwich. She scowls slightly and doesn't respond. I lean toward her and push her hair behind her ear. She turns slightly to look at me. There are storm clouds in her eyes.

"I don't have any questions today," she murmurs before turning back to her plate.

"I fucked up last night," I admit.

She huffs as she puts a fry in her mouth. "I didn't realize you could admit such a thing."

"Kenz—"

"Drop it. Please."

I stare at her profile for several seconds before exhaling deeply and picking up my sandwich. I'll drop it for now, but once I give her a few days to process whatever memory she had. Then I'm getting answers.

Chapter 12

McKenzie

I look up from my book and watch Phoenix as he works. Since the memory I had a few days ago, he's been hovering. He hasn't gone to his office in the city, instead he's been working here. Today he's keeping me company in the library instead of working from his office across the hall. Maybe he's nervous after last time. That I'll leave again and this time not come back. But I made the decision when I came back that I wouldn't be leaving again. Ever.

The memory I had the other night showed me who was behind taking me the first and second time. It wasn't my father. Part of me is angry at Phoenix for this grudge he has against my father, but I understand. The one person he's wanted to please the most has manipulated him his whole life.

I've been contemplating these past few days on how to handle this new information. Do I tell him or not? I'm demanding honesty from him; I should do the same in return. Will he believe me? I have this sinking feeling it's going to be difficult for him to give up a lifetime of belief.

His eyes find mine over his laptop like he could feel my eyes on him. One side of his mouth tips up as I climb off the swing and walk toward him. I've missed his touch, his kiss, the feel of his skin beneath my hands. His eyes travel down my body, his gaze landing on the anklet I found the day I came back and haven't taken off since.

I'm wearing a light blue dress that stops right above my knees. I have a lot of dresses that are comfortable and make me feel beautiful and sexy. And the way Nix looks at me in them makes me want to wear them every day. I stop in front of him and he places his laptop on the end table next to the sofa.

"What are you working on?" I ask him. He leans back, spreading his legs wider so I can step closer. He leans his head back against the sofa pillows as he stares up at me. His tattooed hands clench against his thighs before he relaxes them.

"There's a fight this weekend. I was reading the stats of each fighter," he answers. My eyes widen in surprise. I forgot about the fights. He mentioned it months ago, but nothing since. I lean forward and place my knee between his legs on the sofa. His eyes drop to the cleavage on display, my lips, then back to my eyes.

I lick my lips as I inhale deeply. "Will you take me?" He smirks, his hands rubbing up and down his thighs, like he's trying not to reach out and touch me. I wish he'd give in.

"Yes."

He has respected the boundaries I've put up. But I want him. I want him to distract me. To remind me why we're so good together. I want *him*. I straddle him and his smirk turns into a full-blown grin.

His hands rub up my thighs, to my hips, and grip my ass as he pulls me into him.

"I was wondering..." I trail off, losing some of the nerve I had. *What if he turns me down?* His grip on my ass tightens as he rocks me against him again. His hardness presses against me and I have to bite the inside of my cheek to stop myself from moaning.

"You were wondering?" he prods.

I run my hands along his shoulders, his black T-shirt stretched tight along his chest and biceps. *He's so sexy.* "I was wondering, did you ever have fantasies of doing things in the library at Brighton?" I swallow. "With me?"

His muscles tighten beneath my hands and I swear I feel his cock twitch against me. He sits up, bringing his chest against mine, his hands rubbing up my back. One hand cups the back of my head and the other comes around to hold my throat loosely.

"I did."

My breathing increases as he confirms what I think I may have already known. "Tell me," I whisper, scared to break the spell.

His hand tightens slightly around my throat. "One fantasy was me crawling under one of the tables and making you come on my tongue as you read one of your books. Reminding you if you made one sound I wouldn't let you come." He arches an eyebrow as I rock against him. "We were in a library after all." I huff a laugh.

He licks his lips as his eyes fall to mine, but he still doesn't lean forward to kiss me. "Another fantasy was pulling you back into the stacks and fucking you against one of the bookshelves. Kissing you breathless to silence our moans as you came all over my cock."

I close my eyes and tilt my head back, imagining doing that with him. He could have done anything to me and I would have let him. Even now, I'd let him. He runs his hand through my hair, down my back, and back to my ass, pulling me against him again. This time he rocks into me and I swear I feel his piercing through his sweats and my panties.

He finally leans forward and kisses me just below my ear, the hand that was around my throat drifting down to cup my breast, his thumb circling my nipple. "You always thought the only interesting thing about you was your hair," he murmurs against my neck. I tilt my head, giving him better access as he sucks the skin between his lips and teeth.

"I love your hair, but I always felt like your beautiful brown eyes could see the depths of my soul. Your slender throat was made to be marked by me and me alone. Your long legs were meant to be wrapped around me as I thrust into you. Your strength and heart called out to my black heart and made it beat again."

I lean back and stare at him. His ice-blue eyes connect with mine and I see the truth there. Phoenix means every word. He's not the kind of man that says things he doesn't mean. He's never painted this picture of himself as the hero. No. He's the villain and I know without a shadow of a doubt he would tear this world apart to find me. The decision I've been playing with the past few days clicks into place.

I lean forward and take his mouth with mine. I need him more than the air I breathe. He sucks my bottom lip into his mouth and I moan. The sound breaks whatever leash he had on himself. His hands grip the back of my thighs and he lifts me, flipping me onto my back on the sofa and settling between my legs.

His lips trail down my neck to my cleavage. He runs his tongue along the seam of my dress. "I've missed you so fucking much," he murmurs against my skin, his finger hooking under the strap of my dress and pulling it down my arm. I'm on fire, but goosebumps break out along my skin. I open my mouth to tell him I missed him too, but he starts talking again before I can.

"I'm sorry." He leans up to stare down at me, pushing my hair behind my ear. "I'm sorry for how I acted when I first bought you. I'm sorry I forced you to marry me. I'm sorry for being a total asshole those first six months. I was trying my best to keep you at arm's length, thinking I was protecting you."

He leans down, kissing me again, his tongue sliding against mine. My legs are still wrapped around his waist. I leverage myself so I can rub against him. He groans into my mouth, breaking the kiss he breathes hard against my mouth as he rubs his covered cock against me. I clutch at his back, fisting his T-shirt, then push it up.

He leans back and yanks it over his head. I rub my hands along his heated skin, his muscles flexing beneath my hands. We stare at each other for a long moment, my mouth tips up into a small smile.

"We can protect each other from now on," I tell him. He returns my smile, his thumb trailing from my forehead, to my cheek, and to my ear, his hand cupping the side of my neck. I lean up and capture his bottom lip with my teeth, releasing it slowly. The blue of his eyes is barely visible, as desire shines brightly down at me. "Now, I know this isn't Brighton, but it is a library. So.." I lift one shoulder and smile at him.

I don't need to give him any further encouragement. He stands, pulling me with him, and walks to one of the bookshelves that has a ladder. He places me on the ladder and makes sure I'm steady before he drops to his knees. His hands snake under my dress and pulls my panties down my legs. I step out of them carefully so I don't fall off the ladder.

Nix wraps one of my legs over his shoulder and looks up to wink at me, then his head is beneath my dress. I grab it and hold it against me so I can watch him. My stomach quivers in anticipation as he looks at my pussy for a brief moment before closing his eyes and licking me.

My head falls back against one of the steps on the ladder as I get lost in the feeling of the swipes of his tongue. I grip his hair, moaning as he hitches my leg higher so he can thrust his tongue inside me. He stops immediately. My eyes pop open and I look down at him.

He gives me a wicked grin. "You have to be quiet, love. We're in a library." He brings his middle finger up and circles it around my clit. I bite my lip, trying to stop myself from crying out.

"I can't." The words come out in a groan as he slides his fingers through my folds.

"Then I'll have to stop."

I suck in a breath and glare down at him. He arches an eyebrow in response, waiting for me to agree. I nod once and he unleashes on me entirely. He sucks my clit into his mouth as two fingers enter me, crooking them just so. I see stars with how tight my eyes are closed.

I clutch his hair and pull my lips between my teeth so I don't let any sound escape. My abdomen quivers from the onslaught.

Wanting to ride his face, I try to buck against him, but it's impossible in this position. He rakes his teeth over me and I slam my hand over my mouth as I come so hard he has to wrap his arm around my waist to stop me from crumbling to the floor.

He stands to his feet, not giving me time to recover as he quickly pushes his sweats down. I eye his cock, my eyes feasting on his piercing. Pulling my bottom lip between my teeth, I remember what it felt like in my mouth.

He chuckles as he wraps his hand around his cock and swipes the head against my pussy, giving me a chance to feel his piercing. "Later you're going to ride my face while you suck my cock, but right now I need to be inside you." Our eyes collide as he lines himself up with me and slowly sinks into me.

I wrap one leg around his waist and watch as his mouth drops open and his eyes become half hooded. "Fuck, you feel so good," he says as he bottoms out. He leans his forehead against mine as he rocks into me slowly. "I'll never get enough of you. Never," he whispers before he pulls almost all the way out of me, his cock teasing my entrance, and thrusts back into me.

I gasp, but have enough self control to stop myself from moaning. A growl rumbles in his chest, but he doesn't completely release it as he keeps a steady pace within me. My head falls forward into the crook of his neck as I meet each of his thrusts. His thrusts are hard and oh so good. He wraps his hands around the back of my thighs, lifting me so my ass is resting on the rung of the ladder.

I cling to him as he adjusts me just enough that he is rubbing against my g-spot with every thrust.

"Oh god," I whisper as I allow him to take over. His arms are shaking, the muscles in his neck and arms taut. I clutch at his shoulders as I eye what I consider my spot. My spot to mark him. Leaning forward, I latch onto the skin just below his ear.

He grunts. "Fuck, Kenz," he moans.

I release his skin slightly and nip at his earlobe. "Shush. We're in a library."

He chuckles as I take his skin between my lips again. I try to focus on marking him, but his thrusts are becoming more pronounced and I know I'm going to fall off the edge I'm on. His chest quivers against mine as he makes his thrusts more shallow, zeroing in on my spot. My nails rake down his back as he rocks into me over and over again, his piercing touching that bundle of nerves.

I clamp my mouth shut and push my face into his neck as I come. It's so good. He's the only person who will ever make me feel this way. After a few seconds, he begins to lift me up and down on his cock. He leans back slightly, watching as he pounds into me over and over again.

"So. Fucking. Hot." He enunciates each word with a thrust, then he's throwing his head back and coming inside me. Another growl rumbles through his chest, but other than that, he doesn't make a sound. He slowly releases my legs, making sure my feet are on the ground as he pulls back.

Immediately I feel empty and want him again, but my legs are shaking so badly, I'm not sure I could do it again. He tucks himself back in his sweats and places his arm under my legs and the other under my neck, cradling me as he walks back to the couch.

He sits and settles me in his lap. Wrapping my arms around his neck, I lay my head on his shoulder. He rubs lazy circles along my back as we both catch our breath.

"Nix?" I whisper. He hums in response. "Let's not keep things from each other anymore. I know I still have memories that will come back. Hopefully. But from this day forward, let's be honest with each other."

He pushes me back slightly to look at me. His eyes change to different shades of blue as he thinks it over. It's amazing to watch and know when he comes to a decision. He nods. "Okay."

I take a deep breath. "There's something I have to tell you."

Chapter 13

Phoenix

I stare at Kenz, waiting for her to tell me what she needs to say. My stomach tightens as I wait. The strap of her dress falls off her shoulder, so I fix it, trying to keep my mind and hands busy. I didn't even undress her. But taking her against the ladder in the library has been a fantasy of mine for years. Even when we finally decided to not stay away from each other, it wasn't something we ever did. The main place we played our fantasies was at the auctions. That's where we played.

When I got Kenz back the first time, she was different. She was more assertive but aloof. Like she was trying her hardest to not let her walls completely down. And I never tried too hard to make them come down. We were never completely ourselves with one another. Maybe now we can be.

So, her asking if we can be completely honest with each other; I mean it when I say yes. She pulls her bottom lip between her teeth and takes another deep breath as she tries to climb off my lap, but I won't let her. She settles and leans her back against the arm of the chair, her legs draped over my lap. I rub the palm of my hand along her silky soft skin as I give her time to figure out what she wants to say.

"I know who took me the first time," she admits. My hand stills on her leg for a second before I resume its trek up her shin to her knee.

"I thought you did."

She tilts her head at me. "You did?"

I nod. "I can tell when you're lying. When I got you back the first time I asked you and you told me the same thing you did last week. They put something over your head before you got a look at them." She opens her mouth to say something, but I hold my finger up, telling her to wait. "But both times you couldn't look me in the eye when you said it."

"Why didn't you push me on it?"

I look away from her and stare out the window. "I should have. Because I'm pretty sure the person who took you the first time is the same person who took you the second time and I could have stopped it if I had known. I didn't push you on it last week because I decided to give you some time, but I wasn't going to let it go like I did before. I was going to ask you again, and if you refused to tell me, I wasn't going to let you leave the house until you did." I look back at her and she frowns.

"I should have told you back then. I wish I knew why I didn't tell you, but I still can't remember everything after I was taken. I've gotten small memories back, but that's it." She looks down at her lap as she interlaces her fingers. "So, you know when I lie to you."

It's a statement, but I nod anyway. She lifts her head and looks me in the eye. "It was your mother who took me."

Every muscle in my body locks into place as her words ricochet in my mind. "My mother?" My words are low, but she nods. That was the last person I expected her to say. I gently push her off my lap and sit forward, leaning my elbows on my knees as those words repeat in my mind over and over.

She sits next to me; her knuckles turn white from how hard she's clinching the sofa by her thighs. I feel her eyes on me, but I don't look at her. I stare down at a spot on the carpet, trying to remember the last time I saw my mother. I was fourteen, and it was Christmas time. I went home for the holiday break and I remember thinking things were strained at home.

My parents barely spoke to each other and my mother barely spoke to me. My dad said it was because she was struggling with depression, but deep in my gut, I knew something wasn't right. But being the self-centered teen I was, I blew it off. I run through the summer before high school, how we searched everywhere for her.

My dad and mom started going to auctions; it had been my mom's idea, and he agreed. They had planned on going to the auction in the spring that year, but my dad didn't want to because it was going to be my first weekend home. Mom went anyway, and it was the last time he saw her.

"Nix?" Kenz whispers my name, but I don't respond. *This can't be true. It has to be someone else. She's never met my mother.*

"It had to be someone else saying it was my mother," I finally say. She's quiet for a long moment.

"Maybe. I've never met your mother, but..." She trails off and I finally lift my head to look at her. Her lips press together in a slight grimace.

"But what?" I ask. She wrinkles her nose and tries to smile at me, but it wavers.

"She told me to tell you she wasn't taken. She left."

I curl my hands into fists, my heart beating so loud I can hear it in my ears. I snatch the T-shirt I threw on the ground earlier and pull it over my head. Standing, I place my hands on top of my head. Kenz stands and rubs her hands down her dress. I'm sure my cum is dripping out of her now, but I can't bring myself to walk her upstairs and clean her up.

"Nix—"

"Don't," I snap. She closes her mouth and runs her hand through her hair, her fingers shaking slightly. "I need some time alone." I turn on my heel and walk out of the library. Placing my hands in my pockets, I grimace when I touch McKenzie's panties I pocketed earlier.

Walking into the kitchen, Phillip greets me. I give him a half-hearted smile and walk outside. I head toward the hydrangea garden McKenzie requested when we first started building here. I hired a landscaper and didn't spare any expense. After I got her back, I was determined to move us out of our house in the city to somewhere that was more secluded.

I met Larry one night at one of my bars. He got so drunk instead of me calling him an Uber, I had Rex drive him home. I rode along to make sure he was okay. On the way, he told me about how he lost his wife five years earlier and that day would have been their fortieth anniversary. We developed a relationship over the next few months, and he told me he owned almost two hundred acres of land.

Developers had been hounding him to sell so they could turn it into lake houses, but he liked his privacy and the land had been in his family for three generations. But it was too much for him and he didn't have any children. He asked me if I would buy it and let him stay in his house. He didn't know what I did, but he knew I had contacts that would leave him alone if I bought it. So, I bought the land for almost a million dollars.

We did updates on his house while we built our house. I bought the land while I was still looking for McKenzie after she was taken the first time. Sitting on one of the benches in the middle of the garden, I watch the bees and butterflies as they fly around. I knew Kenz wasn't comfortable in my house in the city from the comments she made and I wanted her to be comfortable. I wanted her to have a home that she helped design and decorate.

I was in my office downtown when all hell broke loose. Rex and a few of the security guys we had back then were notified something had been dropped off in front of the building. I was going to go down and see what it was, but Rex made me stay in my office until they figured out what it was. It wound up being McKenzie. She had been tied up, put in a brown rucksack, and knocked out with some kind of drug.

We scanned every surveillance footage around the area available to us and no one could tell who it was that dropped her off. It looked like a man. It definitely wasn't a woman. This whole time I thought McKenzie's father took my mother, and I thought he took McKenzie.

Grabbing my cell phone out of my pocket, I pull up my father in my contacts.

He answers on the third ring. "Hello?"

"I need you to meet me downtown in thirty minutes."

"Son—"

"I don't want to hear any of your fucking excuses. Be there."

Chapter 14

McKenzie

I want to go after Phoenix, but I know the bomb I just dropped on him isn't something he was expecting. So, I'll give him space. For now. After sitting in the library for another thirty minutes, I decide to go take a shower. Maybe when I get out, he'll be ready to talk. I stop by the kitchen when I hear Phillip and Clara's voice. They both glance up, smiling at me.

"Miss Kenzie, how are you?" Phillip asks as he places a glass dish in the oven. It looks like some kind of casserole. I haven't baked anything since I've been back. Maybe after I take a shower, I'll make Phoenix some cookies.

"I'm okay. Have you seen Phoenix?" I ask. He and Clara share a look.

"We saw him briefly. He went outside for a little while, but he and Rex just left to go to his office in the city," Clara answers.

"Oh." My stomach drops. *He didn't tell me. What does that mean?* I pull my bottom lip between my teeth before forcing myself to shake it off. "Well, how are you two?" I ask them. I haven't talked to either of them much since I've been back. I've been so preoccupied with deciding on telling Phoenix or not I was stuck in my own world.

Clara walks over and offers me a smile. "We're doing fine."

Phillip turns and looks at me as he leans against the counter. "I sure miss you in the kitchen with me."

"I was just thinking that. Nix is having a bit of a bad day, so I thought after I take a shower I'd make some cookies." Clara and Phillip both nod in agreement. I wave at them and make my way up to our bedroom. *I hope he makes it home in time for dinner.*

I pull the last batch of chocolate chip cookies out of the oven. I went a little crazy and made almost a hundred cookies. Maybe Phoenix can take me to Larry's house and I can drop some off for him, too. I clean up my mess as Phillip puts some homemade biscuits in the oven.

"Once these are done, dinner will be ready," Phillip says. Phoenix isn't home yet and I haven't heard from him all day. I tried to call him earlier, but it went straight to his voicemail.

What if he doesn't believe me? What if he doesn't come home? What if he tells me to go back to Larry's?

I swallow a few times until the lump finally goes away. I finish cleaning when the timer for the biscuits goes off. I want to cry, but I inhale deeply and force myself to stop thinking about it.

"I'll go get Anna," I murmur.

I glance down at myself. I'm wearing a long black maxi dress. I thought it looked good with my silver hair and red lips. I wanted to look nice for Phoenix. Knocking on Anna's door, I open it when she tells me to come in.

She looks up from the book she's been reading and smiles at me. "You look pretty," she says. I lift one side of my mouth, trying to smile. At least she noticed. I've noticed she rarely leaves her room and I don't like it. I did the same thing when I first got here, but after a while I couldn't stand it anymore.

But she doesn't seem to want to leave. It's not healthy. "Thank you." I gesture behind me. "Dinner is ready. It smells really good."

She closes her book and sets it on the table next to her chair. "Oh, I'll eat in here."

I interlace my fingers together in front of me as I study her. "No. You'll eat in the kitchen with me." I'm being firm, but I think she needs it. She needs help to get out of this bubble she's created for herself.

She blinks several times before leaning back in her chair. She runs her hand down the arm of the chair and glances outside. "Could we eat in the breakfast nook instead?" she asks.

I tilt my head at her, trying to hear what she's saying without saying it. "Why?"

She swallows and looks down at her lap. "The kitchen is so big," she whispers. I walk to her and kneel down in front of her, grasping her hands.

"Oh, Anna." I don't know what to say. "You don't like big spaces?" I ask.

She clings to my hands and squeezes her eyes shut. "There's all those windows, then the different hallways that lead to the kitchen, and the living room. There's so many spaces for someone to come in and me not see them." A blush creeps up her neck and she covers her face with her hands.

I lean forward and wrap my arms around her waist, holding her tight in a hug. She returns my embrace, her cheek on top of my head. "But you were in the living room that night Phoenix and I came home. You even asked to go out with us."

She shrugs. "I have good days and I have bad days. That was a good day. And as soon as I said that, I regretted it," she admits.

I lean back and sigh. "I hate the people that did this to you. I'm going to find them and kill them."

She sniffs. "Can I help you?"

I chuckle. "Definitely. We'll kill them, then have a party." A tear slips out of her eye and I wipe it away with my thumb. "Do you remember who took you?" I ask her.

She leans back, her hands clutch at the arms of the chair. I stand and sit in the other chair, giving her space. "I'm pretty sure Regina had something to do with it."

I try to think if she's ever mentioned Regina before, but can't think of anyone. "Who's that?"

"She was the wife of Steve, the man who bought me. But I'm not entirely sure." She takes a deep breath and brings her thumb up to her mouth, biting on the nail. She leans forward. "I think Dr.

Chamberland was there," she whispers. Adrenaline floods my nerves so fast my hands and fingers tingle. "The dean from Brighton was there and some woman with eyes that remind me of Phoenix."

My ears ring as I think back to what Phoenix told me about the dean wanting to buy me and how he had bought other girls. *Did he want to buy Anna too, but lost her as well?* And Dr. Chamberland. I didn't tell Phoenix about that memory that had returned.

"Did..." I trail off as I try to shuffle through the rapid thoughts going through my mind. "Did they hurt you?"

Anna pulls her legs up into the chair and wraps her arms around them. "The dean... he did things to me." Anna's fingers turn white because of how hard she's clutching her legs. "I always felt uneasy around him at Brighton." Her voice catches and she closes her eyes for a few moments. A tightness forms in my chest. I bring my hand up to rub at it, hoping it will go away, but it only gets worse.

"Dr. Chamberland never touched me and he always had a mask on, so at first I didn't recognize him when I got here. But one day he said something that reminded me of being in that container and I knew it was him. I told Rex I didn't want to see him again." She sucks in a breath.

I bring a hand up, covering my open mouth as she continues.

"The woman. She never hurt me, but she would sometimes watch while the dean did things to me. And she loved to taunt me and tell me how much she was going to sell me for. But she never did. She kept me in that container. They'd move me every few weeks to a different container like they were trying to cover their tracks, but

I know other girls were put in containers and sent away on ships. I could hear them crying."

A sob escapes Anna, and it's taking all I have to keep it together. We sit quietly for several minutes. I don't know what to say. My mind has gone completely blank. All I can think is how much I want to make these people suffer. I remembered Dr. Chamberland the other night. After they had hosed me off and chained me back to the bed, he was talking to Nix's mom and told her he was going to adjust the dosage of whatever drug they were giving me.

Whatever it was would affect my memory and I wouldn't remember any of what they did to me. He told her it was time to begin thinking about this because Phoenix was close to finding me. Dr. Chamberland is the reason I can't remember. He's probably also the security breach. Phoenix fired all his security guys, and it was Dr. Chamberland the whole time.

"One night," Anna continues. "A man opened the container. I could tell he wasn't expecting to see me. I don't remember what he looked like. I don't think I ever saw his face; it was so dark. He closed the door, but came back a little later with some food and water. The next day, Rex and Phoenix showed up and rescued me."

I blink as I digest what Anna told me. "Why didn't you ever tell Rex?"

She wipes at her face and I realize she's wiping her tears away. "I wanted to. There were a few times I almost did, but I felt like he didn't want to hear what happened to me. Since I've been back, the majority of conversations have been surface level. Anytime it would begin to get deeper, he runs off to do some kind of errand." She shrugs and slowly drops her legs back to the floor. "I finally stopped trying."

I lean forward in my chair and rest my hand on top of hers. "I'm so sorry."

"You don't have to say that. You've been through your own horrors." She squeezes my hand and offers me a sad smile.

"I had some memories return a few days ago." She tilts her head at me as she waits for me to continue. "The woman with the eyes that look like Phoenix." I take a deep breath. "That's Phoenix's mother. And I remember Dr. Chamberland drugging me so I'd lose my memory." Anna's hands cover her mouth and her eyes flick over my shoulder.

"What the fuck?"

Chapter 15

Phoenix

I pace back and forth in my office downtown. My phone rings, and McKenzie's name pops up. I'm about to swipe to answer it, but my father walks in at that moment.

It's strange that I look more like my mom than my dad, but the older I get, the more I see the resemblance to him. His hair is sandy brown, he has a mustache and beard, and he has green eyes. I have a similar build to him, but that's about it.

He walks in like he has better things to do than be here, and it pisses me off. I have felt he's been hiding something from me for years now and after what McKenzie told me, I'm wondering what it is.

"What's so important, son?" He doesn't sit, instead he stands by the door, hands in his pockets, like he's already ready to leave. I gave Rex instructions to stand outside the door and not let him leave until I give the okay.

Standing in front of my desk I lean back against it, crossing my arms across my chest acting like I don't have a care in the world when that is the furthest thing from the truth. "Where's mom?" I ask.

His eyes widen slightly, the only show of surprise he shows. He tilts his head and arches an eyebrow. "How should I know? We've been searching for her for eleven years."

I lower my head and narrow my eyes at him. *If this man has been lying to me all these years, I'm going to beat the shit out of him.* "Let's look back over the past eleven years," I say. He gestures to me with his hand as if saying *go on then*. I grind my teeth, but continue.

"Mom wanted you to go to an auction with her in the early summer, but you didn't want to go because I would be home that weekend." I watch him and wait.

"Yes," he says, sounding annoyed.

"And you just let her go?" I ask. I've never asked him that outright, but I've always wanted to know how that conversation went. I know if McKenzie told me she wanted to go to an auction without me, it wouldn't happen.

"You know how your mother is." *Is* not *was*. "She threw a tantrum when I told her we weren't going to go that weekend. She was finally beginning to act like herself again, so I told her to go."

"Why did she have to go? Why couldn't she miss one?"

"It was her auction. She never missed any."

The hair on the back of my neck stands on end as I tilt my head at him. "Her auction?"

Dad blinks rapidly as he sucks in a sharp breath. "I…uh…" He exhales and pulls his hands out of his pockets.

"What the fuck, dad?" I ball my hands into fists, forcing myself to stay where I'm at.

He runs his hand down his face. "She didn't want to tell you until you graduated; then everything happened." He stumbles over his words, saying them as quickly as possible. "I didn't want to tell you after that."

I huff. "If it was her auction, how the hell would she have been sold at it?"

He grimaces and pinches the bridge of his nose. "Son," he murmurs.

I step forward until I'm only a couple of feet away from him. "Was she sold?" I say through my teeth.

He shakes his head. "No." I pull my hand back and punch him in the face. He grabs his nose and falls back against the door. I want to punch him again, but I walk away. Shaking my hand at the slight sting, I walk to the window and look over the river. Rex comes bursting in, but I keep my back to him and my dad.

"Sir?" Rex says.

I look at him over my shoulder then glance at my father who's taken a handkerchief, *a fucking handkerchief*, out of his pocket and put it against his nose, trying to stop the bleeding.

"Fucking hell. I think you broke my nose." His voice is muffled as he glares at me.

I shrug. "Be glad you're still alive." I look back at Rex. "We're okay for now, but be prepared to get rid of a body, just in case." I eye my father again and he snorts, then moans. Rex turns and leaves, closing the door behind him.

"I need to go to the doctor." I roll my eyes. *I'll get Dr. Chamberland to check him out in a little while.*

"Stop being a little bitch. You're not going anywhere until you tell me everything." I walk to the chair behind my desk and sit staring at him until he finally sits in the chair on the other side.

"She wasn't sold or taken. She left."

My father talked for almost an hour, telling me everything. Things I had no idea about. McKenzie's father never started the auctions. The auctions started a year after Brighton Academy was founded. It was used as a breeding ground to raise the next world leaders and sell off their pretty little daughters.

I stop at one of my bars on River Street and order a bourbon. Rex walks in a few minutes later. He made sure my father got medical attention for his nose since I couldn't get in touch with Dr. Chamberland. Any other day I'd be tracking him down, but today he's the least of my concerns.

Rex leans his back against the bar, keeping his eye on the exit. Another one of his security, Jason, stands at the door. "You punched your father." He says it like it's an everyday occurrence.

I down my drink then raise it to the bartender, letting her know I want another. "He's lucky that's all I did." I run my hand along my jaw and shake my head. "He's lied to me for years." The knot that's been forming in my stomach gets tighter. The bartender gives me another drink and I down it too, the warmth of the liquor settling in my stomach.

Rex doesn't say anything. I rarely drink to the point of getting drunk, but I might do just that tonight and Rex would let me. He's the only man I trust with my life. I met him a couple of months before I bought McKenzie. I was working my way up through the ranks of my father's men. One of them got pissed and tried to kill me after one of the fights. Rex killed him instead. I hired him as my security on the spot.

Rex was there looking for Anna or a lead to find out where she was. When he told me about what happened to her, our mission became the same. To take these assholes down. I had no idea my mother was the main asshole. I give Rex a sideways glance, wondering how he's going to react when I tell him. I lift my glass to the bartender again and exhale.

"I've been chasing after the wrong person all these years," I finally say. Rex glances at me and waits. "Marcus Knight never took my mother or sold her at an auction."

Rex stills. He shares a look with Jason and turns to face me, giving me his full attention. "What does that mean?"

The bartender brings me another drink, and instead of downing it, this time I hold it between my hands. "My mother's family started the auctions a year after Brighton was founded. The majority of the girls in the first graduating class were sold. The top twelve girls that were sold for the most, their fathers were considered the founding fathers of the Society and were sworn in as council members."

Rex's eyebrows furrow, and he tenses as he processes my words. When he doesn't speak, I continue. "It was their way of having a way to influence members to do their bidding. They'd hang it over government officials' heads if they needed them to look the other way or pass a bill or law that was in their favor. They'd hang it over those who did illegal business as well, telling them they'd out them and disrupt their entire world."

I down my drink one more time and cut myself off. I have to be coherent when I get home. I know McKenzie is probably worried.

"What are you going to do?" Rex asks. I haven't told him about what McKenzie told me earlier today. I wanted to deny it, but I knew she wasn't lying. Either it was really true or she believed it was true. Until the conversation I had with my father, I wasn't sure if the memory she had was distorted. Now I know it wasn't.

"I'm going to find my mother and I'm going to let Kenz kill her."

The smell of chocolate and brown sugar hits me the moment I step inside the house. All the worry and unease I've felt all afternoon disappears. Even though McKenzie and I never said I love you before I got her back this last time, there were ways we showed each other. Her way was making me chocolate chip cookies.

I confessed to her once after she made them that they made our house feel like a home. Growing up, I always wanted a mom that did normal mom things. Like bake chocolate chip cookies or come watch my lacrosse games. She never did those things, so I tried and tried to do anything and everything I could to please her, to make her love me, but it never worked.

I swallow and push those thoughts aside. The signs have been there all along, and I chose to ignore them. Walking into the kitchen expecting to see McKenzie, I frown when she's not there. Phillip turns to me and offers me a smile that doesn't quite reach his eyes.

"Where's McKenzie?" I ask.

"She went to get Anna a little while ago because dinner's ready, but she hasn't come back." His brow wrinkles slightly as he looks back at the hallway that leads to Anna's room.

"I'll go check on them." Walking down the hallway, the light streams out of Anna's door. As I get closer, I hear them talking. I know Anna is having a hard time adjusting since we've found her. Hopefully now that Kenz is back she can help her more than Rex or I have been able to.

Stepping inside the door, I open my mouth to say hi, but stop at the words Kenz says. "I had some memories return a few days ago. The woman with the eyes that look like Phoenix." *What the hell?* "That's Phoenix's mother. And I remember Dr. Chamberland drugging me so I'd lose my memory." My ears begin pounding as my blood pressure rises. Anna glances at me over McKenzie's shoulder.

"What the fuck?" I growl.

Chapter 16

McKenzie

I stand and twirl around so quickly I almost fall over. Phoenix's neck and face are flushed, his nostrils flaring. I did not want him to find out this way.

"Nix," I murmur. But I don't know what to say.

"Upstairs. Now." His tone leaves no room for argument.

I turn back to Anna, giving her a hug. "Good luck," she whispers.

I touch her cheek. "Eat something," I admonish. She nods once and I turn to face Phoenix. He waves at me to come on, so I hurriedly walk out into the hallway. Rex is standing there with a grim look on his face.

I grab his forearm. "Make sure Anna eats."

His eyebrows draw together, but he nods once. Phoenix places his hand on the small of my back. His touch is gentle, even though I know he's pissed. When we enter the kitchen, Phillip is waiting expectantly.

"Phillip, we have something to take care of. Can you make us a plate?" Nix doesn't give Phillip time to answer as he rushes me out of the kitchen, through the living room, and up the stairs. My stomach churns as he leads me into our bedroom and closes the door.

I turn to face him, crossing my arms over my stomach and rubbing my hands up and down my arms. He doesn't speak right away, instead he stares at me. He changed since this afternoon in the library. I exhale sharply. *Was that just a few hours ago?* He's wearing his classic dark slacks and black button-up shirt.

He unbuttons the top buttons on his shirt, then the cuffs of the sleeves, and rolls them up. I watch as his tattooed skin is slowly revealed. I swallow and think over the day. I should have told him in the library, but he was so upset and I didn't want to overwhelm him and he wouldn't let me.

My breathing is erratic as I watch Nix. He looks like a caged lion. His arms hang at his side, his veins popping against his skin as he balls his hands into fists. His eyes are like glaciers as he stares at me. I swallow and take a step back, but he takes a step forward.

His voice is bourbon over ice. "If you had all your memories back, I'd put you over my knee and spank you." My eyes widen as his hand flexes like he's imagining it.

I take another step back and he takes another step forward. Heat swirls in my stomach, shocking me that I somehow like being the prey and him being the predator. One side of his mouth tips up like he knows it.

"We did that?" My voice is barely above a whisper. He takes another step forward, closing the distance between us further.

"We did." He tilts his head like he's considering his next words. "The auctions gave us liberties to explore, and we took advantage of it."

"Oh." I don't know what else to say. I loved when he bent me over the sex chair at the auction a few months ago. Then I had a memory when he showed me how it worked. I tilt my head at him. "I thought you said the sex chair was specially made."

He narrows his eyes at me. "What?" He steps closer to me again.

"You said it was specially made for me. So it was just right for me, but in my memory there was one already there."

He snorts and shakes his head. "Is that your question for me today?"

I glare at him. "You haven't answered questions in a couple of days, so maybe you should answer more than one."

"That room had been put together for couples to use before I bought you. After I bought you, I moved everything in that room to a different one and that one became ours. Everything in that room was specifically made for us." He takes one more step, effectively caging me against the wall when he places his hands on either side of me. "Now, let's deal with the present situation. Why didn't you tell me?"

I cross my arms over my chest and give my best unbothered expression, even though my heart is pounding in my ears. "When did you want me to tell you? After you told me you needed some time alone and walked out on me? I didn't even know you left until Phillip told me after I sat in that library for thirty minutes with your cum still dripping out of me."

I stand up on my tiptoes and get in his space, trying to show him he's not going to intimidate me. His smirk turns lethal when he grasps my throat and lifts my chin. "Tell me everything."

I arch an eyebrow at him, refusing to talk until he gives me some space. He drops his hand and takes a step back. I push his chest, making him stumble back and I side step him to sit on the edge of the bed. He leans back against the windows and stares at me, waiting.

"You know, Nix. I know you're a dangerous man. You've told me you've killed people. You do illegal things. You're one of the leaders of the Society and part of the mafia. But to me, you're just Phoenix. And I'm just McKenzie. Unless we decide to be completely honest with each other, this isn't going to work. Even if the chemistry between us is off the charts."

I comb my fingers through my hair. Nix loosens his muscles slightly as he listens to me. "I don't know why I didn't tell you all of this before, but I'm guessing it's because I was trying to protect you in my own way. Your mother took me the first time and the second time, but..." I trail off and glance away from him.

"But what?" His voice is softer.

I squeeze my eyes shut for a second before opening them again and looking at him. "I think I went with her willingly the second time because she threatened to kill you. When I get those memories back, I'll tell you for sure."

He sucks in a deep breath, his eyes flaring. "Fucking hell." He rubs his hand down his face.

"The memory I had the other night, your mother watched as some guy hosed me down. I was freezing as they brought me back to that room they held me in. Then, Dr. Chamberland walked in and told her you were getting close to finding me and it was time they changed up the drugs they were giving me so I would forget."

My mouth is dry and uneasiness settles in the pit of my stomach. *What if he doesn't believe me? What if he throws me out?* I blink back the tears that want to fall and stare at him. Waiting.

He takes a step toward me, and I lift my chin, waiting. Stopping in front of me, he grabs my hand and pulls me off the bed. He raises his hand and cups the side of my neck. "Fuck, Kenz." He moves his hand to cup the back of my neck and pulls me into his arms. I wrap my arms around him and the tension in my muscles slowly fades away.

"I'm so sorry," I whisper as I hold him tightly.

"Don't apologize, love," he says against my forehead. "I should be apologizing. I've been such an asshole." A tear escapes from my eye and drips on his arm. He leans back and watches as another tear falls. He leans forward and licks it.

"I don't deserve your tears." He cups my cheeks with both of his hands and tilts my head up until his lips are ghosting against mine. "I want you to know we're going to make them fucking suffer, then we're going to kill them."

I sag against Nix. "You believe me?"

He huffs, his breath cool against my warm skin. "Of course I believe you. I told you I can tell when you're lying." He rubs his lips against my cheek. He tilts his head back and blows out a hard breath. "I haven't made it easy, have I?"

I pull my bottom lip between my teeth. "I told you I didn't think it was my father. Even before some of my memories came back."

He walks over to the chair in front of the window, pulling me along with him. He sits and pulls me down in his lap. He wraps one arm around my waist and the other lies on my lap as he grips my hip with his hand.

"My father lied to me." He's gripping my hip so hard it might leave bruises, but I'm the anchor he needs right now. "He knew years ago my mother left, but he planted a seed that your father took her and he never said any differently. He let me believe that for years. Chasing a ghost."

A sharp pain hits me in my chest as my throat tightens at his words. I rub my hand through his hair and massage the muscles in his neck. He looks at me and one side of his mouth tips up as he rubs his hand from my hip down to my outer thigh and back again.

"I can't say I'm completely upset about it, though."

I tilt my head at him. "What? Why?"

He brings his hand up, cupping my face, and rubs his thumb over my bottom lip. "Because I got the girl." I lean forward and capture his lips with mine. In this brief moment, everything falls away. It's just him and me. Not his mother or my father or the unanswered questions lingering between us.

For all the times he's made my pulse race, in desire, in anger, in frustration; I don't know if I've ever experienced this with him. His hand wraps around my throat as he deepens the kiss, his tongue brushing against mine. He pulls me closer as I cling to him. We kiss until we're out of breath, breaking apart briefly, our lips still touching. I breathe in the breath he exhales.

Our souls binding together as one. Whatever may come. Whatever we may face. We'll do it together. His lips trail up my jaw to my ear and he sucks my earlobe into his mouth, making me moan. He increases the pressure on my throat slightly with his hand, forcing me to open my eyes and I'm staring into his beautiful ice eyes.

"I will love you until I breathe my last breath." My heartbeat quickens at his words. It's a promise and a declaration.

I sink even further into him. "It's always been you." He rubs his thumb over my lips again just before he leans up, kissing me until everything else fades away.

Chapter 17

Phoenix

I will never get enough of this woman and every person who has caused her harm is going to fucking pay. Including my mother. But first I need her to know I will always choose her. I will burn this fucking world to the ground to make sure she is safe. I run my hand down her throat, between her breasts, then wrap my arm around her, pushing on her lower back, and she arches into me.

Lifting her in my arms, I turn and place her in the chair so she's sitting before me. Like a fucking queen. She stares up at me, her face and neck flushed. Her tongue flicks out as she wets her lips. I slowly unbutton my shirt and I love how her eyes grow glossy with need as my tattooed skin is revealed.

Pulling my shirt off, I toss it over the other chair and begin unbuttoning my pants. She sits forward and reaches for me, eager to help, but I stop her. She tilts her head to the side and purses her lips.

"I don't get on my knees for anyone but you."

Her breath hitches as I push my pants down and take them off, keeping my eyes locked on her. My cock is hard and ready, but this is about her, not me. I push my boxers down, standing before her completely naked. Her eyes flick to my pierced dick and her mouth parts slightly as her breathing increases.

My girl loves my piercing. Best decision I ever made, even if it did hurt like a motherfucker. I kneel down before her, my cock jutting up and hitting my stomach. She stares at me, waiting to see what my next move will be, her chest moving with every breath she takes.

I place my hands on her ankles and flick the anklet she's wearing with my thumb. "Did you know I bought this for you for our first anniversary?"

She shakes her head. "No." Her voice is raspy with need.

"You'll remember," I promise and I believe it. I've told her that before, hoping she wouldn't remember. Wouldn't remember those first months of us together. How I forced her to walk down the aisle to me. How I ignored her after we were married. Now, I refuse to hide anything else from her.

I rub my hands up her legs, pushing her black dress up as I go. Her head tips back and she sighs as I tease her with my fingertips. When my hands reach her hips, she lifts slightly, knowing exactly what I want without me having to ask. I lean forward and kiss the top of her thigh.

"Such a good girl."

I run my lips up her thigh as I grab her dress and push it up higher. She lifts her arms and I pull it off, throwing it on the floor as I lean back and stare at her. I take in every inch of skin that's on display. Her black lace panties and bra give me glimpses of what's underneath. Earlier it was hot and fast, but right now I'm going to enjoy every inch.

Her chest rises and falls and her lips part slightly. She flexes her hands on the arms of the chair and spreads her legs slightly. I lick my lips, thinking about her taste. Her eyes dart from my eyes to my lips, to my cock, and back again. She wants it so badly, but she's following my lead.

When I told her earlier we experimented after I got her back the first time, I wasn't sure how she'd react. She didn't shy away from what we did at the auction a few months ago, so this part of her wasn't something she was doing just to please me. It's part of her DNA and I can't wait to show her exactly how good we are together.

I rub the back of my knuckles from her knee, up the inside of her thigh, and stop at the apex of her legs. I feel her heat. My eyes drop to her panties and I smirk at the wet spot there. "So desperate for it, aren't you, love?" She inhales a quivering breath and nods.

"Tell me what you want," I demand. I move my knuckle and rub it back and forth over the wet spot that's becoming more pronounced. She jerks and whines as I press harder. My eyes move slowly up her body, stopping on her tits. I rub my other hand up her abs and cup her, then swirl my index finger around her nipple. She gasps and arches. My cock is so hard it's painful. Finally looking up at her, I arch an eyebrow waiting for her answer.

She swallows twice. "You know—" she moans when I press my knuckles harder into her. "You know, you look amazing on your knees." Her words and raspy voice make my cock jump. She slides to the edge of the chair, sitting up slightly and leaning forward. "Now take my panties off and fuck me."

A growl rumbles up my chest as I grab her panties and yank them down her legs. I push her legs apart and insert a finger in her, making sure she's ready. She moans as I hook my fingers, teasing her for a moment before I grab her hips and pull her off the chair and onto my lap.

I place my fingers in my mouth and suck her taste off. She's like my own form of ambrosia. Her eyes flame with desire and lust. Leaning forward, I nip at her ear. "Ride me, love." She doesn't waste any time as she grips my cock, lines it up with her pussy and slowly slides down on me. Her tight heat grips me and I grunt as I'm brought close to coming like a virgin teenager.

She places her hands on my shoulder, lifting up and dropping back down on me. "Fuck," I whisper as I wrap my arms around her, unhook her bra and pull it off her. She tips her head back, her long hair tickling my legs as I lean down and pull her nipple into my mouth.

"Nix," she groans out as she begins to rotate her hips. I place my hands on her hips and help support her so her thighs don't give out.

"That's right, love. Fuck me so good." I lick up her breast and pull her skin into my mouth and between my teeth, leaving a small mark.

"Please," she begs. I pull her close and meet her thrusts. Our chests are slick with sweat as she clings to me, her fingernails raking down my back. I leave open mouth kisses along her jaw, neck, wherever my lips touch.

My balls draw up slightly and I know I'm going to come soon as pressure builds in my groin. Without breaking us apart, I lift her until she's perched on the edge of the chair, pushing her until she's leaning against the back. She continues to buck against me as I circle her clit with my thumb.

"Yes!" Her walls flutter slightly and I know she's close. I increase the pressure and she explodes around me. I grit my teeth, holding off my orgasm until she crests, then I pound into her until the pressure explodes and I come in her tight pussy. I rock into her, prolonging the ecstasy, then fall against her chest as all the tension in my muscles relaxes.

She rubs her hands up and down my spine and wraps her legs around me like she doesn't want me to pull out yet. I drop kisses on her forehead, her jaw, and her lips. After a few minutes, I sit back because I know she has to be uncomfortable. Pulling out, I stare down and watch as our juices mix together.

She huffs and I bring my eyes to hers. "We don't use protection." I stand and offer her my hand. She takes it and I pull her up, leading her to our bathroom. I turn the shower on and turn toward her as we wait for the water to warm up.

"You have an IUD." Her mouth forms an O. I shrug. "You told me you didn't want kids, so I told you I'd get a vasectomy. But you decided you wanted to do that just in case you changed your mind."

I walk into the shower and stand under the heat of the water. She follows me and wraps her arms around me, laying her head on my chest. I cup her face and tip it so she's looking at me. I adjust us so the spray of the water isn't hitting her.

"Are you okay with that?" she asks.

I sigh. "I wouldn't be a good father, Kenz. So, I was okay with it. That's why I offered to get a vasectomy." She rubs a hand from my back around to my chest and places it over my heart.

"I disagree, but I understand." She snorts. "Our parents really screwed us up, didn't they?"

I run my fingers through her hair. "From the stories you told me about your mom, she seemed pretty great."

She smiles and nods. "She was, but she died when I was fourteen. The one thing I remember the most is baking with her." Her eyes light up. "I made you cookies today!"

I chuckle and lean down, kissing her softly. "I know. I smelled them as soon as I walked into the house."

Her stomach growls and her cheeks turn a pretty shade of pink. "I forgot we haven't eaten yet."

I turn around and grab her body wash and loofah. "Guess I need to feed my wife." I motion for her to turn around so I can wash her back first.

"I love the sound of that," she murmurs as I pour the body wash in the loofah and begin washing her.

I hum in agreement. "We'll eat first, then you're telling me everything."

Chapter 18

Phoenix

I head downstairs while McKenzie dries her hair. Phillip has gone home, but he left a note saying the food is in the oven warming and to not forget to turn the oven off. I grab a tumbler for me and a wineglass for Kenz. I pour myself some bourbon and some wine for Kenz. We both need it.

I take a sip from my glass and lean against the counter. The signs have been there the whole time that my mother was not a good person. I wanted her to be something she wasn't. So, I latched onto the idea that Marcus was the villain in my story. I rub my hand down my face.

I'm so pissed at my dad. He's lied to me for years. He allowed me to buy McKenzie as revenge against her father. He has no idea the feelings I developed for her over the years; I kept that to myself. Anytime I talked to him, I always made it seem to be part of my grand plan. If he had told me back then he had nothing to do with my mother disappearing, I still would have bought McKenzie.

Which brings up the next question. Why did he sell her? Why was he concerned for her safety? I was able to push him out of the council within a year of buying McKenzie, but he didn't fight too hard to stay. I think back to the last conversation I had with him.

We had words because I was convinced he took her the first time. He never denied it, but he said one day I'd find out the truth and he told me I better take care of his daughter and that was the last time we ever spoke. He still comes to auctions once or twice a year, but he keeps his distance. I exhale sharply and turn around to face the counter, placing my palms down to lean against it. I hang my head, trying to think back through every scenario with him.

He knew what I thought of him, and he knew why. Why didn't he correct me? Why didn't he try to defend himself?

Small hands rub from my shoulders down my back and around my waist. Kenz places her cheek on my back and holds me tight from behind. "Nix?" she whispers.

"Your father knew I thought he took my mother. He never denied it. Why?" Kenz doesn't answer right away.

"I don't know."

I turn around in her arms and wrap mine around her, holding her close. She looks up at me and she raises one shoulder.

"I made sure you and I were in every class back at Brighton." I've never told her this, but like she said, it's time we're honest with each other. "Our senior year I was only in two of your classes, so I went to the dean and made sure he changed it. He was new."

She nods. "I remember."

"You remember?"

She bobs her head. "I remember the dean being new, but I didn't know you did that with our classes. Why?"

I rub my thumb along her throat. “I’ve been obsessed with you from the very first day I saw you.” She leans back slightly, like she can’t believe it. I shake my head and kiss her forehead. “So oblivious,” I whisper against her skin. “I found out your father helped Dick get a job there.”

She snorts. “Dick?”

“That’s what I called the dean. It’s short for Richard.” She laughs, and it eases the tightness in my chest. “I was pissed I didn’t know.” I take a deep breath. “My mother’s family started Brighton Academy. Alexander Brighton, my great grandfather, was the founder. My mother was supposed to be the dean, but she disappeared before that could happen.”

McKenzie’s mouth is open in surprise. “How did I not know that? Did I forget?” she asks. A sharp pain lodges in my chest.

“No, love. I’ve never told you that before.”

She swallows and steps back. She grabs the glass of wine and takes two big gulps before setting it back down. “Why didn’t you tell me?”

“I don’t know. Things are different now. Things have been different since I got you back this last time. After the first time, we had chemistry, we experimented, but you were always on guard. You wouldn’t allow yourself to fall in love with me. And who could blame you when I was never completely honest with you?”

She walks away, but turns back around to face me. “But I did.”

“What do you mean?” I take a step toward her.

“I did love you. The memory I told you about. I asked you if I was taken from the house and you said I wasn’t, but I was.” I shake my head before she finishes. "Yes, I was!" She stomps her foot, getting frustrated with me.

"You weren't home when you were taken."

She growls at me. "I know what I remembered. Your mom told me if I didn't come with her she'd kill me, but first she would kill you and she'd make me watch. So, I went with her because the thought of something happening to you made me physically ill. And she said she knew I loved you. She had a boat at your dock and I got in."

My mouth opens and closes, remembering back to the day she was taken. We went down to River Street, but I had to go into the office. She said she'd go to some of the shops. Even though they were tourist traps, she always loved them. Rex stayed with me, and one of my other men stayed with her. I ball my hands into fists.

"Do you remember anything else?"

Her eyes become glossy as she shakes her head. "I wish I did, but I don't remember what happened before that or after that. The only thing I've remembered is what I told you earlier."

I sigh and step forward, wrapping my hand around the back of her neck and pull her into my chest. "I'm sorry I didn't believe you. When you remember more, tell me so we can piece all this together." She sniffs and nods.

"I hate this, Nix. I hate not knowing everything. Missing these big gaps is so frustrating." She stumbles over her words. "I don't even know how to explain what it feels like. Like a part of me is missing." I hold her tighter. "What if I don't get all my memories back?"

"I'm going to call Dr. Pearl tomorrow." She stiffens against me. "I'll have Rex run another background check on her and follow her for a few weeks, then I'll call her." She relaxes against me again.

"I want to kill Dr. Chamberland," she murmurs against my chest.

"We'll do it together," I promise her. I don't know if she's kidding or not, but I'm serious. He's a dead man walking and has no idea. I pull back and kiss her softly. "Let's eat."

"Okay," she whispers. I grab an oven mitt and pull the food out of the oven. I place the plate in front of her.

"Don't touch," I warn her.

She gives me a soft smile as I place my plate down as well. Turning the oven off, I sit next to her and we dig into the food. It's some kind of chicken and broccoli casserole. McKenzie hums, doing a small dance in her seat. I chuckle.

"I don't think I've had anything that Phillip has cooked that hasn't been delicious," she says before she takes another bite of food. She moans and my cock twitches slightly. *Jesus, this woman.* "I still think my favorite is his pancakes, though."

I shake my head at her as I take another bite. "One of my restaurants on River Street has this salad that's your favorite." I smile as I remember the number of times she would call me and beg me to bring her one home and Phillip would fuss at her, telling her he was there and could make her one.

"Really? Can you take me to try it again?"

"We'll go tomorrow," I tell her.

She glances at me. "Tomorrow?"

"There's a fight tomorrow night. We're going. Then we're going to kill Dr. Chamberland."

Chapter 19

McKenzie

Why does it excite me that he's telling me we're going to kill someone? And getting the chance to go to one of these fights sounds fun. I'll get to see a side of Phoenix I've never seen before. Well... unless I have and don't remember.

"Have I ever been to a fight with you before?" I ask him.

He smirks and gives me a sideways glance. "You have." I narrow my eyes at him. *He's not saying something.* "I promise we'll have fun."

"That's not what I'm worried about. I'm looking forward to seeing this side of you." Something like sadness flashes in his eyes. "I mean, I know I've seen this side of you, but I don't remember." A lump forms in my throat and I swallow, trying to get rid of it. He leans close to me and places a kiss on the side of my head.

"You will," he promises again.

He sounds so sure, but I'm beginning to doubt. It's been almost nine months. How long will it take? Before I can say anything, Rex and Anna walk into the kitchen. There's a light in Anna's eyes that wasn't there earlier. It makes me breathe easier.

"Can Anna go?" I whisper.

He shakes his head. "She's not ready, but we'll go out to eat beforehand and she can go with us." I smile at him pleased he's willing to make a compromise.

Anna greets us. "Hi."

"Hey. How are you feeling?"

She takes a deep breath as she looks around the large kitchen, pulling her bottom lip between her teeth. "Okay."

Rex places his hand on her back and whispers something in her ear. She nods once and steps further into the kitchen, Rex staying right beside her. She must have told him how she felt about large spaces and he's doing what he can to make her feel more comfortable.

I take a sip of my wine. "Phoenix said we can go out to eat tomorrow night. Do you think you're up for it?" I ask her. Her face brightens, and she looks at Rex. He gives her an encouraging smile.

"Yes! I think getting out of the house will help me." It's going to take years for us to get through all this trauma, but we'll do it together. Anna twirls her blonde hair around her finger. "Ummm..." She pauses and takes a deep breath. "I'm pretty sure Dr. Chamberland was involved in my kidnapping. I told Kenz earlier he always wore a mask, but he would check in on me randomly. He said something one day when he was checking on me here and I realized who he was. That's why I asked to not see him anymore."

Phoenix's hands grip his silverware so tightly his knuckles turn white. Anna looks out the windows and closes her eyes. "When you walked in earlier, I had just told Kenz that there was a woman there with eyes that looked like yours. She said it was your mother."

Phoenix drops his silverware, making Anna jump slightly as they clatter against the counter.

I place my hand on his thigh, offering some type of comfort. I know it can't be easy when the one person that's been on a pedestal your entire life is knocked off in one night. Phoenix doesn't take his eyes off Anna, giving her his full attention. His face is a perfectly created mask. I know that expression well. He wore it a lot when I thought I was his prisoner.

Anna clears her throat and rubs her hands along the counter. "The dean from Brighton..." She closes her eyes. "He would do things to me and she would watch."

I glance at Rex. His face is a mask as well. I'm sure he's already heard this, but I know this can't be easy for him either. He was her security guard. The little I know about him, he probably blames himself.

Phoenix stands slowly, every move calculated. He walks to Anna and hugs her. My heart melts a little at how gentle he is with her. This man can kill someone with his bare hands, but he knows how to be soft as well. He leans back, gently holding her shoulders.

"I promise they'll all pay."

Anna glances at me with a small smile playing on her lips. "McKenzie promised we'd kill them, then have a party."

Phoenix's head snaps in my direction, his mouth tipping into a mischievous grin. "Did she?"

I lift my shoulder and return his grin. "It's a promise I intend to keep."

Rex laughs as he and Phoenix share a look. "Sounds like a plan to me," they say in unison.

The next day I feel a little nauseous and worried about how the night is going to go. Nix and Rex are currently meeting in his downstairs office to plan the night while Anna and I sit in the library. My book is open in my lap, but I haven't read a page yet.

"Are you nervous?" Anna asks me.

I take a deep breath and look over at her. "Is it that obvious?"

She chuckles. "Well, you haven't flipped a page in a while and you keep chewing on your thumbnail."

I pull my thumb out of my mouth and grimace. "I don't know what to expect. I hope Nix prepares me for tonight." I give her a sideways glance. "Are you sure you don't want to go to the fight?"

She's shaking her head before I finish. "I'm nervous as it is going to a restaurant. Even with Rex and Phoenix there knowing they'll protect me. There are too many things that could happen at the fight."

"Okay. I don't want you to feel like we're intentionally leaving you out."

She pats my hand and we face each other more fully, both of us sitting on the couch. "I don't feel that way. It's going to take me some time to begin feeling any resemblance of normalcy."

"And that's okay. The things you went through... Do you ever think about the other girls we went to school with and where they might be now?" I ask her. Anna nods as she picks at a loose piece of thread on her jeans. "I remember seeing one of the girls from school at the auction Nix took me to after he bought me." I pull my legs up to my chest. "What if they didn't have anyone looking for them?"

"Maybe they got to stay with the person who bought them," Anna murmurs.

"That's true, but what if they didn't want to be sold? You didn't. I didn't. Nix told me to be in the council you either have to sell your first-born daughter or buy someone else's daughter."

Anna brings her fingers to her lips and shrugs. "I don't know." Her words are barely above a whisper. I can tell from the frantic look in her eyes my questions are making her anxious, so I drop it.

"What are you going to wear tonight?" I smile at her, trying to ease her mind.

"Rex said to dress casual, but what does that mean? I don't think I've ever seen him or Phoenix leave the house in jeans."

I chuckle. "I think their idea of casual is dress pants and a button-up shirt, no tie."

She laughs and nods. "What are you wearing?"

"I'm wearing jeans, a lacy camisole, and heels. Nix said it gets warm in the warehouse, so I thought that would be the safest bet."

She arches an eyebrow at me. "You're wearing heels to a fight?"

"Nix told me he wanted me to look fuckable. So everyone will be jealous knowing he'll be the only one fucking me tonight."

Anna covers her mouth and giggles. "You two are so cute." I shrug one shoulder, not disagreeing. "I don't have a lot of things. Could I wear something of yours?"

"Of course."

I hop up off the couch and grab her hand, pulling her with me, excited to have something else to think about besides what could happen tonight. We head upstairs and I stop in front of the bedroom door. *He told me once this was our space, and no one was allowed in. Did that mean Anna?*

Turning left to the other room I stayed in, I take her to the walk-in closet. There are still clothes in here. I'll have to ask Phoenix why, but it works out in my favor for tonight. I motion to the clothes. "Take your pick. My outfit is already picked out and waiting for me in my bedroom."

Anna walks around the closet, her fingers grazing across pieces as she goes. She pulls out a black jumpsuit that's strapless. She shows it to me before holding it against herself. "What do you think?"

I smile. "I think it will look perfect on you. I have some black Louboutin heels you could wear with it." She squeals a little and does a little dance. Anna always loved this type of stuff. She liked getting dressed up. I learned the majority of my style from her.

"Go ahead and get dressed. I'll be right back. I need to ask Nix something. Will you be okay?" She smiles and nods. She's venturing out more, but I don't want to assume she'll be okay by herself. I turn, heading back downstairs and to Nix's office. His door isn't closed all the way, but I hear him and Rex talking, so I knock.

"Come in," Nix calls out.

I walk in and give a small wave. Nix leans back in his chair and smiles at me. He has no idea what he does to me when he smiles at me like that. His gaze sweeps over me, and my stomach quivers. I'm wearing tights and a T-shirt, but the way he looks at me, I could be standing here in lingerie.

"Hey, love. Are you and Anna done reading?"

I walk further into the room and smile at Rex. He nods slightly with an amused look on his face. "Yes. She didn't have anything to wear, so I told her she could look through some of my clothes. I just..." I'm not sure if I should say this in front of Rex or not, but Nix isn't telling him to leave, so I continue. "I remembered you saying our room was ours and no one was allowed in our space, but I wanted us to do our hair and makeup together—"

Nix holds his hand up, stopping me. "That situation and this one is different. Of course she can go in there and you two can have fun getting ready. I'll get Phillip to bring you two snacks and some champagne."

I break out into a big smile and close the distance between us. I intend to kiss him quickly and leave, but he grabs the back of my head and lingers for a few seconds longer before pulling away slightly. Our eyes connect and for the first time since I woke up here all those months ago, I feel a connection with him I didn't realize we were missing.

It's like now we're on the same team and no longer fighting each other. I lean forward one more time, giving him another kiss. "I love you," I whisper against his lips.

He flexes his hand in my hair and grins at me. "I love you too, love." I know at this moment if I never get my memories back, I'll be okay with that.

Chapter 20

Phoenix

I inhale deeply as Rex and I wait in the living room for Kenz and Anna to come down. I walked into our bedroom about thirty minutes ago to the sound of them giggling. I called out to McKenzie, but she ran to the door of her closet and shut it, telling me I wasn't allowed in. I had half a mind to kick the door open, throw her over my shoulder, and remind her who she was talking to. But I'll take care of that later. I knew at that moment they needed their time together. It's the first time Anna has let loose since we rescued her.

Rex looks at his watch and scowls at me. I shrug. "What are you going to do? This is the circle of life."

He snorts and rolls his eyes. "Boss, I never thought you'd be whipped."

I open my mouth to snap at him, but voices come from above us, drawing our eyes to the stairs. I told Kenz this morning to wear something that made her look fuckable. What she doesn't know is that anything she wears makes her look that way, but I'm intrigued to see what she picked out.

When she comes into view, I immediately regret my words. *How the hell am I going to make it through this night without fucking her?* She's wearing black strappy heels, the straps wrap around her ankle and stop just below her dark-colored jeans. Her jeans are tight and have rips in strategic places, giving me glimpses of her knee and thigh. She's wearing a red lacy top, which might as well be lingerie.

Her silver hair hangs in waves around her shoulders. I flex my hand, imagining grabbing it as I thrust into her from behind. Her bright red lips lift into a smirk, as if she knows exactly what I'm thinking. I adjust myself, not hiding how she affects me, and her smirk turns into a full-blown grin.

She stops in front of me and arches a perfectly shaped eyebrow at me. "What are you thinking, Nix?"

I've completely forgotten about Anna and Rex as McKenzie demands my full attention. I bring my fingertip up and trace the edge of her top that's low cut and leaves little to the imagination. "I'm thinking about all the different ways I'm going to fuck you later."

Her cheeks turn a pretty shade of red, but she doesn't shy away from me. Her lips tip up into a seductive smile as she takes another step toward me. Unable to keep my hands off her any longer, I wrap my arms around her waist and pull her into me.

"I never would have worn anything like this before you," she admits.

I tilt my head at her. "What's changed?"

She pulls her bottom lip between her teeth, but quickly releases it like she remembers she's wearing lipstick. "You make me feel sexy and confident."

I rub my knuckle down the side of her neck and she shivers at my touch. "You are sexy and you should definitely feel confident. You're beautiful. Inside and out."

She looks to the side, a smile playing on her lips. "Doesn't Anna look great?" she asks. I finally pull my gaze away from her and look at Anna. I smile at the healthy glow of her skin. She looks genuinely happy. Anna is standing before Rex with a small smile on her lips as she looks up at him.

I raise an eyebrow as I stare at them. Rex runs his hand through his hair. "Jesus, Anna. You look..." He trails off at a loss for words. "Gorgeous," he finally says. McKenzie turns in my arms and leans against me.

"She is, isn't she," McKenzie says. Anna is wearing a black, strapless jumpsuit with black heels and gold jewelry. She has on a gold choker, gold bracelets, and gold earrings. She does look beautiful and happy.

I glance down at McKenzie, noticing her naked throat. "Kenz, I have a present for you." I've had this for months now, but I've been hesitant about giving it to her, unsure how she would respond. But, now, I no longer care. I'll give her a choice, but I hope she chooses to wear it. Especially when we're away from the house.

Kenz turns back around and tilts her head as she gazes at me. "What is it?"

I pull the long box out of my back pocket. Rex takes the hint and ushers Anna outside, giving us a moment. I hand Kenz the box and she slowly opens it. She doesn't react, just stares at it for a few seconds before bringing her finger up and rubbing along the smoothness of the necklace. It's a sterling silver choker necklace with black accents and a small diamond heart in the front. The clasp is what makes it unique.

She glances up at me with a small smile. "It's beautiful." *Will she think that once I tell her its purpose?* I lift it out of the box, put my hand in my pocket and take out the small key, unlocking the clasp so I can put it on her. I watch her face the entire time. Her eyes widen and she takes a small step back. "What kind of necklace is it?"

"It's a discreet submissive collar."

Her eyebrows furrow, the lines around her eyes crinkling. "What does that mean?" She glides her finger along the necklace again before looking up at me.

"When you're in a Dom/sub relationship, the submissive can wear a necklace showing she belongs to her Dom." This is the first time I've mentioned this to her since I got her back. The only time we ever played like this before was at auctions. "It's completely your choice if you want to wear this or not."

She looks from the necklace to me, and back at the necklace. "What's the purpose of the necklace?"

"To give some peace of mind." I point to the diamond. "I had this specially made for you. There's a tracking device in the necklace, so if anything were to happen to you again, I would know exactly where you're at." I show her the latch on the back and the key in my hand. "And it can only be taken off by using this key in the lock."

Her mouth forms a small O. She doesn't speak for several moments as she thinks over the explanation I just gave her. "Do I wear it all the time?"

"I would prefer you did, but you can take it off when you go to sleep, take a shower, or even when we're both at home." I think to the day she got in that boat and found herself at Larry's house, but I force the uneasiness about that happening again down. After all those months chained up, I'm not going to treat her like my prisoner. If she decides she doesn't want to wear it all the time, I'll have to be okay with it.

"I…uh…"

"Kenz, you can say no. This is your decision." I want to say more, but I shut my mouth because I don't want to influence her answer one way or another.

"Can we try it out tonight and let me think about it?" She touches the necklace one more time. "That way I can see how it feels?"

"Of course, love." She turns around and lifts her hair up. I place the necklace on her, latch it, and lock it, then place the key in my pocket. She turns as I'm placing the key in my pocket.

"What if you lose the key?" she asks. I take the key back out of my pocket, grab my wallet out of my back pocket, and place the key in a hidden slot. She smiles and takes a step back. "So, how do I look?"

My eyes zero in on the collar around her neck, my cock twitching. The only thing that looks better around her throat is my hand. I lean down and kiss the crook of her shoulder, flicking it slightly with my tongue. She sucks in a breath as I finger the collar around her neck.

"Like you're mine," I say, desire evident in my voice.

She smirks and turns with a swish of her hair. "I am."

Chapter 21

Phoenix

Dinner was fun. McKenzie and Anna enjoyed themselves and both were tipsy by the time we finished eating dinner. McKenzie and Anna are walking to the SUV, both giggling and fighting not to trip in their heels. Rex and I walk closely beside them so we can catch them, just in case they do fall.

No longer able to keep my hands off her, I wrap my arm around Kenz's waist and pull her in close to my side. "Are you enjoying yourself, love?" I ask her when there's a lull in whatever conversation she and Anna have going on. Trying to listen to them is like coming in halfway through a movie and having no idea what's going on. She nods before turning her attention back to Anna.

"Do you remember that time Kelly's hair turned blue?" Anna asks Kenz. I press my lips into a thin line.

"Yes! I forgot about that. I still have no idea how that happened. She swore I did it to her." Kenz blows a raspberry. "Like I'd have done anything like that back then. I would definitely do it now, though."

"I did it," I say simply. All three sets of eyes turn to me. Rex has a bemused look on his face, but doesn't say anything.

"What?" Anna and Kenz say at the same time. Kenz slaps my arm.

"She gave me shit for weeks because of that!" she exclaims. "Why did you do that?"

She's about to learn how obsessed I was with her. "She was making fun of you after a parent's weekend saying some really mean things to you."

A distant look comes over McKenzie's face like she's trying to remember, then she nods when it comes back to her. "She was always mean to me, though."

"I know, and I got sick of it. So, I put something in her shampoo that would turn her hair blue. I wanted her to know what it felt like to be made fun of. I also made sure that she was made fun of the entire time her hair was blue."

Anna's mouth is open and McKenzie is smiling as she shakes her head like she can't believe I did that. "You really did have a thing for me."

I raise an eyebrow at her and lean down, kissing her on top of her head. "No, love. It wasn't just a thing. I was obsessed." Her cheeks turn pink, but she smiles. We make it to the SUV. Rex holds the front passenger door open for Anna as I open the back door for Kenz and slide in beside her.

"Sir, I'll drop you and Miss Kenzie off at the warehouse, take Anna home, and return. Jason will stay with you two until I return," Rex says as he leaves the parking lot and turns in the direction of the warehouse. I nod in acknowledgement and pull McKenzie into my lap.

"What are you doing?" she whispers, her gaze flicking up front. My fingers trace the edge of her top, then the collar on her neck. I rock against her so she can feel how hard I am.

"I'm not going to be able to wait until we get home to fuck you," I whisper against the skin just below her ear. She exhales sharply. "Seeing this collar on you and knowing I can pull up the app on my phone at any time and know exactly where you are is so hot." I pull her even tighter against me and place my hand high on her thigh. She lets her legs fall open.

"Such a good girl," I whisper, and cup her with my hand. Her hands clutch my forearm and she jerks her hips toward my hand. When Rex makes a left turn, I know we're a few minutes away from the warehouse. "Do you think I could make you come in the next three minutes?" I ask her. Her gaze darts to the front again, then up to me.

My lips tip up into a smirk. She would let me, but as much as I want to feel her pussy pulsing around my fingers, I'm not going to do that to Rex or Anna. I lean forward and kiss her, licking into her mouth. She returns my kiss with enthusiasm as I rub my hand against her pussy hard. She whines into my mouth, but I don't do anything more.

I wrap my hands around her waist, kissing her one more time, before lifting her off my lap and putting her next to me. She looks up at me with disappointment. I wink at her and adjust myself. Again.

I'm going to have fucking boxer burn by the end of this night with how much she's turning me on tonight.

We're a few hundred feet away from the warehouse and my stomach clenches. She doesn't remember seeing this side of me. Hopefully she'll love it as much as she did the first time. McKenzie may have been the sweet, innocent girl in high school, but she's come out of her shell since I bought her at the auction. My goal at one point was to corrupt her, but it seems like this part of her was there all along. She just needed someone who let her explore it.

Rex stops in front of the warehouse, and Jason steps up immediately opening the door. McKenzie says bye to Anna, leaning over the center console to give her an awkward hug.

Rex and I share a look. "Text me when you're back." He nods once and I step out of the SUV, turning to help Kenz out.

There are already people in line. The front of the warehouse looks like a club, and the top floor *is* a club. Those who know about the fights and have received an invite will come to the roped off area, give the secret password for the week, then be escorted to the underground portion where the fights are held.

I wrap my arm around McKenzie's shoulders, holding her close to me, while my eyes dart all around us aware of my surroundings and anyone who is close to us. Jason clears our path as we walk into the club. The fights don't start for another forty-five minutes, so I lead Kenz to the bar and order us drinks. She hops up on the stool and I stand next to her, my back leaning against the bar watching everything.

The bartender drops our drinks off and Kenz sips at her rum and diet Coke. "That's the last drink you're getting tonight," I inform her as I sip my bourbon.

She tilts her head and looks up at me. "Why?" Her voice is sassy. I smile. I glance at Jason to make sure he's watching, he silently nods so I turn to give McKenzie my full attention.

I rub my finger along the collar around her neck. "Because you had three glasses of wine at dinner and you're already a little tipsy. So, I'm cutting you off."

She purses her lips and arches an eyebrow at me. "I believe the last time I checked, I'm a grown woman and I can make my own decisions."

I lick my lips, and her eyes immediately latch onto my mouth. I lean down so we're at eye level. "Tonight you're not making decisions. I am."

Her eyes darken as she looks at me under her eyelashes. She leans forward, her lips touching mine slightly. "We'll see." I lean forward to suck her lip into my mouth, but she leans back and turns toward the bar. She grabs her glass and downs her drink in two swallows, then lifts her glass to the bartender to get another.

She cocks her head and looks up at me as I stand to my full height. *Oh, this is going to be fun.* "That won't be necessary, Eli," I tell the bartender as he sits another drink in front of McKenzie. I take some bills out of my wallet to pay for our drinks, including the one she will not be drinking.

I lean down, lift McKenzie out of her chair, and drop her over my shoulder. "Nix!" she gasps and slaps her hand against my lower back. Eli gives me an amused look. Jason doesn't bat an eye. He falls in beside me as I make my way toward the VIP area only meant for us. Jason stops by the roped off area.

I step further into the area. There are two couches, both closed off from view by two wall separators, so no one can see into this area of the VIP section, giving us privacy. I drop Kenz on the couch furthest away from the roped off area. Her back hits the couch, and she immediately tries to sit up, but I'm faster than her. I straddle her waist and place my hands on either side of her head.

She swallows and stares up at me. Her gaze drops to my lips, betraying how turned on she is by this. "Now love, I'm going to have to punish you."

Her eyes widen and her hands clench into fists. "What? Why?"

I tilt my head at her. She knows exactly why, but I'll appease her for now. "You were being a brat by ordering another drink."

Her mouth opens and closes. "It was just a drink."

"It was *not* just a drink. In about an hour, we're going to go downstairs where you'll need all your senses. Having more to drink will only make me worry more about you. Understand?"

She nods, shame and embarrassment flashing in her eyes. I climb off her and she presses her hands against her cheeks as she blinks her eyes. "I'm sorry," she murmurs. I offer her my hand and help her up. She stands in front of me, her arms hanging limply at her side.

I wrap my arms around her, pulling her in close to me. "Now you know, but next time, listen." She returns my embrace and nods against my chest. I kiss the top of her head and pull away.

"Go sit on the other couch." Her eyes dart to the other couch and her shoulders droop a little, but she does as I say. She sits down and looks up at me expectantly.

I sit on the couch she was lying on and she purses her lips. Her eyes squint at me. I spread my legs slightly and stare at her for several seconds. "Now, let's address what your punishment will be."

Chapter 22

McKenzie

My chest tingles with excitement and a little apprehension. I chew on the inside of my cheek as I stare at Nix and wait for his next words. He leans back, his legs spread wide as he watches me. I break eye contact with him, it all becoming too much as I glance around the VIP room.

What will he do to me? Here, where anyone could walk in on us.

We're hidden by the wall separators, so people could only see if Jason let them past the roped off area. "Eyes on me, love." My eyes fly back to him as heat rises up my chest, to my neck and cheeks. I bring my finger up and play with the collar around my neck, tracing the heart of the diamond as I gaze at him.

I love this necklace and the idea of it. What it represents. It's so strange how much things have changed between us. When I remembered he bought me at the auction, the thought of him owning me... My thoughts trail off. *Well, this is different. He's giving me a choice on whether I wear it all the time or not and it means something different. It's his way of keeping me safe. His way of marking me as his own.*

"Get on your knees and crawl to me." His words bring me back to the present and I freeze. *Crawl to him?* I glance around again. "Keep your eyes on me, love," he says again.

"I…" I pause and wipe my sweaty hands down my jeans. "I can't do that."

He leans forward and arches an eyebrow. "You can't? Or you won't?"

I gesture at the roped off area. "Nix, what if someone walks in?" I whisper-yell.

He leans back again and drapes his arms across the back of the couch. "I promise you no one will walk in. This area belongs to me and you. No one is allowed back here unless I've ordered something from the bar. We have complete privacy."

I bite my lip and stare at him for a few seconds. *What will he do to me after I crawl to him? Is the crawling punishment or something else?* I swallow and take a deep breath. Scooting off the couch, I fall to my knees. I'm surprised at how soft the carpet is, but pleased it won't be too uncomfortable. I fall forward on my hands, keeping my eyes on Nix the entire time.

He keeps one arm laid across the back of the couch like he doesn't have a care in the world, but he lifts a hand and rubs his lip with his thumb as he watches me intently. My face is hot, but I'm not sure if it's because of embarrassment or because of the way Phoenix is looking at me. I move forward, my breasts swaying with the movement.

Nix leans forward with his elbows braced on his knees and his hands hanging loosely between his legs. His eyes are glued to every sway of my hips and breasts. "Fuck," he murmurs the closer I get. "You look like a fucking goddess."

I suck in a breath and try to wet my dry throat. This doesn't feel like punishment. His words, the way he's looking at me, like I own him just as much as he owns me. I stop between his legs and he leans back, staring at me. Thinking back to the second auction he took me to, I remember his instructions.

I lean back, put my feet together and spread my legs, placing my hands on my thighs. Nix's lips lift into an approving smile. He doesn't do anything right away besides stare at me. His eyes take in every part of my body, tracing along my neck, my arms, my cleavage, to my outstretched hands and back up.

A lump forms in my throat out of nowhere, and my eyes begin to sting with unshed tears. Nix notices immediately and leans forward, reaching his hand out and rubs his knuckles along my jaw. "What is it, love?"

I swallow and blink, trying to stop the tears from falling, but one falls anyway. He watches as it treks down my face. I squeeze my eyes shut, sure he's going to lick it, but he doesn't. He kisses it. I open my eyes in surprise. He tilts his head at me, waiting. "It's silly," I whisper.

He shakes his head. "It's not."

I huff. *He doesn't even know what's wrong.* I inhale, trying to give myself some courage. Being vulnerable with him is something I'm going to have to practice. "You're the only person that's ever made me feel wanted. Important."

He sighs and rubs his thumb along my cheekbone. "You are important." I smile at him, remembering when he said those very words to me the day my father didn't show up for a parent's weekend.

"Well, you make me feel it," I say. He kisses me softly before leaning back and resuming his laid back stance.

"I want you to remember that," he says. "Now, I want you to unbuckle my pants and take my cock out."

I narrow my eyes at him, but do as he says. Unbuckling his belt and unbuttoning his pants, I remind myself of what he said earlier about no one coming in here. I push his pants down slightly and he lifts his hips to help me. He's already hard, but I rub my hand along his covered length anyway before pushing his boxer briefs down and getting my first glimpse of his piercing.

Nix's breath quickens as I rub my thumb along his piercing. I want to lick him, but I lean back and wait for his next instructions. He grips himself and rubs his hand up and down his cock. I lick my lips and he smirks. "Your punishment will be sucking my cock."

I snort. "That's not a punishment."

He arches an eyebrow. "You didn't let me finish." I motion at him to continue, and he shakes his head slightly. "You're going to make me come down that pretty throat of yours, but you're not going to be allowed to come." He crooks a finger at me. His way of telling me it's time. "And I know how much sucking my cock turns you on."

My mouth pops open. I want to say something smart, but nothing comes to mind. I lift one shoulder like it's not a big deal, but by the look in his eyes, I know he's not buying it. I drop my gaze to his cock. He settles in, his eyes hooded, as he watches me.

I grip his cock, and he hisses. Grinning up at him, I lean forward and kiss his piercing. His jaw tightens and his pupils are so large the ice of his eyes is barely visible. I suck his tip into my mouth, wondering what he'll do. Swirling my tongue around him, the salty taste of him hits my tastebuds. He hums and grips my hair in his fist.

"We don't have a lot of time, love." I drop down on him and he grunts. "Kenz," he moans, and I love it.

I want to rub my legs together, but the way I'm kneeling, there's no way I'm going to get any kind of friction or pressure. I pull up on him and can't stop myself from jerking my hips and my clit rubs against the seam of my jeans. I'd gasp if I didn't have a mouthful of cock.

Nix clicks his tongue at me and I glance up at him under my eyelashes. He lifts one side of his mouth. "What did I tell you, love?" I swirl my tongue around him again, my pussy growing wetter. *Why did I get the other drink? What was I trying to prove?* "I'm going to take control," Nix says. "If it gets to be too much, just tap my shin the same way you would your wrist. Understand?"

I nod the best I can, but he sees. I loosen my jaw and let him guide my head. He thrusts up slowly, hitting the back of my throat. I have a stellar gag reflex because it doesn't affect me at all.

"Take a deep breath." I do as I'm told. He pulls back out and when he thrusts back in, this time it's with more force. He hits the back of my throat, but he stays there instead of moving. "Swallow."

My eyes fly to his and I swallow. He hisses and begins to do short thrusts. I breathe through my nose as saliva pools in my mouth and dribbles down my chin. "So. Fucking. Sexy." He says each word with a short thrust and it makes me feel like the goddess he called me earlier.

He has complete control now, but I decide not to be just a silent participant. I bring my hands to his shins and rub up to his thighs. His breathing is becoming erratic and his muscles tighten beneath my hands. He tilts his head back as he continues to rock into my mouth. I know he's seconds from coming, so I move my hand to his balls and massage them.

"Fuck!" He doesn't shout, but he's loud. Although the music in the club drowns him out. He holds me down on him and he's coming in hot spurts down my throat. It's so much this time I'm not able to catch my breath, but it doesn't scare me. I've always loved the thrill of holding my breath as long as I could until I couldn't anymore.

This isn't any different. I'm just not underwater. My vision begins to blur around the edges, but I still don't tap his shin like he told me to. He pulls me off him just as I think I might pass out, and I suck in gulps of air. His eyes fly to my face, full of concern, then he's putting his hands under my arms and lifting me onto his lap.

He grabs a napkin off the side table and wipes my mouth and neck. "What the hell, Kenz? I told you to tap my shin."

I shrug and lay my head on his shoulder. "I liked it," I whisper, my voice raw from how he used my throat. He rubs his hand up and down my back.

"Jesus. What is it with you and holding your breath?" He holds me close. "You always scare the shit out of me when you do it."

Huh, guess this is something I've done before. "It must be something I do often," I say. He pushes me back slightly, looking me over like he's trying to make sure I'm okay.

"No, not often. That's why it scares the shit out of me. You'll go a long time without doing it, so you'll catch me off guard when you do it. This you've never done before." He kisses my forehead. "I should have been paying more attention. Sometimes you make me lose my head, but that's no excuse." I smirk, and he narrows his eyes at me. "What?"

"I like the thought of you losing your mind because of me." He smiles and shakes his head.

He pats my ass and gently pushes me so I'm standing before him. I rub my legs together, completely turned on, but he doesn't even acknowledge it. I want to stomp my foot, but I take my punishment with as much grace as I can. "The fight starts soon. So, we need to head downstairs. I need to make sure everything's in order." I take a few steps back as he grabs his cell phone and texts someone quickly.

"I should probably freshen up." I want to go to the bathroom and take care of myself before the fight.

"You can do that here," he says as I turn to grab my purse.

I look at him over my shoulder. "I need to go to the bathroom."

He tucks his shirt back into his pants and makes himself presentable again. "Alright, I'll go with you." There's no room for argument, but I want to anyway.

"What? Why?" I ask as I turn around and face him.

He steps forward and wraps his arms around me, pulling me into him. He smirks at me. “Because when I said you don’t get to come, I meant it.”

I huff and turn to walk out of our area just as a server walks in with a tray of drinks. “Mr. Stone, the drinks you ordered.” He places two waters and two cokes on the table. Nix thanks him and gives him a tip as he leaves.

“One is to give you a little sugar and caffeine, the other is to hydrate.” I scowl at him and grab the coke first.

“I can’t believe you won’t let me go to the bathroom by myself.” He shrugs and takes a drink from his cup. I gulp down the coke, remembering how dry my throat is. I place the glass back down and tap my foot, ready to go to the bathroom, but Nix grabs the glass of water and hands it to me.

“Hydrate Mrs. Stone, you’re going to need it.”

Chapter 23

Phoenix

I put McKenzie's arm on mine and guide her down to the basement of the warehouse. Her attitude is in full force and I smirk. I let her go to the personal bathroom attached to my office and stood inside while she relieved herself. I did give her some privacy. I faced the door since I'm not a complete ass. Kenz didn't agree and she told me so.

I chuckle at the memory, and she glares up at me. I lean down and kiss the side of her forehead because she turns at the last minute to look straight ahead. I release her arm and wrap it around her waist, then grope her ass. She bites her lip and sucks in a quick breath. *My girl is turned on.*

Leaning down, I whisper in her ear, "I love when McFeisty comes out to play." I cup her ass again and make sure when I do, my middle finger gets close to her pussy just to tease her a little more. She tenses a little, then pushes back into my hand. I remove it immediately and she huffs. This is what I've missed over the past several months. This side of her.

What she doesn't know is I'll make sure she's satisfied tonight and I don't think I'll be able to wait until we get home. There's a crowd beginning to form at the entrance, but no one has been allowed in except the fighters. Rex pushes through, guiding us in, and Jason follows us. I hold Kenz close to me, looking at every face we pass. I wonder if my mother shows up at these fights.

I still have a lot of questions for McKenzie. How did my mother get into auctions and I didn't see her? Granted, we wear masks, but I would think I'd recognize my own mother. But I lost her not too long after McKenzie lost her mother, so maybe I wouldn't. It's been over a decade since I last saw her. She may look completely different now. Still, I continue to look for her dark blonde hair and eyes the same color as mine.

People move out of our way, recognizing who I am. The vibe down here is completely different from the one upstairs. Excitement is in the air. There's laughter; some from enjoyment, others from the high they're getting off whatever drug they just took. People are dressed comfortably, but more skin is showing.

We walk past a group of guys that are throwing punches in the air, but they all stop when they spot McKenzie. She doesn't notice at first because she's taking in all the sounds, noise, and smells. I have to remind myself that this is the first time she's been here. At least that's what she thinks. She doesn't remember the other times I've brought her. After a few seconds, she realizes it got unnaturally quiet, and she looks toward me, but pauses when she sees the group of men staring at her.

She's a sight to behold in her ripped jeans and red top that hugs all of her curves. To top it off, the collar around her throat makes me want to fuck her right here, right now. Her fingers come up and touch the collar and the men's eyes follow. The disappointment that's evident in each of their eyes makes me smirk. She seems to realize they're disappointed and her mouth tips up into a small smile.

As we pass, she shrugs at them. "Sorry, boys," she says in that sexy raspy voice of hers. I enjoy watching them watch her. Like I told her, I don't mind others looking, but if they touch, I'll make sure they won't be able to touch anything ever again. I stop when we get a little ahead of the guys and McKenzie looks up at me with a question in her eyes.

I lean down and kiss her; long, hard, and dirty. Wrapping my hand around her throat and my other arm around her waist, she sucks in a breath and kisses me back with enthusiasm. I force myself to pull away and she gives me a curious look. I run the back of my knuckle from her temple, down her cheek, and jaw.

"Such a good girl." She beams up at me, loving the praise. I kiss her one more time, then grab her hand, interlocking our fingers, and lead her to the locker room. There are fighters getting their hands wrapped while others are warming up. I greet those who greet me and continue through until we get to my office.

Felix is waiting for me, sitting in the chair in front of my desk. He's sprawled back, his ankle crossed over his knee as he looks through some papers. Felix is a tall skinny guy with hair as black as a raven. He looks like a young James Dean, but with black hair. Many of the girls would love for him to take them home, but he doesn't pay any of them any attention.

When he notices me, he raises his hand to greet me as he continues to leaf through the papers. He doesn't look up until I sit in my chair and pull Kenz into my lap. He does a double take when he sees her.

"Kenz, doll! I was wondering when I'd see you again. Feeling better?" I stiffen, hating myself for not warning her about him.

But McKenzie doesn't flinch. She smiles broadly at him. "I am. Thank you for asking." She leans back into me and I pat her thigh lightly so she knows I'm proud of her.

"Felix," I say his name so McKenzie will know it and she relaxes a little when she realizes it. "Who do we have tonight?"

He leafs through his papers again like he wasn't just looking at them. He knows all of these fighters inside and out, but he still studies their papers just in case. He's good at his job, that's why I hired him. "The one to beat will be Bill. Everyone is placing bets on him."

I nod. He'll win unless we have someone off the streets that hasn't made a name for themselves yet. It's happened. That's how Bill got here. He came in one night and upset so many people because of the thousands, some millions, they lost. But since then, he's earned them so much more.

I glance at McKenzie. I didn't prepare her enough, but I can't back out now. "How many girls are here?" Kenz doesn't react, which surprises me a little. I did tell her a little about this months ago, so maybe she's going to take this better than I'm giving her credit for.

"Twenty. Shay won't be here, though. She sent a text saying she wasn't feeling it tonight." He shrugs and reaches into his pocket, pulling out a cigarette and lighting it. He takes a pull before speaking again. "I think it's time to talk to her. She hasn't been here in a while. If she doesn't want to do this anymore, maybe she can work somewhere else?"

Kenz moves and I glance up at her and she arches an eyebrow at me. She wants to know if she should know who Shay is. I give a slight nod. She pulls her lips between her teeth. She wants to say something, but she'll wait. I rub her thigh. She's doing so well. She just got punished, but I'm definitely going to reward her for how well she's doing.

"I agree. When's the last time you saw her?" I haven't been to a fight in a few months. Not since that night I left on my motorcycle and I stared up at McKenzie in her room. Felix takes another pull from his cigarette as he thinks.

"Shit, it has to be going on three months, maybe four." He puts the cigarette out in the ashtray next to his chair and stands. "I'm going to tell the guys to begin taking bets. We'll be ready for the first fight in thirty minutes or so." He gives us a small salute and walks out, closing the door behind him.

I kiss McKenzie's neck. "You did so well, love." She smiles at me, but I can tell she wants to say something. "Go on." I encourage her.

"Who's Shay?" She asks. I look away. I hate that she can't remember, but it's not her fault.

"Shay was one of the first girls we rescued." McKenzie's eyes widen slightly. She twists her lips to the side.

"We rescued her? How?" I rub my hand up and down her thigh.

"One of the reasons I forced you to marry me is because if you're married, you can choose not to have sex with the person you buy. I forced you to marry me when I did because I was told there would be someone from Brighton being sold at the next auction, but I learned her father decided he couldn't go through with it. It was my intention to rescue her, but I wasn't having sex with someone that wasn't you."

Her mouth opens and closes several times. "Why didn't you tell me that? Instead of forcing me?" She finally asks, her eyes narrowing. "I remembered you telling me if you're married you don't have to have sex with the person you buy. But I wasn't sure if it was because you cared about me or not." She pulls her lips between her teeth and glances away.

I shake my head and inhale sharply. Wrapping a hand around the side of her neck, I pull her down until I can rest my forehead against hers. "I was an asshole." She snorts in agreement. I kiss her just below her ear. "You're the only one I've ever wanted. If I could go back and change the way I acted those first months with you, I would."

She smiles and kisses me. It's short and quick, but I needed it. "We're going to be okay." I run my fingers through her hair and pull her to me, kissing her long and slow. She whines and pulls away. "Nix." I chuckle and she huffs.

"I promise I'll take care of you." Her eyes brighten, but I push her off my lap. "Later."

Chapter 24

McKenzie

Phoenix guides us back through the locker room. He checks in with Felix one more time, who gives him a thumbs up and continues taking bets. "How much do you make on these fights?" I ask as we weave through the crowd. There's a ring in the middle of the room and there are already a couple of guys in it preparing for their fight. Rex and Jason are already up front waiting for us. I'm assuming there are other guys around us following us as we make our way to our seats.

Phoenix sits and pulls me into his lap. "I charge a thirty-dollar entry fee. And I get ten percent of the winnings. And people bet crazy amounts at these fights." I'm not sure how to reply. What's a crazy amount? Guess I'll find out tonight. "Felix will bring me the numbers soon. We cut off betting five minutes before the first fight." He glances at his watch. "Which starts in fifteen minutes."

"Is everything done in cash?" I wrap my arm around his neck to get comfortable.

"Yes, the fights are illegal. So, we then take the money and put it into the businesses around the city." Before I can ask anymore questions, Felix slides in and shows Phoenix the numbers. I don't pay attention, not really caring about that part of all this. Instead, I look around trying to take everything in. This is a lot more organized than I was expecting. I don't know why, everything Nix does, he does it to the best of his abilities.

At the same time, the excitement and anticipation are thick in the air, making it feel a bit chaotic. There's shouting, laughter, people pretending to fight, and there are women weaving in and out of the crowd that have a different air about them. They're here working, waiting for the excitement and energy to turn into desire and lust.

I think about Shay, this faceless woman Nix and I rescued. It doesn't make sense that we would rescue her and she still wound up doing this. I guess here she gets to choose who she has sex with. The announcer gets into the ring and announces the names of the men fighting and the winning pot of the bet for the two of them.

I try my best to focus on the fight, but I can't stop thinking about Shay. Felix said it's been three or four months since she's been here. *Did something happen to her?*

"Nix?" I talk directly into his ear so he can hear me. He tilts his head to let me know he's paying attention. "What if something happened to Shay? Do you send guys to check on these women if they don't show for a while?"

His muscles tense beneath me, obviously not having thought of that. He twists his head so he can talk into my ear. "I've been preoccupied. I haven't thought about it," he admits. *He's been preoccupied with me*. Guilt swirls in my stomach even though I know it's not my fault what happened to me.

"We can talk about it later," I tell him. "Maybe get Rex or one of the other guys to look into it." Nix nods in agreement. He grips the back of my head and pulls me in for a hard kiss. He releases me before I'm ready, but I don't pout like I did earlier. He promised he'd take care of me, so at least I have something to look forward to.

There are four fights. The winner of each fight spars the next guy on the docket, and whoever wins the third fight gets to go into the ring with Bill. It hardly seems fair. The guy that gets in the ring with Bill is sweaty, bloody, and obviously a little tired. But he sits in his corner waiting for Bill to be announced.

Nix leans up and presses his lips to my ear. "Dr. Chamberland will be with Bill," he says, and I stiffen. My heart beats faster and I feel a little nauseous. Nix rubs his hand up and down my spine as he feels my discomfort. He points just as the doors in the back open.

"Why is Dr. Chamberland with him?"

"Dr. Chamberland told Bill about the fights. He was struggling financially and a good fighter. So, he came in one night and has been the guy to beat for almost a year." I nod slightly as I try to swallow so I can dampen my dry mouth. The hair on the back of my neck lifts as I watch the corner of the warehouse.

Although my attention is glued to the corner of the warehouse, trying to get a glimpse of this mysterious Bill. I have this feeling someone is watching me. I turn to look over my shoulder, glancing through the aisles and rows of people. It's hard to see anyone since we're seated and the majority of everyone else is standing and cheering for their guy.

I inhale sharply through my nose, trying to calm my racing heart. It's so hot in here with all these people. When I don't see anyone watching me, I turn back around just in time to see Dr. Chamberland stand at the corner of the ring and hold up the ropes to let Bill climb in. My heart stops beating when Bill stands and raises his hands over his head.

I sit forward and grip one of Nix's thighs as I study Bill's features. My ears ring and I can feel my pulse throughout my body. "Kenz?" Nix's voice sounds like it's coming from far away. He shakes me slightly to get my attention, but I can't take my eyes off Bill. "McKenzie!"

I'm being pushed off his lap, and he places me on the seat as he kneels in front of me, cradling my cheeks. I can't focus though, his face is blurry, and it occurs to me it's because I'm crying. I squeeze my eyes shut as memories assault me.

"No! I swear when Phoenix finds out he's going to fucking kill you!"

I shake my head, trying to stop them. I don't want to remember.

His arm on my chest, trying to hold me still as I fight him off. His rough hands as he pushes my panties down my legs. Dr. Chamberland walking out with a shake of his head. Phoenix's mother standing in the corner laughing.

"McKenzie, please!" Nix is gripping my biceps gently, but I can't see him. I can only see William above me, a gleam in his eye as he gets off on hurting me, but now he's called Bill.

"He..." I trail off, unable to speak because my breathing is so erratic. A bottle of cold water is pushed into my hand.

"What's wrong with her boss?" I think Felix is asking, but Nix doesn't respond. Instead, he takes the top of the water bottle and helps me drink a few sips.

"Come on, love. Please talk to me," Nix begs.

"Should I get a doctor?" Rex asks.

Nix lifts me in his arms, cradling me to his chest as he walks out of the warehouse. I close my eyes and let my head fall against his shoulder. It's so loud in here, everyone shouting Bill's name. There's a loud crunch from the ring and people cheer, but I squeeze my eyes shut, refusing to look up there. We finally get out of the main arena and into a hallway.

There's still some laughter and talking, but it's not as loud or as suffocating. "Breathe, love," Nix whispers. "Did you have a memory?"

The lump in my throat grows larger. *Why is he here? Why did Dr. Chamberland bring him here?* I finally open my eyes and look over Nix's shoulder and there she is with a hateful smirk on her blood-red lips. I should say something. Tell Phoenix. But I can't. My heart is beating so hard it's painful.

She lifts her hand and gives a little wave before turning and walking away. Her fake red hair swinging as she saunters off. Nix walks us through the locker room back to his office and he places me gently on the edge of his desk. Holding me so I don't fall over. He cups one side of my face and stares at me, his eyes beseeching and begging for me to say something.

I lick my lips and look around the room quickly, making sure Felix didn't follow us back here. It's only Rex and I see Jason through the small window in the door standing there, guarding. I finally look back at Nix. This is going to break his heart.

"Bill..." I suck in a breath and Nix's eyebrows lower and the creases around his eyes become so pronounced I want to touch them to try to ease the blow I'm about to bring. "He raped me."

Chapter 25

Phoenix

The only thing I see is red. McKenzie's red lips to be specific because everything else in my vision is blurry. I remove my hands from McKenzie's face so I don't hurt her by accident because of how angry I am. No, this isn't anger. This is rage. *That motherfucker has been fighting at my club since McKenzie first went missing.*

I stand and put my hands on top of my head as I pace.

He was fighting here almost every weekend while I was looking for her. He had drinks with me in celebration while he was raping my wife. MY WIFE!

I don't think as I walk to the door and yank it open. Jason jumps back in surprise as he calls my name. But I don't stop. I walk down the hall toward the noise of the crowd screaming. It's a celebration. Bill won again.

I'm going to yank him off that fucking stage and kill him. I'm going to beat his head to the ground until his brain is mush.

Someone jumps in front of me and I'm about to push them out of my way when I recognize it's Rex. He puts his hands on my shoulder. "Phoenix stop." His voice holds no room for argument, but I don't give a fuck. The fabric of my shirt rubs uncomfortably against my skin, so I unbutton it and rip it off, throwing it at him.

I'm about to get bloody, so I'll save myself from having to clean the blood out of that shirt. I step around Rex, but he gets in my face. I ball my hands into fists. "I'm about to knock you on your ass if you don't get out of my way."

"Phoenix!" It's McKenzie which makes me stop short. Turning to look over my shoulder, I see her running down the hall in those heels. *Jesus, she's going to break her fucking neck.* I turn around and face her as she launches herself at me, throwing her arms around my neck. I grab her and she lifts her legs to wrap them around my waist. I place a hand under her ass to support her so she doesn't fall.

She buries her head in my neck and kisses my bare shoulder. "I'm sorry." Her voice cracks. "I'm so sorry." I deflate a little, my tight muscles loosening some. Here she is saying sorry to me when she's the one who went through it.

"Love, don't you say sorry. This is not your fault." I'm such an asshole. I allowed my anger to take over instead of comforting her. She was having a fucking panic attack, and my first thought was to kill that son of a bitch. I rub my hand from her head and down her back, trying to comfort her.

Jason stops in front of me, his eyes flicking from me to Rex while deciding what to do. He handled the situation well. He didn't chase after Rex and me; instead, he stayed with McKenzie. I turn back to Rex, tightening my hold on McKenzie. "Get Bill and Dr. Chamberland. Tell them we're going to have a celebratory drink before they head upstairs. You know where to take them."

Rex nods once and motions for Jason to follow him. I turn and press McKenzie to the wall so I can lean back and look at her. She has slight black smudges under her eyes from crying. Her cheeks and neck are red. She's still a sight to behold, though. "You had a memory." She nods and opens her eyes slowly to look at me.

"As soon as I saw him." Her voice cracks and she shakes her head like she wishes she could unsee everything. "And when you were bringing me back to your office, I saw your mother."

"What?" I look down the hallway from where we came like she's going to be there.

"I should have said something, but I couldn't. It was hard to breathe." She sobs and puts her head in my neck again. "Why does she keep showing up? It's like she's intentionally torturing me."

"What do you mean she keeps showing up?"

McKenzie stiffens a little in my arms, but she leans back up to look at me. "I've seen her at auctions as well. The one you took me to before I got my memories back she was there. I didn't realize it was her until I got my memories back, but it was her. It's like she's always in the background waiting to pounce."

How have I not noticed her being around? Why hasn't my security noticed? What the fuck is going on?

People begin to pour out into the hallway, so I slowly release McKenzie. I keep my arm around her so she doesn't fall and so I can feel her. She's the only thing that will keep me from going crazy.

"Nix, your mother. She changed her hair color. It's red now."

I take in a deep breath. Of course she changed her appearance. I don't say anything, instead I interlace my fingers with McKenzie and begin walking to the room Rex will bring Dr. Chamberland and Bill to. It's in a hallway that's guarded. No one is allowed down here. It's been a rule since we started doing fights here, so no one even tries anymore.

It's dark, so it turns people away naturally. Walking down a long black hallway turns even the bravest person around. Especially when they don't know what could be lurking around the corner. I stop in front of a door and place my thumb on the keypad. Opening the door, I walk in and pull McKenzie in behind me. I wrap my arms around her and hold her close, taking advantage of the quiet moments before Rex shows with Bill and Dr. Chamberland.

She rubs her hands over my bare skin and kisses my left pec. "I hate what I remembered."

I lean back to look at her, gripping the back of her neck slightly. "I know, love. I'm so sorry that happened to you, but they will pay."

She pulls her bottom lip between her teeth, looking off to the side before she looks back at me. "You're going to kill them." It's not a question. She knows what's going to happen.

"I am. You can stay, go into the other room, or you can kill them and I'll watch." She pulls back slightly and mulls it over in her mind.

"I wish Anna was here." That's not what I was expecting her to say.

"Why?"

She lifts one shoulder. "Because I promised her we'd do it together." She sighs. "I don't know if William or Bill did anything to her, but Dr. Chamberland did. Well, he didn't stop it."

I kiss her forehead and pull away from her completely going to the cage that holds my weapons. "We found Dick the dean. Well, Rex found him. He's leaving tomorrow to go track him down, so we'll let her kill him."

She snorts and nods as she watches me. "Are you going to torture them first?" she asks as I put some tools on a silver tray.

"Yes." They will pay. She walks over and stands next to me, her hand shakes slightly as she rubs her finger along each tool. I rub my finger from her shoulder down to her elbow. "You don't have to stay in here while I do this, but those men are going to pay for what they did to you, Anna, and probably countless other women."

She puts her face in her hands. "I want to kill him. I do, but I don't know if I can." I grip her biceps and turn her to face me.

Leaning down, I look her in the eye. "There is nothing wrong with that, love. It doesn't make you weak."

She nods, but doesn't look convinced. "I want to stay until Rex brings them in. I want them to be forced to face me. To know they got caught." I pull her into my arms and kiss the top of her head.

"Whatever you want, love. It's yours."

Chapter 26

McKenzie

Phoenix takes my hand and leads me to a door I didn't notice. It leads into a room that looks similar to the VIP room we were in earlier tonight. It has a self-serve bar off to one side stocked with all the drinks that you could want. There's also a wine refrigerator, and a stainless steel refrigerator maybe for snacks. There are couches and chairs placed strategically throughout the room.

"This is the celebration room, so they won't suspect anything." Phoenix's jaw clenches and inhales deeply. "The amount of times I've had drinks with both Bill and Dr. Chamberland in this room and they smiled and joked with me, all the while abusing you."

My hand flutters to my throat, and I finger the collar. My stomach dips as I realize what he means. "Bill started fighting here while I was kidnapped?" I ask. Nix nods, his neck and face red with rage. "I'm never taking this off," I whisper.

His eyes collide with mine. There's hope and relief in them. "Are you sure? You can take it off when you're at home." I love that he's making sure I'm okay with this.

"But I was taken the second time from our property." I can tell Nix wants to argue, but his phone vibrates, so he looks at the screen.

"They're on the way."

I gesture to his naked chest. "You're still not wearing a shirt. It's very distracting."

He chuckles and walks over to a wardrobe. Opening it, he grabs a white button-up shirt that looks exactly like the one he had on earlier and puts it on. He grabs my hand and walks me over to the bar. "Want a rum and coke?"

I scowl at him. "You said I couldn't have any more alcohol."

He snorts. "Things have changed significantly in the past couple of hours. But that was also because I wanted your mind clear while we were watching the fight."

I twist my lips to the side as I think. "Do you know what I'd rather have?"

He steps in close to me, wrapping his arm around my waist. "What's that?"

I can tell by his expression he already knows what I'm going to say. "An orgasm."

He grins at me, but his eyes are full of concern. "Even after the memory you just had?"

I bite my bottom lip and lift my shoulder. "I'd like for you to take that memory away," I admit.

He leans forward and kisses my hairline. "Anything you want, love."

I sag into him and he supports my weight. This man. He has no idea how amazing he is. I open my mouth to tell him, but before I can, the door opens. I stiffen in his arms and his grip on my waist tightens slightly. My back is to the door, so I don't see as they enter. I glance up at Nix as my heart begins to race. He rubs his thumb along my cheek and leans down, kissing me softly.

He pulls away slightly, his lips still brushing mine. "Act naturally in the beginning. You'll know when you can confront them." I nod once and he gives me one more kiss before tapping me lightly on the ass, and turning me around to face my nightmare.

I force myself to keep my face neutral, even though all kinds of emotions are roaring through my veins right now. Dr. Chamberland looks the same as he always did, but he looks exhausted and unkempt. I wonder if his lifestyle is creeping up on him. He has his hair slicked back, but it looks like it's slicked back from grease, not product, and he has dark circles under his eyes. He rubs the back of his neck and unbuttons the top button of his shirt. His eyes flit around the room, not staying on one person too long.

Bill, I can only glimpse at. I know if I look at him any longer, I won't be able to contain my emotions. He's bald, has various tattoos along his chest and arms, and his eyes look almost black. Like he's possessed, and it freaks me out. One side of his mouth tips up slightly and his eyes wander down my body like he's remembering all the things he did to me and I have to look away. I smile at Rex, and he gives me an encouraging smile in return.

"Your wife is here to celebrate with us tonight," Bill says. He begins to walk toward us and I internally freak out, afraid of what he's going to do. Nix wraps his arms around my waist and pulls me against his chest. His warmth invades my senses, and it helps me calm down slightly.

"Yes," Nix responds. "This is McKenzie." Bill extends his hand in an attempt to shake mine, but I only stare at it. I will not touch this man and he will never touch me again.

He arches an eyebrow. "No handshake?" I shake my head no. "That's rude."

Nix comes to his full height and maneuvers me so I'm slightly behind him, but can still see everyone in the room. "Don't speak to my wife that way. If she doesn't want to shake your hand, she doesn't have to. Do you touch women against their will often?"

Bill takes a step back and raises his hands in surrender, his eyes narrowing slightly. Dr. Chamberland's shoulders pull back and he watches our interaction more closely than he was. "Sorry, man. I didn't mean anything by it."

"Make sure it doesn't happen again," Nix snaps.

Bill nods and offers a smile that he might think is placating, but only looks creepy. "So, are we celebrating or what? I'm ready to go get my girl for the night." The way he says that it makes my stomach clench and brings every nerve in my body to attention. Trying my best to play it off, I walk over to the drinks, Phoenix not too far behind me.

"What will you have?" I ask.

"Beer for me," Bill responds.

I open the fridge and Phoenix grabs a bottle of Corona. He pops the top and grabs a lime, putting it in the top, but I notice before he puts the lime in he drops some powder. I glance at him and he nods at me slightly.

"What about you Dr. Chamberland?" I swallow past the lump in my throat. My heart is beating erratically. I might pass out tonight if I keep putting my heart through all this.

"Red wine for me, whatever is open," he replies.

I glance over my shoulder and notice him and Bill sitting on one of the couches next to each other. Rex is talking to them, keeping them distracted. Nix hands me a small paper container that looks like a small pixie stick candy.

"Pour that in his wine. Can you do that?" he asks. I nod slightly. Grabbing the only bottle of red wine that's open, I pour him some and quickly pour in the powder Nix gave me. I swirl the liquid in the glass and turn with Nix. We walk to them and with every step, the beat of my heart becomes louder in my ears.

These men are about to die, and they have no idea. Nix hands Bill his beer and I hand Dr. Chamberland his wine. I kind of wish I had taken that rum and coke now. I need something to calm my nerves. Nix walks back over to the bar and I swear my heart stops in my chest. Rex moves where he's closer to me and I breathe again.

Something Bill said earlier clicks in my head and I tilt my head to gaze at him. He's halfway through his beer, but Dr. Chamberland has only taken a few sips of his wine. *What if they react differently to whatever it was Nix gave them?* I mentally shake my head, not worried about that right now.

"Which girl are you going to get tonight?" I ask Bill as he's about to take another pull from his bottle. Nix comes up next to me and hands me a glass of dark liquid. I'm sure it's rum and coke, so I give him a grateful smile. Nix puts another Corona on the table in front of Bill. I turn my attention back to Bill to watch him closely.

He finally shrugs. "Whoever I want. I'm the reigning champion. Any girl will be happy to go home with me." He drinks the rest of his beer and grabs the other beer Phoenix brought. I wonder if that one is drugged too.

"What about Shay?" I remember what Felix said earlier and I want to ease my mind that Bill didn't do something to her. I don't even remember Shay, but apparently I know her and if I do, I would be concerned about her wellbeing.

"What about her?" The smirk on his face tells me all I need to know. Nix places his hand on the small of my back, communicating with me he'll take over. I take a sip of my drink and savor the taste.

"We haven't seen her in four months. Have you seen her recently?" Nix asks. Rex makes a small move, so he's closer to me, but it seems I'm the only one who notices.

I wonder where Jason is. What if things go badly? Bill can fight. What if he hurts Nix or Rex?

"I can't remember when I saw her last. Why?"

I tilt my head to look at him. *I think he's had one too many punches to the head.*

"Because we haven't seen her in four months," Nix replies slowly. Dr. Chamberland watches this exchange as he sips from his wineglass. Part of me wants to tell him to drink it quicker. *What if Bill gets affected first?* I size Dr. Chamberland up. *He isn't the bigger threat, so maybe it will be okay.*

Bill stands quickly, and I flinch slightly. Nix wraps his arm around my waist and pulls me into his side. Bill sways slightly on his feet, and he puts his hand to his head. "I stood too fast." His words are slurred slightly.

"Shay?" Nix presses.

Bill rolls his eyes. "I had some fun with her a few months ago. Yeah."

Dr. Chamberland drinks the rest of his wine and continues to remain quiet. He probably thinks it's in his best interest. No one says anything. It's unnaturally quiet in the room as Bill sways again. Dr. Chamberland puts his head in his hand like he's beginning to feel the effects of the drug as well.

"But..." Bill's words slurring. "I didn't do anything to her she wasn't asking for." I bite my tongue so hard I taste copper. Rex moves even closer to me, and I know whatever they have planned is about to happen.

"What about my wife?"

Chapter 27

Phoenix

Dr. Chamberland's head slowly lifts, the drug taking an effect on him. I put more in his wineglass, knowing he'd only drink one and drink it slowly. Bill's gaze slides to McKenzie, but I step in the way.

"Don't look at her. Look at me."

Bill's eyes widen and he backs up slightly, running into the couch, then he stumbles and falls back. Dr. Chamberland jerks slightly from the sudden movement. Bill tries to stand again but sways, so he puts a hand out to catch himself.

"What did you give us?" Dr. Chamberland asks, but I ignore him.

Bill stands again, and he rotates his head to look at Dr. Chamberland. Their movements are so slow it would be comical if I wasn't filled with rage at what they did to McKenzie. I nod at Rex and he walks to the door, letting Jason in. They both grab Dr. Chamberland and escort him into the room McKenzie and I left earlier.

"What's going on?" Bill asks, falling back on the couch again. The drugs I gave them cause temporary muscle paralysis. Bill is our top fighter for a reason, so I had to do something to put him at a disadvantage.

McKenzie hasn't said anything in a few minutes, so I glance at her to make sure she's okay. Her eyes are brimming with tears and something akin to hatred shines in her eyes as she looks at Bill.

Bill turns his head slightly like he's going to look at her again, but I step in front of her so he has to look at me. "You remember?" His head lifts, trying to see over my shoulder. McKenzie steps beside me and clutches my bicep, her nails digging into the skin.

It reminds me of the night I bought her when I told her to dig her nails into my forearm. Her eyes narrow at Bill and she nods. Bill's mouth turns up into a demeaning smile. "The best fuck I ever had." I whip my head around to look at him, and Bill turns that smile on me. "All that time you were looking for her and I had her."

I take a step toward him, trying to decide if I kill him now or torture him longer than I planned. But a streak of silver flies past me. McKenzie grabs a beer bottle, pulls her arm back with such fierceness it makes me proud, and breaks it across his cheek, screaming the entire time.

Bill's face jerks with the force of her hit, a shard of glass sticking from his cheek. Blood pours down his face to his neck. He doesn't react to the pain I know he must be feeling. The drugs I gave them paralyzes them, but it doesn't block the pain. I did that intentionally, especially for Bill, because he's a strong fucker. He slowly turns his head back around and gives a bloody smile.

McKenzie still has the bottleneck in her hand and she pulls her hand back to strike him again, but I put my hand on her shoulder gently. She whips her head around pissed I stopped her. I lift my hands. "All I'm asking is that you don't kill him. Not yet."

"I wasn't going to." She snaps and turns back to glare at Bill. "What did you do to Shay?" My girl is still worried about someone else.

Bill's head lags against the back of the couch. "She's chained to my bed."

My hands ball into fists. *Fucking shit! This is a hard lesson learned.* I'll begin conducting check-ins with all the girls from now on.

"Which arm is his strongest?" McKenzie asks me. I know she's doing it to taunt him and make him think he'll get out of this alive.

I nod toward his right. "He's good on both sides, but his right side is his dominant." Before I'm done with my sentence, she sinks the remainder of the bottle in his right bicep and twists it, shredding flesh and muscles. Bill screams, blood dribbling out of his mouth. The scream is filled with pain and the knowledge he'll never win another fight again.

Rex and Jason come storming through the door, guns drawn, but they stop short at the sight of McKenzie standing over Bill as she breathes hard. She spits on him and turns away, tears spilling down her cheeks. She has blood splattered on her arm, neck, and chest, but she doesn't notice. She falls into my arms, sobbing.

I hold her and motion to Rex and Jason to get Bill. While they take care of him, I pull Kenz to the other side of the room. Sitting in an overstuffed chair, I pull her down on my lap and try to soothe her, while she lets go of all the emotions running through her. Some of the blood that was splattered on her rubs off on my shirt. That's why I keep a wardrobe here. Grabbing my phone, I call Felix.

"Hey boss." He pauses for a moment. "Everything alright?" I'm sure he hears McKenzie, but I don't care right now.

"Do you know where Bill lives?"

"Yeah."

"Go to his place and get Shay. He's got her chained up there."

"What the fuck?!?" Felix shouts so loud I have to hold the phone away from my ear. "I'll kill that motherfucker."

"Don't worry, that's being taken care of." I promise him, rubbing my free hand up and down McKenzie's back.

Her sobs have turned into hiccups and she's clinging to me. *I'm going to make them pay.* And the fact my mother was here tonight too is unbelievable. What the hell kind of game is she playing? Why is she always lurking? All the years I wasted looking for her and it seems she's tried to sabotage me at every corner.

"Tell me where you bury him so I can go piss on his grave. I'll head to his place now."

"Make sure to watch your back. He had help." It's all I can tell him for now, at least until I can figure out what to do about my bitch of a mother. I hang up and wrap my arms around McKenzie, holding her until her muscles lose some of the tension.

"I want to kill him," she whispers. I lean back and push her hair away from her face. I study her, my eyes narrowing and my lips pursing as her eyes lock with mine.

"Kenz—"

She shakes her head. "He violated me in the worst way imaginable and he laughed about it. How many other women has he done this to?" Her voice cracks on a sob. I cup her face with my hands and rub my thumbs over her cheeks. A small speck of blood smears as I do it.

Her face is flushed, and her pulse is beating hard beneath my grasp. "I'm sorry I didn't find you soon enough," I murmur. She grips the sides of my neck with her small hands, her skin cold even though she's flushed.

"It's not your fault, Nix." Her lips brush over mine as she speaks.

My heart beats heavy in my chest with guilt. "It is. I was so focused on my hatred of your father. I never considered someone else took you, let alone my own fucking mother." I squeeze my eyes shut, wishing I could do things differently. Wanting to kill my father for not being honest with me. "If I hadn't received a tip of where you were, I don't know if I would have ever found you."

She leans back slightly and tilts her head at me. "You received a tip?"

I heave a sigh and brush my lips over her forehead. "Yes, an unaddressed envelope showed up at my office with your rings inside and the address of the place you were being held at."

She shifts and sits back, her lips twisting to the side. "Who sent it to you?"

"I don't know. We tested it for fingerprints, but nothing came back." I swallow as I feel a hole opening in my chest that aches. "I assumed it was your father toying with me."

Kenz pushes off my lap and begins to pace. "I need to find my father. Does he go to the auctions anymore?"

The last thing I want is for her to go looking for her father. He may not have been behind her being taken, but I still don't trust him. He still sold her. He still trusted a man that shouldn't have been trusted. I scoff inwardly. Not that I'm any better. I trusted my father. I trusted Dr. Chamberland. I knew Bill was unhinged, but didn't realize how unhinged. I push my hands in my pockets as the pit in my stomach grows more pronounced.

"He hasn't been to one in a while. He might go once a year. I used to think it was his way of reminding me he was still around, but knowing what I know now, it was probably so he could check on you and make sure you were okay."

Before she can respond, Rex comes back into the room. "Everything is ready, sir." I nod at him and extend my hand to McKenzie. She stares at it for a long moment. I wouldn't blame her if she didn't take it. After all the shit I've put her through, I wouldn't blame her if she walked away from me and never returned this time.

But she does put her hand in mine. Then she looks up at me with those big brown eyes of hers and gives me a small smile. "We'll make it through this. Together." Relief courses through my veins.

"Together."

Chapter 28

McKenzie

Nix and I follow Rex into the room we were in earlier. Bill and Dr. Chamberland are chained to chairs. The chairs look like the kind at a dentist's office. The silver tray Nix was preparing is on a rolling cart between the two chairs. Dr. Chamberland's eyes are wide with fear as he watches us walk in, hand in hand.

Bill is sweating profusely, blood still running down his cheek from the shard of glass sticking out. I glance at his arm and notice the bottle is right where I twisted it. I had no idea I had that in me. Pure rage filled my veins when he laughed at what he did to me and taunted Nix, but when he said Shay was chained to his bed, I lost it.

I wonder how many women he's sexually assaulted. How many women has Dr. Chamberland drugged? Bill doesn't seem right in the head, but Dr. Chamberland he seems normal. I sigh and shake my head. *I guess you never really know someone. Not really.*

That thought tickles something in my brain. Something that's just out of reach. Something that's right there on the edge and if I could just touch it, I'll be able to pull it out of the blackness in that part of my brain that has forgotten so many things. When it doesn't come out of that darkness, my shoulders sag in defeat.

I'll remember. I will. Rex steps up beside me, concern evident in his eyes. He hands me a wet washcloth and I realize it's to wash off the blood that sprayed on me from what I did to Bill. I give him a grateful smile and wipe it off. It's so strange. I thought I'd feel some twinge of guilt for what I did to Bill, but I don't.

Maybe I am my father's daughter. I can do unimaginable things without it causing any type of guilt. It could also be because I did it to someone who deserved it. Perhaps the men my father did it to deserved it as well. Hope is beginning to swell within me that my father is the man I remember as a young girl.

The one that would sneak me a cookie and push me in the swing. Until my mother was killed. That feeling comes back. The one where I know I'm forgetting something. Missing something.

"You okay?" Rex asks me.

I realize I zoned out, and Nix is walking from the wardrobe at the side of the room. He's taken his shirt off again. I take in his tattoos, his abs, and the V that disappears below the waistband of his pants. I remember earlier tonight crawling to him, taking him in my mouth, and being reminded he tattooed the very spot I gave him a hickey for the first time.

He stops in front of me with a small smile on his lips, like he knows what I'm thinking. "I'm okay," I tell Rex, not taking my eyes off of Phoenix. Bill and Dr. Chamberland are being unusually quiet, but I don't question it. Maybe Rex gagged them. "It's weird," I begin to say as I take a step closer to Nix and rub my right hand over his pec and shoulder while tracing the lines of his abs with my left hand. He sucks in a breath and I tip my lips into a slight smile.

"What's weird, love?" he asks as he allows me to continue to explore him.

Right, I was going to say something. How easily he distracts me. "It's weird how turned on I still am." His muscles tighten beneath my hands. "I want you to erase the memory of him, but it's not just that. It's you protecting me, your dominance, the way you love me, everything." I step even closer to him, my breasts pressing against his chest. "I still want that orgasm you promised."

He wraps a hand around the back of my neck and pulls me closer. He leans down and kisses me long and hard, with his tongue brushing against mine. "You'll get it." He steps away and turns to look at Dr. Chamberland and Bill. "As soon as I kill these motherfuckers."

Dr. Chamberland begins to mumble something. I look closer and see the strap wrapped around his head. He *is* gagged. Bill thrashes against his chains. Nix rubs his hands together. "I see the drug is wearing off for you." He walks over to his metal tray, ignoring the mumbling still coming from Dr. Chamberland.

He picks up an injection needle and turns to me. "Should I give them more, love?" I stare at him. I have no idea what the right answer is. "If I give them the injection, it will completely paralyze them, but they'll remain awake. I'll be able to torture them and they'll feel everything, but since this one is more potent, they won't be able to scream. With the powder, they could still scream."

To prove his point, he grabs the bottleneck that's still sticking out of Bill's arm and twists it. Bill screams behind his gag, saliva and blood dripping down the corners of his mouth. Dr. Chamberland's eyes shift to the right, as his body trembles and tears stream down his face. I walk toward him and place my hands on the arms of his chair.

"Do you know what you're feeling right now, Dr. Chamberland?" He's struggling, trying to swallow only for drool to spill out of his mouth, down his chin, to his throat and disappearing behind his buttoned up shirt. "It's what I felt every time you drugged me, not knowing if that dose would kill me or if I'd wake up. How many girls have you drugged? How long have you worked with her?"

I don't mention it's Phoenix's mom because I don't know how much Rex and Jason know, and it's not my place to tell them. His eyes seem to say he's sorry, but is he sorry because he got caught or because he really feels remorse?

I glance over my shoulder at Rex. "Can you take his gag off?" Rex hesitates for a moment before doing what I asked. When the gag comes off, Dr. Chamberland begins to sob.

"McKenzie, please forgive me. Please!"

Phoenix snorts from where he's standing between the two chairs. "Why should she forgive you?"

Dr. Chamberland's eyes shift to Nix. "I told you where she was. I helped you find her."

My heart beats heavy in my chest and before I can blink, Nix is standing in front of Dr. Chamberland with his hand around his throat. He squeezes so hard I know it's cutting off the doctor's air supply.

"It was you? You sent me her rings?"

Dr. Chamberland begins to thrash, his eyes bugging so hard it's almost fascinating when a blood vessel bursts in his eye and a bright red spot appears at the edge of his eye. I place my hand on Nix's shoulder. "Don't kill him yet, Nix." Nix holds on for a few more seconds and I wonder if he'll actually let him go, but he finally does.

Dr. Chamberland takes in huge breaths, a bruise already forming on his throat where Nix held him with all his might. Surprisingly, Bill has stayed quiet during this entire exchange. Maybe because he's in so much pain, he doesn't care, or he knows it's in his best interest to keep his mouth shut right now.

Nix turns and looks at Rex. "I need a drink." Rex nods once and walks toward the other room where the small bar is. He turns to me before he opens the door.

"Do you need anything, Miss Kenzie?"

My throat is dry, and I never got to finish the rum and coke Nix poured me earlier. "Water and the rum and coke Nix made me earlier." Rex nods and walks into the other room. I lift my hand to push my hair out of my face, my hand shaking slightly. Nix appears in front of me, blocking my view of the two men.

"Kenz, if you need to stop it's okay." I smile at him.

"I love how you have always looked out for me. How you've always protected me. Even when I didn't realize that's what you were doing." I lean up on my toes and kiss him softly on the lips. "I'm okay Nix. Yes, this is a lot. But these men have taken so much from so many women, not just me. I want them to pay, and I'm going to help."

My voice leaves no room for argument. He nods once and kisses me on the forehead. Rex enters the room with our drinks plus a few bottles of water. Nix walks over to him to grab both our drinks, and he hands me mine. I take a sip of it, relishing the coldness in my hot, dry mouth. Nix downs his in one gulp and places it back on the tray Rex brought them in.

Nix turns and faces the men, rubbing his hands together again. "Let's get this party started, shall we?"

Chapter 29

Phoenix

I turn and look at the two men while the alcohol warms my veins slightly. The amount of respect I had for Dr. Chamberland completely vanished. All the times I admitted to him how worried I was about McKenzie and the whole time he knew where she was.

"Phoenix, I'm sorry," he whispers. Tears and snot dripping down his face.

I lean over him again. "I don't want to hear it, doc. You knew. You fucking knew I was going out of my mind and you lied to my face." The blood in my veins begins to bubble from rage. I want to skin him and make him feel every bit of pain I felt for those months she was missing.

"I know," he croaks. "I know I deserve what you're going to do to me. But I loved her. I would have done anything for her."

I stand to my full height. "My mother?" I shake my head and Bill snorts. "It looks like she's deceived all of us. She used you."

The truth shines in his eyes. "I know," he murmurs again. "That's why I finally told you where she was. I couldn't do it anymore. I knew she was using me. I knew she didn't love me. So, I finally told you where she was." He sucks in a shaky breath.

I look at McKenzie. She has her hands covering her mouth as she listens to him. "Don't feel sorry for him, love. He had a choice. I understand being crazy in love. Trust me. But not to the point that you're hurting someone else."

She looks at me. "I'd never ask you to do that."

"Exactly."

Understanding dawns in her eyes. She knows I wouldn't do it if she asked, but she would never put me in that position to begin with. Dr. Chamberland should have known my mother didn't love him. The more I learn about my mother, the more I loathe her.

The woman I've had up on a pedestal my entire life wasn't just pushed off, she's been incinerated.

I turn my attention back to Dr. Chamberland. "What about Anna? If you felt so bad, why didn't you do something about her?"

Dr. Chamberland takes in a shaky breath. "I left her container door open on purpose, so someone who was working the dock would look in it to inspect it and find her." He squeezes his eyes shut. "I hate myself for everything I did. I realized it too late."

"Yes, you did." I check in with Kenz one more time to make sure she's okay. She nods slightly, letting me know she's fine.

I walk to the silver tray and grab my gun. I back up and stare at Dr. Chamberland. Bill begins to buck against his chains, the drug having lost its effect on him already. I nod at Rex to take care of it and focus on Dr. Chamberland again.

Within a few moments, Bill's bucks lessen. I don't know if Rex gave him the entire syringe or not. Right now I don't care. I want Bill to suffer for what he did to McKenzie. I have a little more sympathy for Dr. Chamberland. He was deceived by mother just like I was.

I don't have enough sympathy for him to let him live, though. The moment I found out what my mother did and had time to process it, I chose McKenzie. I'll always choose McKenzie. "Close your eyes, love, if you don't want to watch." I glance at McKenzie over my shoulder, but she doesn't close her eyes.

She stares at Dr. Chamberland, who gives her a sad smile. "I'm so sorry, McKenzie. I wish I could change it."

"Why did you give me drugs to make me lose my memory?" she asks.

"I was trying to spare you. I didn't want you to remember everything that was done to you. I…" He swallows. "I don't know what all was done to you. I refused to watch, but I was trying to help, so you didn't have to live with it for the rest of your life."

McKenzie steps forward, with tears streaming down her face. "That's a bunch of shit and you know it. You were saving yourself, so you wouldn't get caught. All you did to me was give me these gaps in my life I can't remember. And even the memories that have come back, I don't trust them. Not completely. It still feels like something's missing." She shakes her head and wipes her hand across her face.

She motions to me to finish it. Dr. Chamberland looks at me with understanding in his eyes. I raise my gun and shoot him between his eyes. McKenzie flinches at the gunshot and Bill's eyes widen slightly. I turn and grasp McKenzie's shoulders lightly.

"Are you okay?"

Tears are still streaming down her face and she sniffs. "Yes. Why do I feel sorry for him?"

I pull her into my arms and hold her tight. "Because you're good." She wraps her arms around my neck and holds me tight. I lift her slightly. "You're better than me; the best person I've ever known."

She kisses my neck, my cheek, my ear. "You're good. You're so good," she whispers in my ear. I'm not, but I'll let her believe it. When she loosens her grip, I set her down and kiss the top of her head. Turning my attention back to Bill, his eyes are looking toward Dr. Chamberland. He's unable to move.

Without giving him time to process what I'm going to do, I grab the switchblade in my pocket, flip it open, and plunge it into his thigh. He groans and his eyes widen to the size of saucers. McKenzie squeaks in surprise. I look at her and she's staring at the knife sticking out of his thigh.

"Is there anything you want to do to him?" I ask her.

Bill looks from me to her. I'm sure when he got here tonight, he didn't think it would be his last night alive. He probably thought that he'd get to party upstairs, then go home and fuck Shay who he has chained to his bed. And next weekend he'd get to come back for the next fight, all the while keeping me in the dark. Why he thought he'd be able to get away with this forever is beyond me. He's obviously been hit too many times. But now he's going to meet the man people are afraid of. The man people won't cross because they know what I'll do to them. McKenzie grabs the drink that Rex brought her and gulps it down.

"No," she finally answers. "I just want to kill him."

I glance at Rex and Jason. I don't think Bill ever touched Anna, but you never know. "What about you Rex?"

He shakes his head. "I'm saving my revenge for Dick." Jason smirks, and I nod in approval. He hasn't been to an auction since I bought McKenzie. He probably knows better. I made sure he got fired from Brighton. Photographs of him buying those girls were mailed to each board member with a threat that if something wasn't done swiftly, they would all be fired as well.

I turn my attention back to Bill. "Guess you're all mine." I grab the forceps and click them in front of Bill's face. He sucks in a breath and I think he attempts to shake his head, but nothing happens. I could pull the beer bottle out of his arm. I wonder if he'd bleed out. We don't need that. Not yet.

I grab the hand on his unhurt arm, put the forceps under his thumbnail and yank it off. He moans against the gag in his mouth. I walk behind him and unhook the gag, taking it off him. I'm not sure if he'll be able to scream or not, probably not, but that's why this room is soundproof. No one will be able to hear him.

I remove the rest of his fingernails one by one, talking to him as I do it. "You know, I bought McKenzie at an auction." I look at her to gauge her reaction, but her eyes are stuck on Bill and what I'm doing to him. Bill groans as I yank another finger nail off, tears, sweat, and blood streaming down his face. I reach up and yank the shard of glass out of his cheek.

He screeches slightly, and I hum. Not quite screaming yet. "I made it clear when I had to have sex with her in front of all those people they were to stay behind the boundary I created." I have four more nails to go. "Five men didn't respect that boundary and tried to get closer. Of course, Rex took care of that. Later that night, we came to this very room. I cut their dicks off, stuck it in their mouths, sewed their mouths shut and left to go grab something to eat."

I'm done yanking his fingernails off. I grab my hammer and without any kind of warning, bring it down on his left hand. The bones in his hand shatter instantly. McKenzie turns away at that, so I stop and walk over to her. I don't try to turn her around or get in front of her. I have some blood on me and I don't want to upset her.

"If you need to go to the other room and take a break, you can," I whisper behind her. I wrap my hand around her hair and lift it off her neck. She's flushed and sweaty, but maybe this will help cool her off slightly.

"I'm okay, Nix. The sound was worse than watching it," she whispers.

"Rex can get you some earplugs if you want."

She sucks in a breath and nods slightly. Rex goes over to the wardrobe I have in the corner of the room and opens one of the drawers. He comes back with some earplugs.

"You twist them slightly and put them in the ear canal, then they'll expand," he explains. She opens the packet and does as he instructed and turns back around to face me. I study her, making sure she really is okay.

"I'm okay. This is a lot." She shrugs slightly and I nod.

I won't keep this going much longer. I can tell she's exhausted and ready for it to be over. As much as I'd like to extend his torture for hours, maybe days, I know Kenz won't be able to handle that. And after all the hell she's been through, I'm not going to make her. I kiss Kenz's cheek and turn back to face Bill.

"Anyway, as I was saying." I walk over to the side of his chair and adjust it so he's leaning back like in a recliner. I reach for his jeans that he changed into and unbutton and unzip them. He knows what's coming with the portion of my story I've already told. I yank his pants down along with his underwear. "Tighty whities? Come on man, are you three?"

I put gloves on because I'm not touching his dick. Anger courses through my veins at the thought of it being inside McKenzie. I was supposed to be the only man she ever slept with and this asshole ruined that. I take the sharpest knife I have, grab his dick, and chop it off. He screams this time. Taking advantage of his open mouth, I shove his dick in his mouth. He gurgles around it, his eyes bulging so much he looks like a cartoon character. Rex is at my side, handing me a needle and thread. He holds the top of his head and the bottom of his chin, keeping his mouth closed.

I sew a few stitches, but not like with the other men. Only enough to give McKenzie time to kill him. Stepping back, I stare at him. He's still moaning, blood pouring from his face, his arm, his fingernails, and now his groin. He's a mess, so I bask in it for a moment.

Before I can say anything, my phone rings. Yanking the gloves off that I put on, I grab it and see it's Felix.

"Yeah," I answer.

"I got her boss. She needs a doctor. Do you think Dr. Chamberland is available?"

I glance toward the slumped body of the doctor. "No, he's not. He's no longer on my payroll. Take her to the Medical Center and ask for Dorothy."

"Got it." He hangs up, and I pocket my phone.

"We got Shay. You deserve so much worse than what you're getting, but my wife wants to kill you and I'm going to let her."

I turn to McKenzie. Her breathing has quickened and her eyes are wide. She's not looking directly at Bill. She's looking over his shoulder. I study her concern flitting up my spine.

"Kenz?" I say loudly so she'll hear me. Her attention snaps to me.

She removes one of her earplugs. "I'm ready. I want to do it, then I want to get out of this room."

"Kenz, this is something you'll never be able to take back or undo. If you don't think you'll be able to handle it—"

"Phoenix, I can handle it. I'm sick of men telling me what I can and can not do. I'm sick of being lied to and taken advantage of. I'm sick of it and I want him to pay for what he did to me and Shay and probably other women." She gestures to Bill, but I know I'm included in that sentence. I've lied to her and taken advantage of her feelings for me, but somehow she still loves me. I don't deserve her.

She puts the earplug back in her ear. I hand her my gun and she takes it, weighing it in her hands. "You know how to shoot. I took you to practice quite a bit after the first time you were taken, so instinct should take over even if you can't remember it. Aim between his eyes and shoot."

She nods once and steps forward, standing in front of Bill. Rex has moved behind us and I stand next to McKenzie, letting her feel my support and also letting her know I'm here if she decides she can't follow through with it. She stares at Bill for several seconds. "I hope you rot in hell." Then she lifts the gun, points it between his eyes and shoots twice.

Chapter 30

McKenzie

My body sways slightly and I open my eyes enough to see Phoenix lifting me from the SUV. I lay my head on his shoulder and wrap my arms around his neck as he carries me into the house. I'm exhausted and feel so dirty. No one speaks as we enter the house, and Phoenix carries me up the stairs. He walks into our room and directly to the bathroom.

He sits me down gently on the bathroom counter and kisses my forehead. "I'm going to warm up the shower." He keeps his voice low as he steps back, making sure I don't crumple from exhaustion. He yanks the T-shirt off he put on before leaving the warehouse and throws it in the laundry basket.

His muscles ripple beneath his skin as he leans into the shower and turns it on, closes the door, and walks back over to me. He grips the camisole I wore tonight, so I raise my hands as he takes it off and throws it on top of his shirt. His fingers trace the collar around my throat before reaching inside his jeans and taking the key out of his wallet.

I recoil at the thought of him taking it off. In such a short amount of time, I've become attached to it. "I'll put it back on after we take a shower," he promises. I nod once and sit up so he can unlock it. Exhaustion and sadness overwhelms me as tears begin to stream down my face.

"If only I had it before." I choke on the words and Nix gathers me in his arms, trying to comfort me. When he realizes my sobs aren't going to stop anytime soon, he pulls back slightly and finishes undressing, then helps me out of my jeans. He lifts me in his arms again and walks into the shower with me. He puts us directly under the stream of the water.

I sag into him as the warm water washes away the grime, sweat, and blood. My body shakes with the sobs wracking through my body. I'm not crying over what we did to that asshole. I'm crying for innocence lost, for all the women he hurt, and for the memories I still don't have.

Nix is like an anchor in the middle of my storm. He holds me tight and doesn't waver. Our relationship may have started on rocky ground, but he chose me. That's all I wanted. He chose me over his mother, even over his own morals. Morals he swears he doesn't have, but I know him. He is good. I don't care what he says. He is good and I will spend the rest of my life showing him that.

My sobs finally lessen, and I look up at Nix. My husband. The love of my life. He returns my gaze, those piercing blue eyes focused solely on me. "I love you." The relief in his eyes breaks my heart. I lift my hand and rub it along his jaw. "You checked in with me multiple times tonight. You have no idea how much I needed that. And you got rid of two men that did awful things to me and so many other women. You chose me."

He rests his forehead on mine and pushes my wet hair over my shoulder. "I'll always choose you. Always." He kisses me softly.

When he pulls away, I slump even more in his arms. Exhaustion is going to pull me under any moment now. Nix grabs my shampoo and turns me around. He washes my hair while massaging my temples. Then he grabs my loofah and body wash and proceeds to wash me. He massages my spine and shoulders, trying to ease the tension in my muscles.

I sink into his touch, enjoying how he works the knots out of my muscles. When he's done, I return the favor and wash him from head to toe. When we're finished, he turns the water off and grabs our towels. He wraps his around his waist and dries me off. I need to dry my hair because it will be a nest in the morning if I don't, but I don't feel like it.

"I'll braid it for you," he murmurs, reading my mind. I wrap the towel around me and stand in front of the mirror as he steps up behind me. Grabbing the hair brush he runs it through my hair a few times before plaiting it.

"How do you know how to do this?" My voice is barely above a whisper. I don't want to break the atmosphere we've created.

He glances at me through the mirror. "You taught me how." Disappointment settles in my stomach.

"I didn't know." I swallow and close my eyes, sighing deeply.

He kisses my exposed shoulder. "You will," he promises. I open my eyes and give him a soft smile. He's so sure I'll remember. I wish

I felt as sure as he did. When he finishes, he wraps a hairband around the end of my braid. We brush our teeth, then he leads the way into our bedroom.

I grab a T-shirt out of his drawer and pull it on. I don't bother with panties as I crawl into bed. Phoenix is right beside me, not bothering to put any clothes on. He settles on his back and I climb onto him. My head tucks beneath his chin and he wraps his arm around my waist. He doesn't complain about how needy I'm being. I just want his arms around me and his body heat surrounding me.

I wonder how he'd feel about spooning and being inside me without actually having sex. Before I can ask, sleep pulls me under.

I step out of the candy store with a bag of banana runts, because they're the best and this is the only place I can get just that flavor. It's hot and humid. Some days, the humidity is so bad it feels like walking through a sauna or a really hot shower. Nix had to go into the office today, so I joined him. I love walking down River Street while he works.

Usually after he gets done, we'll go to the piano bar or his rooftop restaurant. I know River Street is touristy, but I love it. I love watching the people, the kids, and the families. Everyone seems so normal. So different from me. I'm married to a man that will probably never love me. Not really. Not like I love him.

I'll never admit that to him or anyone. He already has so much sway over my decisions and emotions I can't give him anymore leverage. I walk over to the waving girl statue and sit on a brick wall, watching the River Cruise ships and the people. I take a few pictures for people.

A couple walks up to me and smiles. "Can you take our picture?" The girl asks. I nod and grab her phone. I take several of them in front of the statue and also in front of the water.

"Are you celebrating something?" I ask as I hand her the phone back. They smile at each other, obviously basking in their love. My chest and stomach burn at the look they share.

"We're on our honeymoon. We're taking two weeks to travel the eastern states," the man replies.

I force a smile. "Congratulations."

The girl looks down at my hand, and I realize she's looking at my ring. "How long have you been married?"

"Three and a half years," I reply.

"Are you still in the honeymoon phase?" She looks positively giddy. I swallow past the lump in my throat and nod enthusiastically. We can't keep our hands off each other, so maybe we are still in the honeymoon phase even though we've never actually been on a honeymoon. Out of the corner of my eye, I see Dr. Chamberland speaking to one of the security that constantly follows me around.

I sigh in relief, ready to leave this conversation. "I need to go. Have fun." I offer a slight wave they return as I head toward the doctor and Clyde. When they spot me, they both turn and offer me smiles. I wave as Clyde steps forward.

"Mr. Stone had an emergency and asked me to drive you home." My eyebrows cave in. That's odd. Usually Nix would call or text me. I grab my phone, but nothing. So, I send him a quick text. Maybe I'm being overly cautious, but after what happened all those years ago, I feel like I'm constantly looking over my shoulder for Nix's mother.

He still doesn't know it was her. He's still convinced it was my father. I still haven't relayed the message she told me to tell him all those years ago. For months after, I would try to get the courage to do it, but I never could. After a while, I finally stopped trying. Nix doesn't answer, which is unusual, so I nod at the men and follow Clyde to the car.

Dr. Chamberland says he has to go help Nix, so we say our goodbyes and I get in the SUV. I stare at my phone, waiting for a reply or something, but nothing comes. I want to call him, but I don't want to come off as desperate. When we get back to the house, I tell Clyde I'm going to walk down the lake.

"I'll let Phillip know we're back. Do you want some food?" he asks. I sigh, realizing I won't be eating with Nix today, so I agree. I walk down the hill toward the lake and stop at a bench I love. Sitting for a few minutes, I think back to the couple that was on their honeymoon. That's what I want. Love, not just lust. I want Phoenix to choose me over everything else.

Lead settles in my stomach. Maybe I'm asking for too much. Maybe I'm going to wind up just like my mother. In love with a man that won't love me the same way. I glance toward the water and stand. Whose boat is that? I've never seen that boat in my life. Before I can turn around and run back up the hill, an arm wraps around me and pulls me against a hard chest. Before I can scream, a hand slams over my mouth.

Nix's mother steps out from the trees. Fuck! She jerks her head and the man holding me against his chest walks down the hill. I don't make it easy for him, though. I jerk in his arms, trying to make him drop me, but his grip on me is strong. I finally get a good kick in and hit his shin. He almost drops me that time, but his hold stays true.

Nix's mother swirls around as she glowers at me. "If you don't come with me, I'll kill you, but first I'll kill Phoenix and I'll make you watch." I swallow and breathe heavily against the hand that's still on my mouth. The thought of the world being without Phoenix is not something I can fathom. I squeeze my eyes shut and stop fighting.

"I knew you loved him." I glare at her. I hate that she's right. I hate that I love him. But I do love him and there's nothing I can do about it.

"Come with me and nothing will happen to him." The man lifts his hand off my mouth when he senses the fight leaving me, but he still stands at my back, just in case I try to run.

"What did he ever do to you? He's been looking for you for years." I haven't seen her at an auction since the one where she took me. But I could feel her watching, lingering, and I still never told Nix. I'm such an idiot.

She smiles at me, it's menacing and I want to look away but I force myself to stay focused on her. "If I wanted to be found, he would have found me. Now, don't make me tell you again. Get in the boat." I exhale in defeat and climb into the boat, looking up at the house one last time. The house of my dreams that he allowed me to design. He wouldn't do that if he didn't love me, would he?

"Let's see if he'll come for you." She snorts like she doesn't believe he will.

I straighten my spine and narrow my eyes at her. "He will come for me. He always comes for me." She throws her head back and laughs, but I continue to glare at her. "When he finds out the evil bitch you are, he's going to kill you."

She laughs harder. "He would never kill me. Never."

I arch an eyebrow at her and turn away. "You'll see." It's a whisper and a promise. One I hope is true.

Chapter 31

McKenzie

I sit up in bed, covered in sweat. That day is so clear in my mind now. How sad and lonely I was. How badly I wanted Phoenix to admit he loved me. I glance over at his side of the bed, but he's not there. I fell asleep on his chest. *When did he wake up? How did I not feel him get up?* Glancing at the clock, I realize it's four in the morning. It feels like we just went to sleep.

Stepping out into the hallway, I glance toward his upstairs office, but the light isn't on, so I walk downstairs and go to the kitchen. He isn't in here either, so I grab a bottle of water out of the fridge and walk down the hallway to the library and his downstairs office. He isn't in any of those rooms either.

Walking further to the theater room, I don't see him, so I turn back around and head to the other side of the house. He's probably in the gym. There's another hallway next to the one that leads to Anna's room. Walking down that hallway, I hear the thumping sound of Nix hitting the punching bag. Stopping inside the gym, I lean against the door and watch as he lands blow after blow to the punching bag.

He's like a moving work of art. He's in shorts, so every tattoo he has is on display. The tattoos along his thighs, arms, and shoulders ripple with each punch and bounce. I lick my lips and push away from the doorway, walking further into the room. I'm only wearing the T-shirt I put on when I went to bed and I'm very much aware of it now. The edge of his shirt stops mid thigh. When he spots me, he grabs the bag so it stops swinging and stares at me as I walk toward him.

His shoulders move as he catches his breath. He doesn't speak as I get closer to him; his hooded eyes rake over me. When his eyes connect with mine again, the blue of his eyes is barely visible. He holds onto the punching bag like it's the only thing keeping him from launching across the room to me.

If it were any other night, he wouldn't stop himself, but because of everything that happened tonight and what I remembered about Bill, he's holding himself back. I don't want him to. Yes, what I remembered was terrible. But in my head, I can separate him from what happened to me. I know he would never hurt me. Never.

I want to tell him about the memory I had. The one I've had glimpses of for months now, but that was the full memory. I'm sure Dr. Chamberland was working with his mother even then and talked us back into going to the house. I remember Nix telling me we were downtown when I was taken, but why wouldn't Clyde tell him he drove me home?

Unless Clyde was in on it, too. "What's wrong?" he asks. He's still gripping the bag. I take another step toward him.

"I woke up, and you weren't there. I had to come find you."

His eyes fill with concern. "Did you have a memory? I should have been there." He exhales sharply. "I woke up and couldn't go back to sleep."

"It's okay," I assure him. "I did have a memory." He takes a step toward me. "But I don't want to talk about that right now." I stop in front of him and tilt my head to look up at him.

"What do you want?" His voice is rough and deep. He sees what I want in my eyes, but he wants me to say it.

"I believe you promised me an orgasm."

He smirks at me. Finally releasing the bag, he wraps his arms around my waist and lifts me up, my feet dangling as he kisses me. He puts his hand on my ass encouraging me to wrap my legs around him. When I do, the T-shirt lifts and my bare pussy presses against his abdomen. He sucks in a breath and leans back, breaking the kiss.

"No panties?"

I give him a sly smile. "I was exhausted when we went to sleep." Before I can think, he drops to his knees and he leans forward until my back is on the mat. He pushes the T-shirt up until it's bunched up under my arms. His hands cup my breasts as his thumbs circle my nipples.

His cock is hard and peeks out slightly from his workout shorts. If he moves just right, it will slide out enough for me to see his piercing, but he doesn't move. Frustrated, I lift my legs and grab the hem of his shorts between my toes and pull. He chuckles, but doesn't stop me. I sigh when I see his piercing.

He releases my breasts and grabs his cock. He stares down at me as he takes the head of his cock and rubs his piercing through my pussy lips. I hiss and jerk. "You love this piercing, don't you?" I nod as he continues to rub himself along my slit.

He smiles at me and pulls away. I huff in frustration and he laughs. "Roll over and get on all fours." I swallow, trying to wet my dry throat and do as he says. I expect him to take me from behind, but he surprises me when he lays down and pushes back until his face is below me.

I glance down at him through my arms. "What—" I'm cut off when he leans up and swipes his tongue through my folds.

"Sit on my face, love."

I push up from the floor so I'm kneeling above him. I hesitate, so he wraps his arms around my thighs and pulls me toward his face. I sit and he devours me. His hands cup my ass as he thrusts his tongue inside me. I tilt my head back, knowing I won't last long. He uses long strokes, licking from my pussy to my clit over and over again. Before I know it, I'm riding his tongue.

I grip his hair as he encourages me to let loose, and I do. Noises I didn't know I could make leaving my throat. We're far enough away from Anna's room, so I don't think she'll be able to hear us, which is good because at this point I don't care. He inserts one finger, then two, and crooks them enough so he's rubbing against my g-spot. I squeeze my eyes shut so tight I see stars as I come undone.

Falling forward on my hands, he doesn't wait long to climb out from under me. He kneels behind me and lays his chest on my back. "Are you sure?" he asks, his cock teasing my entrance. Checking in with me one more time and I love him even more for it.

"Yes. Yes I'm sure."

He doesn't wait a moment longer as he enters me in one swift move. I gasp at how full he makes me and I buck against him when he doesn't move right away. He wraps his hand around my throat, touching the collar that's there. *I don't remember him putting it back on me after we got out of the shower.*

"I put it back on you before I came down here." He answers my thoughts like he can read my mind. "Open your eyes." I open my eyes and come face to face with us in the mirror. Part of me wants to look away because it's uncomfortable looking at myself completely on display, but when I see the look on Nix's face, it makes me pause.

His eyes are heated with desire as he looks at us in the mirror. His other arm comes around my waist and his hand snakes down to cup my pussy. He pulls out and pushes back into me, his breathing hard in my ear. "So fucking sexy," he murmurs in my ear as his middle finger circles my clit.

I'm still sensitive from the orgasm he gave me just a few minutes ago, but I already feel another one building. I buck against him, meeting each of his thrusts and begin to close my eyes, but he clicks his tongue at me. "Keep your eyes on the mirror, love." I open my eyes and watch. Taking in the way he watches me, how he looks over my shoulder every once in a while to see how flushed I am.

His thrusts become choppy, and I know he's close. He pushes me down again so I'm on all fours and grips my hips. "So beautiful." Thrust. "So fucking sexy." Thrust. "Mine." Thrust. I watch him in the mirror and his eyes bore into mine as he speaks to me, reminding me who I am and whose I am. "I love everything about you." Thrust. "Your mind." Thrust. "Your body." Thrust. "Your heart."

Tears begin to stream down my face. "I will always choose you," he promises, and I come again with a shout and a sob. He comes with me and after a few moments, we both collapse onto the mat. He rolls over onto his back and pulls me onto his chest. Kissing my forehead, my cheek, my shoulder, anything he can touch.

I look up at him and smile. "I love you and I'll always choose you, too." We seal our vows to each other with a kiss and he carries me back to our bed.

Chapter 32

Phoenix

Kenz's head lays in my lap as I rock us on the swing in our gazebo. She told me the memory she had, and we settled into a comfortable silence after. Me mulling over what she told me. I comb my fingers through her hair.

"I need to start believing everything you tell me," I say. She rolls over on her back and stares up at me. I gaze down at her and trace the contours of her face with my finger. "I'm such an asshole. I was so sure you were remembering wrong." She doesn't respond, probably knowing I'm talking through this.

"I never got a text from you, so I don't know if they were able to intercept it or something. And Clyde came rushing into my office and said you went into the Marketplace and he couldn't find you." I run my hands through my hair. "How the fuck did this happen? I ran every single one of my guys. I checked their background, everything."

McKenzie sits up and climbs onto my lap. She takes my face in her hands. "Your mom has been one step ahead this entire time. She probably knew you'd do that and did something so you wouldn't find anything." Dropping her hands, she sighs and looks away for a moment before focusing back on me. "I think we need to go to my dad."

Every muscle in my body tenses at the idea of going to her dad for help, but she might be right. "I'll consider it." She slumps a little, so I lift her chin with my thumb and forefinger. "I've considered him my enemy for years. Give me some time to come to terms with who the real villain turned out to be."

"Okay," she whispers and leans up to kiss me.

We're both exhausted and emotionally drained, so I told her we were staying home today and dealing with everything tomorrow. But after she told me what she remembered, I need Rex to confirm the new guys we hired are trustworthy.

I pull his name up on my phone and call him. He's in the house with Anna, so he answers immediately. "Kenz had a memory. Clyde helped take her the second time, and they *did* take her from the house."

"What? How?" Rex barks. I give him the rundown and he curses. Anna asks him if everything is okay in the background, so he takes a minute to soothe her. "I trust these new guys with my life, but if you think—"

"No, I trust you. But she knows where we live." Dread settles in my stomach. I have to deal with her and soon. "Let them know to be on guard until I get rid of her." He agrees and I hang up.

"We're not going to leave, are we?" Kenz asks.

"No. We moved out of the house downtown because it was my mother's and I knew you weren't comfortable there. You had a hand in everything about our house and this land. She will not take that from you."

Kenz places her hand over my heart. "From us."

"Valentine," Victor answers on the second ring.

"Hey, this is Phoenix Stone."

There's a slight pause. "Phoenix, how are you?"

"That's the question," I reply.

I've met Victor a few times over the past year or so. He and his wife have come to a few of the auctions, but they never buy anyone or participate. It piqued my curiosity last year, and I looked into them. What I found is why I'm reaching out to him now.

"What can I do for you?" Victor asks. I tell him everything that has transpired over the past several years and he listens intently with an interjected question here or there. When I'm done, there's silence on the other end for several moments.

"I'll need to talk to Olivia, but I'm sure she'll agree to help. I'm sorry you and McKenzie have gone through this. Let me get some things together and I'll call you back in a few days."

We hang up and I lean back in my office chair, turning to look out over River Street. McKenzie is down there, walking from store to store again. It's her way of sticking up her middle finger to the memory she had. I love that woman so much and the strength she shows in the face of everything she's gone through.

I pull up the app on my phone that's linked to the tracking device on her collar. She's at the Marketplace. Knowing I can track her whereabouts at any time brings me peace.

Standing, I exit my office and lock up. I nod at Jason in greeting. Anna joined Kenz today, which is a big step for her. I told Rex I wanted him and Luca, one of his other security guys, to stay with them.

"Sir, do you think it would be wise to look into all the fighters before the next one?" Jason asks. I glance at him as we step out onto River Street.

"Yes, I do. I'm meeting with Felix tomorrow to tell him we need to do that. You can join if you'd like to."

Jason nods. "Yes, sir, I would."

Jason is slowly becoming Rex's second, and I understand why. He takes initiative, and he does things the way Rex would. I grab the photo I had drawn up of what my mother looks like now, according to Kenz, and hand it to Jason.

"If you see a woman that looks like that I need you to notify me immediately. Apparently, she changes her hair a lot, so keep that in consideration."

Jason studies the picture and nods. "Yes, sir."

We walk to the Marketplace and I find Kenz looking at some wind chimes. Luca stands a few feet from her, pretending to be checking out some knives, but his eyes are flitting about looking for any threats. He relaxes a little when he sees me, but not completely.

I walk up behind Kenz and wrap my arms around her waist. She lays her head on my shoulder and smiles up at me. We share a kiss that I'd like to turn into more, but we're surrounded by too many people for that. So, I pull away and place my chin on top of her head. "Find something you like?"

"I love these wind chimes." She touches them and the sound they make is beautiful. "They're made of bamboo." The lady standing behind the counter smiles at McKenzie and how much she loves them.

"We'll take them," I tell her.

"Can we have two? One for the porch and the other for our gazebo?" Kenz rarely asks for anything, so I'll give her whatever she wants. I nod, so Kenz points out the other wind chimes she wants. The lady boxes them up, places them in a plastic bag, and hands it to us. Luca walks over and takes it.

Anna and Rex walk over to us. "We're going to go home," Rex says. I place my hands in my pockets and nod as Kenz hugs Anna.

"I'm so proud of you," Kenz whispers. Rex and I share a look proud of both of them for how they're trying to overcome all the trauma they've faced.

"I wish I could stay longer, but I've reached my limit for the day," Anna says.

Kenz leans back and pushes Anna's hair over her shoulder. "That's okay." They hug one more time before Rex walks Anna toward the SUV he's driving.

We spend the rest of the day walking to each shop down River Street and wind up at the piano bar. After we eat our food and Kenz has had two drinks, she settles into me to watch the show. I make her come twice before it's over. I lick her off my fingers as I escort her to the SUV and we head home.

She lifts the privacy window between us and Jason as she climbs on my lap and rides me. We both come just as Jason pulls into our long driveway. She stays on me until the very last moment when she has to get off. I immediately mourn the loss of her warmth wrapped around me.

Rex and Anna meet us inside. Kenz hugs Anna, holding her tightly for a moment. "I couldn't stay any longer," Anna says.

Kenz kisses her on the cheek. "You will. Today was a big step for you. I'm proud of you." Anna smiles at her.

"Thank you, Kenz." They hug for a moment longer before we head upstairs. I give Rex a small salute and he returns it. My phone vibrates as we walk up the stairs. Grabbing it, I glance at the text I received from Victor.

We're in. Olivia is okay with it. I'll send you the address tomorrow then we can call and discuss plans.

"Who's that?" Kenz asks. So, I tell her the plan as we get ready for bed. She crawls into bed in one of my T-shirts and this time I watch. She's not wearing panties. Again. So, I climb in naked and pull her against me; her back against my front.

"I hope this works, Nix," she whispers, voicing her worry and fear.

I kiss the juncture between her neck and shoulder. "It will." I promise her. She's quiet for a long time. I'd think she was asleep, but she's not breathing like she's asleep.

"Nix?" Her voice is barely above a whisper.

"Yes, love." She takes her time replying, but I don't push her. I wait for her to say what she's gathering the courage to say.

She takes a deep breath. "Have you ever wanted to be so close to me, but it doesn't feel close enough?"

I try to decipher what she's saying between the lines, but I'm at a loss. "What do you mean, love?"

I run my hand from her stomach to her sternum and stop at her throat. Circling her throat with my hand she swallows, moving my hand as she does. "Ever since the other night, I want to be close to you in a way that borders on crazy." I huff, but don't interrupt her. "So, I was wondering, could you *be* that close to me? But without it turning into sex? Like what we did in the SUV?"

I run her words through my mind over and over again before it clicks. "Cock warming?"

She shifts against me as I harden against her back at the thought of it. "I didn't know there was a name for it," she murmurs.

"Yes, it can be done like how we did earlier or as something comforting and calming. Like what you're asking for now."

She swallows against my hand again. "Would you want to do that?" She sounds shy and meek. It makes me smile. She has no idea the control she has over me.

"Yes. I could fall asleep like that every night." She giggles and presses her ass against me. I rub my hand up her thigh and lift it so it rests over my thigh. I run my fingers through her pussy to make sure she's wet. She sucks in a breath. "Just checking to make sure you're ready."

I enter her slowly, loving how hot and tight she is around me. Once I settle in, it takes some effort not to pull out and push back in, but I stay perfectly still. Both of us are breathing hard and fast. I push her hair over her shoulder.

"You okay?" I ask.

She hums. "Yes. It feels..." she trails off. "Different." She settles against me and tightens around me slightly, making me grit my teeth.

"Don't be surprised if I wake you up in the middle of the night," I warn. She giggles and I grit my teeth again at the sensation. "It's going to take me a few nights to get used to this."

"You'd be willing to do this every night?"

"I'll give you anything you want. All you have to do is ask."

Chapter 33

McKenzie

"I can't believe you're going to another auction," Anna says. I stare at the clothes in my closet, trying to decide what I need to bring.

I shrug. "This is who I am now, and this plan is in motion, so there's no backing out now." Before she can reply, Clara comes rushing in with a garment bag hanging over her arm.

"It arrived!" she says excitedly. I clap my hands as she hands it to me. Walking to the counter in the middle of the closet, I lay it out and unzip the bag. I pull out the dress and admire it for a few moments before turning it to show Anna and Clara.

"Wow!" "So beautiful!" they say at the same time.

It's the dress I'm going to wear to the auction. The dress is a mermaid fit, the top black lace that will leave little to the imagination, and there are red and black roses that make up the skirt.

Clara walks forward and runs her finger over the silky fabric. "This is going to look beautiful with your skin tone and hair." This is the first time I remember being excited about going to an auction.

Nix said we used the auctions to experiment, so I'm assuming I have been excited in the past, but this feels different.

After this auction, things will be different. Hopefully. "Are you going to try it on?" Anna asks. I walk to the closet and peek into the bedroom. Nix is working from home today, so I close the door.

"I'm pretty sure he'll knock before just walking in." Clara and Anna both snort. I put my hands on my hips. "He's not that bad." They share a look and I chuckle. I take my leggings and T-shirt off, standing before them in my panties and bra. Anna and I were roommates back at Brighton, so this is normal for us and well, we're inducting Clara into the normalcy I guess.

I hand the dress to them and they hold it low while I step into it. It's strapless, so when I pull it up, I take my bra off quickly and wait for Clara to zip it. "It's not as heavy as I was expecting it to be" I say as I walk to the floor-length mirror.

Anna and Clara stand behind me with small smiles on their faces. "It's gorgeous, Kenz," Anna says and Clara nods in agreement. I smile at them and take a deep breath.

"Mr. Phoenix hasn't seen it at all?" Clara asks.

"No, I told him it was red and black because he's picking out our masks and he wants us to match." As soon as the words leave my mouth, there's a knock on the door.

"Kenz?"

I turn around and face them with my hands on my hips. "See?" They start giggling, but the door begins to open. "No!" I yell out.

"What the hell?" Nix says. He doesn't close the door, but he stops.

"I'm trying my dress on and I don't want you to see it."

He huffs. "The girls get to see it," he complains. I walk up to the door and make sure I'm hidden before I stick my head in the crack.

"You can wait," I tell him as he scowls at me.

"Fine, but tell the girls to get out."

"Nix!" I chastise him and he gives me an *I don't give a fuck* look.

"Get out of your dress, but don't put anything else on." My mouth opens in an O just as Clara and Anna walk toward the door.

I step completely behind the door, so Nix doesn't see me. "Phillip said dinner will be ready in fifteen minutes and that was ten minutes ago!" Clara yells as she's leaving.

"I only need sixty seconds," Nix throws back.

I stick my head out the door again. "Sixty seconds?!?"

He arches an eyebrow. "I believe I did that last night, didn't I?" I snap my mouth shut. "Exactly."

I close the door in his face for being so arrogant and to get out of this dress so he can prove himself.

We load onto Nix's plane. According to him, it's mine now too. We're flying to Mississippi to go to the next auction. Victor Valentine will be hosting this quarter's auction. He isn't part of the council, but Nix has been working on getting things changed and finally received confirmation from the council it's okay if non council members host auctions.

They've decided this will be the last auction hosted at someone's residence. They're going to work on opening clubs throughout the country, but for now, there will be four. They'll be located in the northeast, southeast, northwest, and southwest. Nix will be the owner of the one in the southeast.

Everyone is coming on the trip, but not everyone is going to the auction. It took some convincing to talk Anna into coming. When Rex promised her he'd keep her safe, she finally said yes. We all sit; Nix sits next to me while Rex and Anna sit across from us. Anna rubs her hands down her thighs and pulls her legs up to her chest. It's going to take a while for her to get to the point where she's not scared anymore.

Nix made sure word was spread wide about this auction. Our hope is because it's in a different location, it will attract the people we need to come. Nix wraps his arm around my shoulder and pulls me into him. Anna glances at Rex and I see the longing there. Rex only sees her as someone to protect, but maybe one day he'll wake up and see what's right in front of him.

"Victor called me earlier today. He's received almost three hundred RSVPs. It's the largest auction so far. He has security that will be there. Including my security, it will be well protected. Everyone we wanted to RSVP has," Nix tells us.

My stomach swoops knowing who we're about to come face to face with. According to Nix, I've met Victor and Olivia already, but I don't remember. He reminded me they were at the auction we hosted right after he rescued me, but I was living day by day at that time, so it's vague.

"How was he able to get so many RSVPs?" Rex asks.

Nix grins slightly. "There's been a problem with trafficking in his city for a while. He made sure the people in those circles found out about it. What they don't know is the money we raise from this will go toward helping victims of trafficking."

Anna looks out the window and squeezes her eyes shut. Rex wraps his arm around her shoulders and squeezes her. She gives him a grateful smile and lays her head on his shoulder. I wonder if there are people Victor and Olivia want to catch like we do.

Another change Nix made was everyone who is being auctioned tonight is choosing to participate. Every person who signed up to be auctioned had an interview with Nix, Gil, and Victor. They were promised if they decided at the last minute they didn't want to, that would be okay as well. There will also be a few undercover people in the auction. Dick will be there, so the plan is to lure him in with one of the undercovers.

Even more people are participating than before because it's not being controlled by elitist pricks. The bid each person receives goes to them except for ten percent. That goes to the fund to help those who we're trying to help. The flight doesn't take long and before I know it, we're landing.

Nix rented several hotel rooms for all of us, but we're getting ready at Victor and Olivia's house. We stand at their door and wait for them to answer. Their home is gorgeous and inviting. The amount of flowers is amazing.

"Nix, we need to ask them who their gardener is," I say as Victor opens the door, his arm draped around Olivia's shoulders.

"That would be my wife." He smiles down at the black-haired beauty whose cheeks blush slightly.

She shrugs. "Flowers are easier than people," she murmurs.

I chuckle and nod. "One of the reasons I like to bake." We share a look and Victor invites us in. Victor and Nix walk ahead of Olivia and me.

"I know you don't remember me, but we have met a few times over the past few years," she says.

I smile at her and swallow nerves suddenly settling in my stomach. "I wish I could remember."

She pats my arm. "I'm sure your memories will come back when you need them." She sighs. "There are some things I wish I could forget."

I tilt my head at her. Nix said she's had trauma in her past, but he's not sure what. And it's not my place to ask unless she wants to tell me. "So, the auction is going to be somewhere else?" I ask.

She nods and leads me into the kitchen. "Yes. Victor does not want people in our home, especially with everything that is planned for tonight."

"Phoenix is the same way. We have a home in downtown Savannah we use. Where will it be?"

She grabs two champagne glasses, some champagne, and orange juice. "There's a house recently built for special occasions like this. It will be there." She lifts the champagne. "Mimosas?"

"Definitely. How many special occasions are like this auction?" I ask as I take a sip of the mimosa she made me.

She laughs. "It was not built with this in mind, but Connor says he's going to talk to Phoenix and talk him into letting this place be the southern location for the auctions."

I smirk. "I'm sure Nix will be fine with that. He wants this to take off."

Olivia leans in like she's going to tell me a secret. "Well, between you and me, Connor and his wife throw the best BDSM parties." She laughs when my eyes widen.

Laughter sounds behind me, and I turn to see Victor and Phoenix walking in. Victor is laughing with his wife. Nix steps behind me and wraps his arms around my waist while Victor does the same to Olivia.

"Don't let that term fool you," Victor says. "In this case, it stands for burgers, drinks, and salsa music."

Nix and I laugh. "I want to go."

Olivia looks up at her husband. "I'm sure there will be another in a couple of months. We'll be sure to let you know about it."

I glance up at Nix, a question in my eyes. He leans down and kisses me on the forehead. "Anything you want, love." He turns his attention back to Victor. "Shall we discuss the plans for tonight?"

Chapter 34

Phoenix

Victor and I stand at the bottom of the stairs, waiting for McKenzie and Olivia. I inhale slowly, trying to calm my nerves. I never thought I'd have to do this, but here I am. I've been trying to get in touch with my father for days now without any word. I shake my head and roll my shoulders. If Kenz ever decides to have kids with me, I will not be like either of my parents.

I adjust the cuff link on my sleeve and take one more last deep breath. "Tonight will go well," Victor says. I turn my attention to him and nod. "It's perfectly normal to be nervous, though."

I snort. "My whole world has changed in the past several months. This is surreal." He knows I just found out about my mother.

"The man I used to think was a friend turned out to be a complete psychopath, so I do understand some of what you're going through." He pats me on the shoulder. "Our friends will be there tonight. One of them has his own private detective firm and his wife works with him. He's all about doing things the legal way, but he's had his morals tested lately, so I'm sure he'll look the other way where all this is concerned."

I huff. "Obviously I'm not the straight laced guy, so maybe don't tell him what I do."

Victor chuckles. "I'm not so straight laced either." He glances up the stairs, likely thinking of Olivia. He is older than her, but other than that, I don't know much about their relationship. Heels land on the steps above us, which draw our attention to the two women walking down the stairs.

Olivia is in front, wearing a black lace dress. "Jesus," Victor says and I smirk, understanding how he feels. It's one of the reasons I love these auctions. It's me and Kenz's time to dress up and wear something we wouldn't normally wear. Well, her mainly. I always wear suits, but it gives me a chance to match her and wear something a bit more formal. Tonight I'm wearing a red tux with a black vest and tie. The only thing Kenz would tell me was her dress was red and black. She gave me a fabric sample of the color red so I could give it to my tailor to match.

When McKenzie comes into view, I forget how to breathe for several moments. She looks gorgeous wearing a black and red strapless dress. The lacy top giving the illusion it might be see through; it hugs her hips and flares out with black and red roses. The only jewelry she's wearing is the sterling silver collar I gave her and some diamond hoop earrings.

Her hair hangs in soft curls around her shoulders, but she's done a braid around the crown of her head. She looks like the fucking queen she is. She stops in front of me, a small smirk on her mouth. "I love the way you look at me," she whispers. I don't say anything, instead

I wrap my hand around her waist and pull her into me, kissing her hard.

She giggles against my lips and everything in me wants to take her back upstairs and fuck her while she's still wearing this dress. "You look like a queen. My queen," I murmur against her lips. Her eyes brighten as her smile widens.

"And you're my king." Her eyes cloud over with worry, so I pull her close and hold her for a few minutes before we have to leave. Rex will drive us to the house, while Jason takes Anna to one of Olivia's and Victor's other friends that we met yesterday: Caroline and Bass.

They have two young kids and don't want to come tonight just in case things don't go exactly as planned. Anna swears she'll be okay by herself, but I know Rex won't be able to focus tonight if she isn't protected.

After Jason drops her off and assures she'll be safe, he'll join us at the house. Usually those who are security and working the auction wear blue masks to separate them from the rest of the guests, but tonight they'll be there with some of the undercover women that were hired posing as their dates to blend in. When the other girls that work the fight club heard what happened to Shay, they were all willing to help bring my bitch of a mother down.

Maybe she didn't have anything to do with Shay directly, but she empowered Bill so she's responsible in my eyes. Felix wanted to be involved as well, but he didn't want to leave Shay alone. So, he stayed back in Savannah to stay with her. Victor opens the door and gestures for us to leave.

I put my hand on Kenz's lower back and guide her outside to the Hummer Limo that's waiting. I was worried renting this would result in Rex not being able to drive us, but Victor and his partner have a lot of pull in this town, so it wasn't an issue. I am surprised to see the three couples waiting around the limo.

"Friends of yours?" I ask Victor. He told me they had friends coming. I didn't realize they were riding with us. Victor nods and proceeds to introduce us to everyone. They all act like they're family, not just friends. I watch McKenzie as she interacts with them, wondering if she's envious of their obvious closeness.

When we all climb in the car, I pull McKenzie as close to me as possible. "You okay, love?" I ask her.

She smiles and nods. "I really like them," she whispers. She doesn't seem to be envious, just happy. I don't know if I can ever offer her a group of friends like this. She rubs her hand up and down my arm. "Are you okay? You look so serious." I catch one of the guys eyeing me up. I think his name is Julian.

His wife, Bailey, is laughing with the girl with light pink hair, but she notices how he's staring at us and rolls her eyes. She slaps his arm and leans toward us. "Don't mind my husband. This is just his face. He can't help it." He scowls at her, but one side of his mouth tips up. She leans forward slightly and his eyes drop to her cleavage. She winks at us. "I know how to distract him."

McKenzie laughs, and I chuckle slightly. "You have yourself a handful," I tell him.

He sighs good naturedly. "You have no idea." He wraps his arm around her shoulders and drops a kiss on top of her head.

"You couldn't live without me." She flutters her eyelashes at him and he finally breaks into a grin.

"This is true," he says as she leans up and kisses him.

The girl with the pink hair smirks and leans forward. "I'm Bec and this is my husband, Connor. Julian is Connor's brother, but they're as different as night and day."

McKenzie leans forward. "So, you're the one that throws the great BDSM parties." Everyone stops their side conversations and is silent for a few moments before they burst into laughter. They all then proceed to tell us about the BDSM parties. It's a great way to loosen up the atmosphere before the night begins.

Olivia and Victor don their masks and take their place at the front of the house after they've taken us on a tour and shown us everything. McKenzie and I head to the limo so we can all take a ride around town before coming back to keep up appearances. As everyone puts on their masks, I hand McKenzie her mask; it's red and black with a swan on one side. She gazes at it, her fingers stroking over the swan.

"It's beautiful." I help her put it on and she turns back to face me with a smile on her face. "You know how in the movie *Twilight* they have all the graduation caps framed on the wall?" She asks. I shrug, not really remembering if I've ever seen that movie. "Anyway, we'll watch it after all this. But we should do that with our masks. Find a way to display them all."

She motions for me to turn and helps me put my mask on. Mine is a Day of the Dead mask that covers my whole face. It's gold, black, and red. There are some changes in this auction. We're not going with the typical theme of having to wear a certain color mask so people know if you're buying, selling, being bought, or up for sharing.

If the couple is up for sharing or an individual wants to join a couple, they'll wear a gold cuff on their wrist so people will know. I like this new system because it gives more options for masks. With the old system, I never would have allowed myself or McKenzie to wear a black and red mask since that meant sharing was an option. I will never share McKenzie.

I settle back in the seat, mentally putting my game face on. Just as Rex pulls back up in front of the house, my phone goes off. I scowl at the sight of my father's name on the screen.

"Father," I answer, coldness in my voice.

"Whatever you're planning, stop it right now." No hello or how are you. I share a look with McKenzie. She pulls her bottom lip between her teeth, worry evident in her eyes. I bring my forefinger and thumb up to her chin and pull on her lip slightly so she'll release it. I rub my thumb just under her lip so I don't mess up her lipstick, communicating with her that everything will be okay.

"Too late, father." I hang up as he yells my name.

"Nix?" I kiss her jaw.

"Everything will be fine," I promise her, then hand her my mask so she can put it on for me. Everyone climbs out of the limo, McKenzie and I are last. I get out first and extend my hand to her to help her. Wrapping my arm around her waist, we get in line to greet Victor and Olivia.

Let the night begin.

Chapter 35

Phoenix

I keep my head on a swivel, studying every person. Part of me wants to drop my guard a little so I can play with McKenzie, but if I do, it's likely I'll get so wrapped up in her I'll forget tonight's purpose. We sit near the front like we always do, but Victor's friends are scattered throughout the crowd, as well as our security.

I showed them all a picture of Dick, a picture of my mother, and the one I had drawn up of her when McKenzie saw her at the fight. To be safe, I also sent them all a text with a picture of my father and told them he called right before we came in. I don't know if he would come and try to stop us, but it's a very real possibility.

My mother has an uncanny way of making men do crazy things. I grab McKenzie's legs and place them over my thighs so she's practically sitting in my lap. We'll have to turn our head pieces on in just a few minutes and I want some time with her before we do.

She leans forward and licks my neck. My chest rumbles with a moan and she giggles. "So, I was thinking when this is all over, I'd like to get my first tattoo," she murmurs in my ear, her fingers combing through the hair at my nape.

"Oh yeah? What kind of tattoo?" My fingers swirl around the delicate bone of her ankle, tracing the line of the anklet she wears all the time now.

She hums. "I'd like for us to get matching tattoos in the same spot." Her hand rubs down my arm and chest. "But you don't have very many spots left." Her raspy voice and hands are making me hard. I shift, trying to get comfortable and rub against her leg.

She chuckles, her laughter washing over me. "Does the idea of that make you hard?" Her hand on my chest lowers, and I let her cup me over my pants. We're in public, but there're all kinds of foreplay happening around us, so I don't care. Not here.

I turn and face her so she can see the heat in my eyes as I wrap my hand around her throat, squeezing slightly. The vibration of her moan tickles my hand and everything in me wants to lift my mask and kiss her. I'm beginning to regret choosing this mask. Her eyes dance with laughter as she catches on to what I'm thinking.

She leans forward, allowing my hand to press even tighter against her throat. "Where should we get matching tattoos?" Her hand squeezes even tighter around me. She places her lips just below my ear and begins to suck. I loosen my hand around her throat slightly, but she shakes her head, so I tighten it again.

"What about here? It's our favorite spot on each other." She sucks again and I know she's giving me a hickey. I love it when she marks me, her territory. I release her throat and she whines in protest. Later I'll choke her all she wants while I pound into her, but right now I want her soft side.

Wrapping my hand around her hair, I pull on it slightly and she lifts her mouth from my neck inspecting her work before sitting back and looking at me. I rub my thumb just under her ear and smile at the thought of a tattoo being right there where I mark her.

"What kind of tattoo?"

Her smile widens like she's been waiting for me to ask. "I was thinking, a king and queen chess piece or a king and queen crown." My stomach heats with how right that sounds.

"We'll ask my guy to draw both and see which one we like. But I have one small request." Someone rings a bell, letting us know there's five minutes until things begin.

"What's that?"

I rub my thumb across the spot under her ear, imagining the tattoo there. "Yours says *his* and mine says *hers* underneath it."

Her smile is bright and beautiful. "I love it," she exclaims.

"I love you." She leans forward and kisses me where my mouth would be on the mask. I chuckle and shake my head slightly.

She sits up and puts her legs back on the floor. She kisses me on my jaw and lays her head on my shoulder. "I love you, too."

Victor's friend Julian helped hire a few undercover detectives to stay in the back with the girls that are bought to keep an eye on who comes and goes. As soon as someone is purchased, the buyer goes and meets the one they bought, but they are to stay in the back until the time comes for the ritual of having sex with them in front of everyone.

After a very lengthy meeting over several days with the council, many changes have been made that haven't been announced yet. One being, the ritual is no longer a requirement. We're all going to gather downstairs to see who all comes if we don't find my mother and Dick beforehand. All of this is very risky and I'm nervous about what could happen.

Another reason we asked Victor to host the auction is because there won't be a second ritual the council is expected at. When Victor sent out the invitations, he made sure to mention girls that just graduated high school would be attending. Dick's flavor of choice.

McKenzie's spine goes ramrod straight, and she places her hand on my knee, digging her fingernails into it. I don't flinch. I lean toward her, making it look like I'm flirting with her. "What do you see, love?"

She swallows and relaxes a little. "Your mother. She's here."

I force myself to stay relaxed. Running my hand along her shoulder, I run my fingers through her hair, trying to get her to relax a little as well. "I'm not going to leave your side. You're safe." I assure her. She relaxes a little. "Where is she?" She begins to turn, but I stop her. "Don't look. She'll know we're talking about her."

"In the back, near the door." We all have our earpieces in, so I know Rex is listening.

"On it, sir. I'll report back shortly," Rex says.

It's taking a lot of self control not to turn around and see where she's at. What she looks like. But I keep my arm around McKenzie's shoulder and pull her tighter into my side.

"I think I've spotted the dean." I think it's Lincoln that says that. I'm still unfamiliar with everyone's voices.

"Is he bidding?" I ask, leaning toward McKenzie so it looks like I'm talking to her.

"Not yet," another voice chimes in, female this time. His wife, Ansley. There's twenty women and ten men for sale this time. We've gone through five women and three men so far, but the women have been in their late twenties.

"He wouldn't, I suppose. He does like them young." Anytime he bought in the past, the women's age were usually just out of high school. McKenzie was the oldest he ever bid on. When I bought her, he didn't show up again. It makes me wonder about Anna, if she was the one he was always after. Somehow, my mother got her nails in him and let him have her.

"So does Julian," Bailey says.

"And Victor," Bec chimes in.

"Bec!" Olivia chastises her, but she's laughing.

McKenzie laughs and I shake my head. "The difference is their women are willing."

"So willing," Bailey says.

"Jesus," Julian replies.

McKenzie and I share a look, both of us smiling. The auctioneer brings out the youngest woman so far. He says she's twenty, but I made it very clear no one under twenty-one could be bought. Even though the invitation said differently. I sit forward, trying to figure out who she is.

"I told the auctioneer her age was twenty," Jason says in my ear. "Since you said he likes them young, maybe this will encourage him."

"That's one of the UCs," Julian says.

I settle back in my chair. I hate not being completely in control, but everyone is playing their part perfectly.

The auctioneer begins to take bids, starting at half a million dollars. Dick doesn't bid first, but he does follow up with a million. The bid gets up to three million, and I wonder where Dick gets his money. Probably on my mother's payroll with the extra-curricular activities she does. It wouldn't surprise me.

There's some shuffling behind me of someone trying to get to their seat, but I focus on the bidding to see if anyone will outbid Dick. No one bids higher than three million. Dick wins the bid. I suck in a breath as he stands and is escorted out to go meet who he purchased. Now we just have to get my mother and him in the same room.

I rub my fingers along McKenzie's shoulders to her neck, where the collar rests beautifully against her sun-kissed skin. She smiles up at me and it hits me square in the chest; I'm a lucky son of a bitch. I don't deserve her, yet here she is.

"Boss," Rex's voice sounds in my ear. "Your mother just sat right behind you and Miss Kenzie."

Chapter 36

Phoenix

I've trained myself not to react when my emotions are high, but knowing my mother is right behind me is testing even me. McKenzie's nails are digging so hard into my thigh I'm glad I chose a red suit so the blood will blend in. I hate the fear she must be feeling right now. But I will make it right. I will.

We sit through the remainder of the auction. I rub my fingers up and down the inside of Kenz's wrist. Everyone is quiet and on alert. Jason has confirmed he's in the back watching Dick. Victor has a couple of guys back there as well. Luca is standing at the other exit. Everything is covered. My mother is not going to get out of here without being seen.

Once the auction is over, an announcement is made about where the ritual will take place. "I'll follow her and make sure she goes to the correct room," Rex says in my ear. He also opted for a full face mask and his hair is slicked back, so even if my mother has seen him before, hopefully she won't recognize him. McKenzie and I stand to exit. I force my muscles to remain relaxed as I guide Kenz to the aisle.

I wrap my arm around her and lean down as we walk. "Are you okay?" I whisper, so only she can hear and those in our ears.

"My heart is pounding," she replies softly. I place my hand directly over her heart. To others, it looks like I'm flirting with my pet, but I'm trying to calm her and let her know I'm here.

"I'm going to have so much fun with you later, pet," I murmur.

She sucks in a breath, her eyes flying to mine. I wink at her and she exhales deeply. She nods once, understanding I'm trying to get her head back in the game. We follow the crowd downstairs. Some branch off to go have fun of their own and I have to continue to dig deep to stop myself from looking for my mother.

"She's behind the two of you. I'm keeping an eye on her," Rex says.

"Dick is headed downstairs with the girl he bought," Jason tells us.

"My guys will stay at all exits once everyone is downstairs," Victor instructs.

We gather downstairs and wait for instructions like everyone else. Several people were purchased, so they'll begin branching off into the different rooms and areas. The girl Dick bought begins to act out just in time.

"What? I didn't know this was part of this. I'm not doing this." Victor and Olivia step forward with one of their security.

"It's okay," Olivia says softly. "Come in this room over here, both of you, and we'll get this sorted out."

Some other girls begin to protest, which was expected, so the other security that was hired leads them all to separate rooms to help. What they don't know is those rooms will lead them outside.

"Let's go see if Victor needs help," I tell McKenzie.

"I'll talk to her," Kenz says. "I mean, I know how she feels." I know she's saying what she's supposed to, but her words hit me square in the chest. She didn't know what was happening the night her father sold her. She had no idea what was happening. Yet, here she is, by my side.

"She's following you," Rex says.

I interlace my fingers with McKenzie's and squeeze her hand. She squeezes mine in return. Victor and Olivia come out as we're about to walk into the room.

"We talked to her, and she's okay, but she asked if only a handful of people would watch," Olivia says.

Victor gestures. "You four should be okay and us, of course."

I know he and Olivia will not be joining us. I know my mother and Rex are behind us still. This almost seems too easy. We walk into the room and Victor shuts the door. Dick glances around, knowing something is off. Ava, the UC he thinks he purchased, is sitting in a chair in the corner ready to offer assistance if needed.

"What's going on?" He turns toward her. "Get on the bed."

I take my mask off. "I don't think she will."

Dick's eyes widen, his neck and face becoming a bright shade of red. He looks over my shoulder toward my mother, probably hoping she'll do something, but she doesn't say a word.

"Sit," I demand. He swallows, but does as I say. Rex walks over and stands next to him, putting his hand on Dick's shoulder. Ava smirks and waves her fingers at him. He swallows again, but doesn't move. He's already accepted his fate. I know Rex and Ava will handle him if he decides to try something.

I turn, face my mother, and tilt my head. She removes her mask and offers me a snake-like smile, but I don't return it.

"Mother. It's been years," I greet her. Kenz is still squeezing my hand, so I pull her close and wrap my arm around her waist.

My mother clicks her tongue as she stares us down. "What exactly do you think you're doing, son?"

Kenz brings her other hand up and grips my bicep gently. I know she's offering me support. How she ever thought I wouldn't choose her, I don't know. It wasn't a difficult choice. This woman will stand beside me through anything, while the one in front of me is nothing but a narcissistic manipulator.

My gut still clinches at the look in her eyes. She's never loved anyone but herself, let alone me. I force one side of my mouth to tip into a smile. "I'm changing the rules, mother."

She narrows her eyes, causing the creases in her forehead to be more evident. I wonder what she'd do if I pointed it out. Try to stop this conversation to go get botox immediately?

"So, you've made your choice?" she asks. I know she's trying to bait me.

"You made your choice the day you set your sights on my wife."

She snorts and rolls her eyes. "At least one of us gets a Knight." I tilt my head and McKenzie stiffens next to me.

"What do you mean?" McKenzie asks, and I know my mother wanted that question to be asked. She walks over to another chair and sits, adjusting her black dress around her as she gets ready for her performance.

"You see, years ago, in high school, I was promised to a man. A man I wanted more than anyone else." She glances over at Dick, who has kept quiet this entire time, and smirks. "In fact, Richard was friends with this man, gained his trust. Of course, back then Richard was quite the looker."

She sighs dramatically as she stares at him. "You really have let yourself go." Dick doesn't say anything, obviously used to this sort of abuse. "Anyway, my future was laid out before me. I was promised to the most eligible bachelor of Brighton Academy." Her eyes harden and she glares at McKenzie. I pull her closer to me. I want to step in front of her, but I know that will show a weakness and we don't need that. Not now.

"But halfway through our senior year, we had someone transfer in. It was highly unusual for a student to be accepted so far into the school year, especially a senior, but exceptions were made for this particular student." She scoffs and runs her hands down her silk dress. "Her parents had passed away, and she moved in with another family whose children went to Brighton." She rolls her eyes.

"The man I was promised to took one look at her and fell head over heels. I was all but forgotten. My family's empire and his were going to be joined and we would have ruled the majority of the southern states, but he went and ruined it all." She stands and takes a step toward us, but her eyes are glued to McKenzie. This time I do take a step in front of her, but she continues to stare at her.

"All because of your mother. She ruined everything." I spare a glance at McKenzie. She's staring at my mother with tears in her eyes, but she doesn't speak. My mother walks toward Dick, Rex standing behind him, waiting for his opportunity to kill the man that dared touch Anna. She doesn't spare a glance toward Ava, who has almost faded into the background. She does her job well. "So, I started scheming. Richard and I tried to find ways to get rid of Isabel, but we could never get to her."

She turns back around and puts her hands on her hips. "Your father was prepared for what he called my temper tantrum. He protected her. She was fragile, your mother. I thought he'd get bored with her eventually. My father got tired of waiting, so he found your father." She finally looks at me.

"He said I had to marry him or get sold at the next auction. I chose to get married." She runs her hands through her red hair, so different from the blonde hair I remember, and clutches it like she's trying to pull it out by the roots. "I had plans for the auction. I wanted to change things, but I couldn't do that since I was a woman. I had to have a husband." She glances at her red nails. "So barbaric, but I knew my place and did as I was told. I never loved your father. I tried. I really did, but for the majority of my life, Marcus Knight was supposed to be the man I married." She shrugs. "But your father believed I loved him and that's all I needed to begin slowly changing things."

McKenzie steps forward. "You killed my mother." The first thing my brain wants to do is reject this, but I know she's right. I knew where this story was headed the moment mother began talking about the man she was promised to and the girl he fell in love with instead.

"I did." She admits it like she's talking about the weather. McKenzie sinks into me and I hold her tight so she doesn't fall to the ground. "And your father tried to find me. He started coming to auctions. Tried to find evidence, but I was very careful."

"We have a situation out here," Victor says in my ear. I share a look with Rex.

"Handle it," Rex replies.

My mother glances between us and arches an eyebrow. "Issues, boys?"

"Your father is here," Jason says.

I glare at the woman who gave birth to me, but that's all she is to me, I'm realizing. "Dad is here," I tell her.

She sighs and shakes her head. "Loyal to the very end."

I ball my hands into fists as I glare at her. "How are you able to make all these men do your bidding?"

She huffs. "All the men except the one I wanted, you mean?"

Chapter 37

McKenzie

My heart is breaking. It feels like a fissure has started at the top and slowly worked its way down my sternum. My father truly loved my mom. All this time, I thought it was a lie. That he forced her to marry him, but now I'm not sure. As Alice tells her story, revealing the motive she's had all these years, I'm remembering things.

My mom was sick for a couple of months, and instead of taking care of her, my dad started attending auctions. At the time, I didn't realize they were auctions. He always said they were parties, but he would never tell me why he had to attend them. A flash of me sitting on the kitchen floor holding my mom's head in my lap screaming races through my mind. I squeeze my eyes shut. *Did I find her dead? Why don't I remember that?*

"How did you kill her?" I ask.

Alice's mouth lifts into a serpentine smile. "Jimson weed."

I clutch Nix's hand. I think I'm going to be sick. I remember my dad tearing the kitchen apart, throwing everything away.

"Did you drink any of your mom's tea?" He shakes my shoulders, tears streaming down my face.

"No, daddy! I swear."

"You put it in her tea."

"Ding. Ding. Ding."

We never touched my mom's tea. That would explain why she was the only one that was sick. My dad brought a doctor in to look at her, but they couldn't figure out what was wrong with her.

The dean snorts and I turn my glare on him, as do Nix and Rex. "And he trusted me, all the while I was working with her. We had a plan, then *you* had to ruin it," he snarls at Phoenix.

Nix doesn't react, he just tilts his head at Rex, who takes his gun out of his holster and hits Dick over the head, knocking him out and effectively shutting him up.

Alice's only reaction is a shrug. Her attention focuses back on Phoenix, and she lowers her chin, looking at him through her eyelashes. "I was never meant to be a mother, but your father wouldn't listen. He wanted a son, or a little mafia princess. He was always the better parent. When I found out I was pregnant, I cried the whole nine months."

I grip Nix's arm, trying to bring him comfort. This has to be hard to hear. The woman he adored for years turns out to be a narcissistic bitch. But he stands there stone faced, listening. "Nix," I whisper. His gaze finds mine and softens. "Don't listen to this anymore."

He turns and cups my face with his hands. "I need to hear it. I need every seed of hatred to kill her."

Alice scoffs. "You won't be able to go through with it."

I turn and face her, walking toward her, letting every bit of hatred, anger, and loathing course through my veins. "I'll do it. I'll do it for the little girl whose mom you killed, for the man whose wife you killed, for the little boy who wanted a mother, and for the husband and other men you manipulated."

Alice raises her hand, her eyes flashing with anger. I flinch, but Phoenix grabs it before she's able to slap me. "Do. Not. Touch. My. Wife." She tries to rip her hand out of his grip, but he holds fast.

"You're choosing her over me." Her eyes begin to shine with tears and my mouth drops open at how manipulative she is. "Your own mother." She sniffs and I scoff. He pushes her hand away, and she sways slightly. Her eyes slide to mine. "I should have killed you when I had the chance, but that damn doctor. He talked me into drugging you up so you'd forget."

"That doctor is dead now," Nix says. Alice's eyes widen in surprise, but she tries to hide it quickly. "Another one of the men you manipulated to do your bidding."

There's a bang at the door. "Nix, your father has brought other men here. They're trying to get in that room," Victor says. My heart jumps in my throat and my pulse skyrockets.

What will he do? Will he try to save her? How could he after everything she's done to them?

Alice throws her head back and laughs. "Things aren't going quite as planned, are they, son?"

There's shouting outside the door. I glance at Rex, then Phoenix. "Nix, open this fucking door!"

Nix runs his hand through his hair. "Tell him he can come in, but only him. His men have to stay outside."

Rex walks over to the door, standing in front of it as they wait to hear back from Victor or Julian.

"He almost found me," Alice says like this is just a day at the park. She doesn't sound nervous or upset. She still thinks she's going to get out of this alive. Fear grips my chest.

What if she does? What if Nix lets her go? I can't live the rest of my life constantly looking over my shoulder.

"But I was able to disappear for a couple of years, so the trail he was on came up empty." She sits on the bed that's in the middle of the room and crosses her leg. "Then I heard you bought McKenzie, so I came out of hiding. Did she tell you the message I gave her the first time I took her?"

I pull my bottom lip between my teeth.

"She did."

She looks at me, her eyes raking over me. "It's about time."

"You are a nasty human being." I gesture toward Phoenix. "This man loves hard and you've missed out on it, but I haven't. You'll get what's coming to you, whether it's by my hand or his. You will never see another sunrise."

Alice makes a cat fighting noise and smirks. Nix grabs my hand and turns me around to face him, ignoring her. He leans down and kisses me softly. "I love you," he whispers against my lips.

I grip his waist. "I love you."

He exhales, his breath washing over me. "I don't deserve your love." He swallows and closes his eyes.

"You do. You deserve all the love in the world, and I will give it to you for the rest of your life. I promise." I kiss him again.

"I've calmed him down somewhat. I told him he can come in, but only him. He agreed," Victor says.

Nix takes a deep breath and turns to face Rex, giving him a signal to let his father in. Nix pulls his gun out of his holster. *How are they going to do this?* I don't think he'll be able to torture his mother the way he tortured Bill. I don't expect him to.

I glance at Dick. Him on the other hand? I wonder if Nix will let Rex do whatever he wants. When Anna and I were talking last night, I reminded her about us talking about killing him together, but she said she couldn't. She's not ready for something like that yet. I hope once she knows the people who hurt her are gone, she'll be able to come out of her shell a little more.

Nix's father enters, his eyes frantic as he searches the room. His eyes land on Alice and he sucks in a breath. "You're not killing her, Nix."

Nix places one hand in his pocket, keeping the other out as he rests his gun against this thigh. "I am, and there's nothing you can do about it. She has hurt so many people, including my wife. She will pay for her sins."

"Nix, I love her. I can't live without her. If you kill her, you're killing me."

Nix shrugs. "Would she do the same for you, dad? Ask her." Nix's dad looks like he's aged twenty years. He has dark circles under his eyes, the wrinkles around his eyes and mouth are pronounced, like they're etched in stone.

He turns to Alice. "Alice, dear. Tell them you'd save me. Tell them." She gives him a bored look and my heart breaks for him. I cover my mouth. "I've spent over a decade looking for you. I thought—"

"Shut up! You know I left. You made all this up in your head. You knew I didn't love you, but you couldn't let it go. You put this idea in Phoenix's head that it was Marcus that took me, but you chose to be blind. You knew what I did and yet instead of being a man and telling your son, you turned him against a man that probably would have helped him."

My skin tingles like a thousand tiny needles are poking me everywhere as Alice's words sink in. He knew this whole time. It wasn't a recent discovery.

Nix swirls on his father, his face red and his eyes blazing. "Are you fucking kidding me?"

"I told you..." Nix's father stumbles over his words. "I told you she left."

"But you knew what she did. You knew she killed McKenzie's mother, and you did nothing about it. Why did you want me to hate Marcus so much?"

"He had the love of the woman I wanted. That's why! I knew the day she walked down the aisle she didn't love me, but I thought over time maybe she'd love me. Maybe. But she'd go into these depressive episodes, all because I wasn't enough. We weren't enough." He rakes his hand over his beard.

"Then why would you want to save her?" Nix asks softly.

His shoulders slump in defeat. "Because as much as I try not to love her. I do." Dick groans, and everyone's attention snaps to him as he regains consciousness. His eyes widen slightly when he sees Nix's father.

"Him, I don't mind if you kill."

Rex scoffs. "Oh, I will."

Dick swallows convulsively. "But the girl I bought, she won't get her money," he sputters.

"I don't want your fucking money," Ava says from the corner. "It's going to help those who need it." Dick turns to her, shocked she's still in the room. "And one of the assholes responsible for those people will get a bullet in his head." She chuckles and shrugs her shoulders. "Seems like a win to me, don't you think?"

Dick looks around the room like he's just now realizing the situation he's in, and his face goes white. "I'm not in the mood to torture you, though. I just want you dead." Rex walks toward him, slowly raising his gun as he does.

Alice stands from the bed and edges toward the door. The door Rex was guarding, but Nix steps in front of it. "Going somewhere, mother?" She swallows, her eyes darting around the room like she's also realizing the real possibility of not leaving this place alive.

Nix's father takes a deep breath and shakes his head. "Nix."

"Not one more word, father." Nix stands in front of the door and I walk to stand by his side. I clutch his hand as we all face Rex and Dick.

"You will rot in hell for eternity for all the things you did to Anna and any other girl you touched against their will." Rex looks over his shoulder, glaring at Alice. "You too, for allowing it to happen. Watching while things were done to her and to McKenzie."

I squeeze my eyes shut, a flash of Alice's laughter ringing in my ears as Bill is above me. "Breathe, love," Phoenix whispers in my ear, grounding me. Reminding me where I am.

A shot rings out and my eyes open just in time to watch as Dick's body slumps. His eyes still open as he stares unseeing, the gunshot wound to his head seeping blood and brain matter on the wall just behind him. Ava claps her hands in delight and actually giggles. Alice gasps and turns toward Phoenix, her hands raising.

"Nix, sweetheart—"

"Goodbye, mother." He raises his arm and shoots her between the eyes. Nix's father cries out and catches her slumping body before it falls to the ground. I turn in Nix's arms and put my hands on his face, forcing him to look at me. When his ice-blue eyes capture mine, there's torment, pain, heartbreak, and guilt swirling in them.

"I'm sorry," he whispers. He puts his gun back in the holster, wraps his arms around me, and lifts me in his arms. I want to wrap my legs around his waist, but my dress is too constrictive to do that, so I cling to him. "I'm so sorry for everything that was done to you. For not believing you. For blaming your father for all these years. For hurting you."

I kiss his forehead, his cheek, his ear, his mouth. I shower him with all the love and affection he should have had growing up, but didn't.

He clings to me, his head lying in the crook of my neck. "But I can't say sorry for buying you at that auction. I wanted you. I've never wanted anything so much in my life. You're mine. You'll always be mine."

I'm not sorry he bought me at that auction either. "Always."

Chapter 38

McKenzie

We all climb into the limo, and Rex drives us back to Victor and Olivia's house. While we were in the room taking care of Dick and Alice, Victor and Gil took care of letting those who came to watch the various couples do the ritual know that it would no longer be required, unless those who were bought agreed to it. A few did, but others wanted to go off by themselves or leave all together. They led them to a different area of the house, so they wouldn't hear everything that was going on. Rex and Phoenix both used silencers, so that helped hide the noise.

Once we were done, the party was over, and everyone had left. Two separate cleaning crews came in. One got rid of the bodies and evidence of what occurred in that room, and the other cleaned up the mess left by guests. I glance at Julian, wondering if he's upset at the night's events. Apparently out of all of them he's clean cut and straight laced. I'm sure he didn't expect to help a mafia boss. Bailey, his wife, has her head laying on his shoulder and he's combing his fingers through her hair.

He catches me staring at him, but I don't hide my curious stare. "If what happened to you had happened to Bailey, I would have done the same thing," he says.

Bailey opens her eyes and gives a tired smile. "He did kill someone for me," she says. "Him and his brother saved me." She sits up and looks around the group. "They all showed up to help. We're a family and now you're part of it. What you do to make money is your business as long as it doesn't involve hurting people."

"I appreciate all of you helping," Nix says, leaning forward and resting his elbows on his knees. "I don't trust a lot of people, but I do trust you all. Especially after tonight." He sighs and stares down at the floor. He's probably thinking about everything that transpired tonight. About his father.

Rex knocked him out, then Jason and Luca took him out and handed him over to his men. The men didn't seem too upset at the fact that Alice was dead. We ride in silence the rest of the way to Victor's house. Nix has my hand clasped in both of his while I rest my head against him and close my eyes, grateful everything is over. I don't have to look over my shoulder any longer.

After dropping everyone off, Rex takes us to the hotel, so he can go pick up Anna. Nix and I take a shower and fall into bed, both of us mentally, emotionally, and physically exhausted.

"Mom!" I drop to my knees next to her. Her lips are blue, vomit and blood on the floor. I shake her. "Mom! Mommy!" I wrap my arms around her and pull her up so she's in my lap. "Please. Please wake up. Please." Tears are streaming down my face, making everything around me blurry.

"McKenzie?" My dad walks into the kitchen. I have no idea how long I've been sitting here rocking back and forth. Tears and snot dripping down my face. "Oh my god! Isabel?!?"

He drops to his knees beside me, his hands raking along her body like he's trying to find a wound. "James!" James walks in, but I don't pay any attention. "Get the car. We have to take Isabel to the hospital."

I finally look at my father. "She's dead, dad." My voice cracks. We finally look at each other and the heartbreak that's evident on his face causes the sobs to start all over again.

James drops to his knees beside us. "What happened?" It takes me a minute to realize the question is directed at me.

"I don't know. She texted me earlier and said she was feeling better today. We were supposed to bake together, but when I came in, she was passed out on the floor." I motion to the vomit on the floor, the blood from where her head hit the floor, and the broken tea mug with spilled tea next to it.

James takes his phone out of his pocket and begins to make calls, taking charge since my dad isn't in any shape to be doing it.

"Dad? Why? Why did this happen?" Was it the mysterious sickness that's been plaguing her that finally killed her? Did her hitting her head cause her to die?

Dad wraps his arms around me and pulls me into a hug. "I don't know, Kenz. I don't know."

Men come and get mom, taking her to the hospital Dad approves of. He donates to this particular hospital, so they look the other way when his men come in with questionable wounds. James calls someone to clean up the kitchen and get evidence. I'm not sure what that means, but from the fragmented conversation he and my father have, it seems they think someone killed her.

But who? Everyone loves mom. All of dad's men love her, even some of dad's enemies love her. Loved. Another sob escapes at the thought of never getting to bake with her again. Never getting to brush her hair or her brushing mine. She wasn't just my mom; she was my best friend. She accepted me and always promised one day I would meet someone that would love me as much as dad loves her.

I squeeze my eyes shut until we pull up at the house. The kitchen is clean, but I can't bear to go in there. Not now. I wish I had a library to go to and read, get lost in another world, so I didn't have to deal with all the emotions flowing through me. I've asked dad since I was little if he'd build me a library, turn one of the rooms that looks like a museum into a library, but he always says no.

He wants his house to look and feel a certain way. Unfortunately, it feels like something you look at, not live in. When I grow up, my house is going to be beautiful and comfortable. I'll show him you can have both. I go to my room instead, the only place in this house that's comfortable. My mom told him I could decorate it however I wanted, and I did.

I don't leave my room for weeks, unable to bear the thought of not seeing my mom. If I pretend like it didn't happen, then maybe I'll survive this. I miss the smell of her tea brewing and the smell of chocolate chip cookies baking. Then eating them together and me telling her how gross it is that she dunks her cookies in her tea instead of milk.

I finally decide to venture out of my room. I haven't seen my dad since the day we came home. James said he's tearing the city apart trying to find out what happened to my mom. But he's been pretty absent even before mom died. He was always going to these parties that he wouldn't tell me anything about. He always said they were business related. Maybe if he had been home more, mom would have never died.

The autopsy should be back soon, so hopefully we'll know what it was that killed her. Walking down stairs the emptiness of the house resembles the emptiness I feel inside my chest.

There's this gaping hole where my heart used to be. Walking into the kitchen, I stand in the doorway, my lips pressing into a thin line. I try to imagine my mom's laughter, but it doesn't come. Walking to the cabinet, she keeps her tea. I pull it down, fill the kettle with water, and put it on the stove.

I want to bake cookies, but I don't think my heart can take that. Not today. When the kettle whistles, I pull it off the stove, place the tea in the ball infuser, put it in the teacup, and pour the hot water over the tea. I never liked tea. I tried, but never acquired a taste for it. I stare out the window as the tea steeps. I wonder if I'll see my father today.

We've barely spoken since the day it happened. I wonder how we'll be able to survive now. I was always closer to my mom, but my dad and I had a decent relationship until recently. He always made me feel special in his own way, but where is he now? When I need him the most. I walk back to where the tea is steeping, the smell already drifting toward me.

I grab the cup and let the warmth spread to my cold hands. I lift it, so I can smell the tea, debating on tasting it. Before I can bring it to my nose, dad runs into the kitchen, his eyes widen when he sees me. I don't comprehend how he's running toward me. His hand raises and I flinch, thinking he's about to hit me, but he slaps the teacup out of my ha nd.

Tears begin to stream down my face. Why would he do that? What is wrong with him? He grabs my shoulders, his face inches from mine. "Did you drink any of your mom's tea?" He shakes my shoulders, demanding an answer.

"No, daddy! I swear."

He wraps his arms around my shoulders and pulls me into his chest. "Thank god." He rubs his hand over my head and down my hair. "I'm sorry, baby. I'm so sorry." He lets me break, my tears soaking the front of his shirt.

I sit on the couch, my dad sitting next to me. "She was poisoned. That's what killed her. Since she was found with tea, I'm assuming it was the tea. I'm going to send it to get tested to make sure."

"She was poisoned?" I feel numb. I've been through every emotion there is over the past several weeks, and now I'm just numb. "Is that why she's been so sick? Who would poison her?"

Dad runs his hand through his hair and exhales. "Yes. I have an idea of who it could be, but..." He shares a look with James, his main security guy. James' lips are tight and the creases on his forehead look like deep ruts from how hard he's squinting at my father.

"I'm sorry, sir," he says, devastation in his eyes. He blames himself. Why?

"What's going on? Who do you think it was?" I ask.

"Honey, I think it's best if I don't tell you everything."

My mouth pops open, and I stand. "Why? I can handle it. I have to do something. If I can help, please let me help."

He and James share a look and my father sighs. "The less you know, the better, but I do need you to go to Brighton Academy."

I stare at him in confusion. I remember him and my mother talking about that once and she told him he was to never send me there. "Mom said she didn't want me going there."

He rubs his hand along the back of his neck. "I know, honey. But I need you to go. It will help catch the person who killed your mother. If I'm unable to find them, then one day you'll go to one of the parties with me."

"What does going to Brighton have to do with the parties?" I ask.

He shares a look with James again and takes a deep breath. "Just trust me. Okay?" I nod and he leans forward, hugging me tightly. "I promise I'll always protect you." He pulls back and pushes a strand of hair behind my ear. "When you get there, find Phoenix Stone. Stay as close to him as you can, okay?"

I squint my eyes, trying to think if I've ever heard that name before. "Have I met him before?" I ask.

"No, but I've kept an eye on him for a long time. He's your age, and he's a good kid. He'll watch out for you, but promise me you won't tell him I told you this. He isn't too fond of me, so he may not like that I told you to stay close to him."

"Dad, are you sure you can't tell me more?"

He places his elbows on his knees and steeples his hands, bringing his chin to the tips of his fingers. "I need you to stay close to Phoenix Stone. That's all I need you to know."

I swallow and nod. "Okay."

Chapter 39

McKenzie

I suck in a breath, my eyes getting used to the dark. I glance over at Nix to make sure he's still asleep. Rolling over, I face the opposite wall and begin to dissect everything I just remembered. I was under the impression the things I forgot were related to Phoenix.

I can't believe I forgot that. Maybe I chose to forget it. It seems my dad had a plan. Did he use me? Did he really trust Dick and didn't realize he would turn on him? Why would he tell me to stay close to Phoenix? Was he hoping he would buy me all along? I have to speak to my dad.

I try to force myself to go back to sleep, but my mind won't stop. So, I finally get up and walk downstairs. I made some chocolate chip cookies yesterday when we got home. I needed to do something normal. I'm guessing that, along with what Alice revealed, is what triggered these memories to return.

Grabbing a few cookies, I pour a small glass of milk and sit at the island eating them and think back to high school. Small memories begin to trickle in. I squeeze my eyes shut, my head hurting slightly from all the new memories. I was always so shy, but I knew Nix had a soft spot for me. He always says I was oblivious, but I wasn't. My dad told me to get close to him, but I didn't have to. Phoenix was always around, and I loved it. I fell for him. He treated me the way my mother always said the man I fell for would treat me.

He sat with me in the library, walked me to classes, and allowed me to be me. In the beginning, I considered joining the cheerleading squad, but I couldn't. I'm not coordinated enough or extroverted enough. At first I thought that was the only answer to getting close to him, but he was my tour guide on that first day and every day after that, he was always around. Phoenix helped me become comfortable in my skin, so eventually I didn't care what anyone else thought of me.

I close my eyes and let out a long breath. I have to tell him what I remembered. "What will he think?" I whisper.

"Who?" Nix says behind me.

I take a deep breath and turn around to face him. He's standing in the doorway of the kitchen, looking sexy as hell in his pajama pants. He walks into the kitchen and I stare as his muscles flex.

"You," I admit. *Might as well go ahead and get this over with.*

He tilts his head at me. "What will I think about what?"

I close my eyes. "I had a memory." He stops in front of me, placing his hands on my knees as he spreads them and steps between my legs.

"Tell me," he murmurs. I swallow, take a deep breath, and tell him everything.

Phoenix

After McKenzie tells me everything, I take a deep breath and step away from her. I have the same questions McKenzie does.

Did her father use her? Was he really telling the truth that night about Dick? Did he really think I'd keep her safe knowing who my mother was? And if he did, why did he think that?

It seems Marcus was a lot smarter than I gave him credit for. I always had this feeling my dad was never smart enough to outsmart Marcus. He also never seemed to have the courage to go directly for Marcus. *If I ever find out Marcus used his daughter, I might kill him too.* I pause at that line of thinking. *Would I have done the same thing if the roles were reversed?*

If McKenzie told me specifically she didn't want our child going to Brighton, I would have found another way. But from the stories she's told me of growing up, it doesn't surprise me.

"I swear I didn't know, Nix," Kenz whispers.

I take a deep breath and step toward her. "I believe you, love. And even if you did, it wouldn't change anything. I will always love you."

Her shoulders slump in relief. "We need to call my father. I don't understand why he hasn't come around all these years. Why hasn't he tried to find out what's happening? It doesn't make sense."

I huff and shake my head. "Because he knew I'd never let anything happen to you. He knew I'd keep you safe, even against my mother." I wrap my arms around her and pull her into my arms. I don't know why he had so much confidence in me, but he did. Maybe even more so than my own father. "We'll go find him tomorrow," I promise her.

The next day, I get Rex and Jason to find Marcus. They find him in a few hours at the docks, as expected. I let McKenzie know, and she's ready within thirty minutes so we can leave. Anna meets us at the door as we're leaving and gives McKenzie a hug.

"Good luck," she whispers.

I told McKenzie to wear something comfortable. She stops at the sight of my motorcycle and her mouth breaks out into a huge smile.

"We're taking your bike?" I nod and hand her the helmet. She puts it on and I make sure it's on correctly before grabbing mine and putting it on. I climb on and she climbs on behind me. "Have I ever been on this bike before?" she asks through the headpiece in our helmets.

"You have." I grab her thigh and pull her closer. She wraps her hands around my waist and I soak in her closeness for a moment before starting the bike and heading down the driveway. "We've even fucked on it."

She rocks against me. "Nix," she moans, and I chuckle.

"Since you can't remember it, I'll have to remind you later." I'm sure she'll get all her memories back eventually. Now that things have settled down, I'm going to make weekly appointments with Dr. Pearl to help McKenzie. We can finally focus on ourselves and move forward.

I enjoy the ride with her arms wrapped around me, and she points out things she sees during the trip. When we get to the port, Rex and Jason are waiting. I park the bike and help McKenzie off. She grabs my hand and clutches it. She hasn't seen her father since I bought her. That's been four years now.

We greet Rex and Jason and they lead us inside the gate. Marcus is standing there leaning against a forklift, waiting for his daughter. McKenzie stops as she takes him in. He looks the same, maybe a few more gray hairs, but the same as he did four years ago. He pushes away from the forklift when he sees his daughter. His mouth tips into a smile. McKenzie releases my hand and claps her hands.

"Daddy!"

It takes everything in me to stay rooted where I'm at and allow her to run to him. Until I hear his side of the story, I'm not sure I can trust him. Will I be able to trust him even after I hear his side of the story? I wonder if James, the security Kenz told me about, still works for him. Maybe I can talk to him and make sure their stories align. She runs into his arms and he wraps her up, holding her tight. My throat grows tight, a little envious of their display.

She had the parents I always wanted. Marcus pushes her away for a moment to look at her, then pulls her into another hug. When he does, his gaze catches mine. He waves at me. "Come here, son."

I walk toward the two of them, wondering what he's going to say and do. I stop in front of them and he offers me a smile. "McKenzie says she remembers," he says.

I tilt my head at him. *How did he know she lost her memory?*

"Larry and I are very good friends," he answers my unasked question. McKenzie pushes back from him and gapes at him. I'm sure my facial expression looks the same as hers. "I'm sorry, but I had to find a way to keep track of you two. When McKenzie wound up at his house all those months ago, he told me. He also told me how possessive and protective you are of Kenz." He slaps a hand on my shoulder. "I knew you'd take care of her."

He chuckles as Kenz steps back and stands next to me. I wrap my arm around her waist. "I knew Richard, or Dick, as you called him, was on your mother's payroll. I took a huge risk allowing him to bid on McKenzie. I was prepared to kill him if he wound up winning the bid that night, but I knew when you started bidding, he wouldn't win."

"Dad, you came downstairs and watched." McKenzie sounds disgusted.

"I didn't watch. I was in the room, yes, but I promise I didn't watch. I followed you two to the parking lot to make it look believable. Kenz, I'm so sorry for deceiving you, but it was the only way."

"How did you know I would protect her?" I ask.

"Because Richard told me how much you were around her. He even told me once he couldn't believe you allowed her to have a boyfriend." He glances between the two of us. "McKenzie and I wrote to each other, and she talked about you a lot. She said she didn't have to try to get close to you, that it just kind of happened. So, I knew." He chuckles. "Admittedly, I didn't know you two would get married. I do hate that I missed that."

McKenzie and I share a look. *So he doesn't know everything.* I try to communicate with her through a look that it's up to her if she tells him or not, but she shakes her head lightly.

McKenzie huffs. "I don't remember everything. I forgot you told me to get close to Phoenix." She pulls her lips between her teeth. "And I don't remember the letters." I think back to the day Anna gave her the letter and how sad McKenzie looked. *Does she remember that day?*

Marcus gives her a sad smile. "Maybe the accident altered your memories." He glances at me, then back at her. "Maybe someone can help."

McKenzie and I share another look realizing he thinks she lost her memories because of an accident. "Nix called Dr. Pearl. I'll start seeing her next week to help."

"That's good, Kenz. That's good," Marcus says. He looks at me and claps me on the bicep. "How are you doing? I know everything that's happened over the past several weeks. I know you might still hate me, but I'm here if you need me."

"I need some answers," I admit. I have to know what all he was planning before I'll be able to trust him.

"I know you do." He looks between the two of us. "I am sorry I deceived you. In the end, I never found Alice. As hard as I tried. I'm sorry you had to kill her."

I take a deep breath and nod. Maybe he'll turn out to be more of a parent to me than both of mine were.

Chapter 40

Phoenix

McKenzie and I spend the day with Marcus. He tells us he's the one who found Anna in the shipping container and made sure we found out about it. We're sitting in his kitchen and I understand what McKenzie said about this house feeling like a museum. Maybe when he comes to our home, he'll see that you can have nice things and still be comfortable.

"Why did you want McKenzie to stay close to me?" I ask him.

Marcus sighs and runs his hand through his hair. "I knew you thought I took your mother. I knew what your father told you."

I squint, thinking through this. "Then why would you think I'd protect your daughter?" McKenzie looks between the two of us, the same question evident on her face.

"I had a feeling," Marcus says, and I roll my eyes. "I know that's not the answer you want to hear, but I knew you'd find out the whole truth one way or another. I was hoping you'd keep an open mind."

"Why would you think that?"

He inhales deeply and glances between me and Kenz. "I met you when you were about thirteen or fourteen. Do you remember?" I squint, trying to think, but I don't know what he's talking about. I shake my head. "It was right before your mom left. Isabel and I saw the three of you downtown. I kept it short because I knew how your mom felt about Isabel and me, but there was something about that short interaction with you. The way you talked to Isabel." He smiles, remembering back to that day. "A tourist ran into Isabel and you steadied her, but at the same time chastised the tourist for not watching where they were going. I knew you weren't selfish, and I knew you weren't completely wrapped in your mom. Even if you thought you were."

I stare at him for a long moment and sigh, raking my fingers through my hair. I vaguely remember that day.

"You met my mom." Kenz gives me a sad smile.

I kiss the side of her forehead. "I guess I did." I turn back to Marcus. "Why didn't you just come to me?"

"I knew you wouldn't believe me unless you found out the truth yourself."

"Why did you trust Dick?"

Marcus looks out the window as he sits in silence for a few moments. "I'm not sure I trusted him. Not completely. I had an uneasy feeling about him, but I didn't have any concrete evidence he was going to stab me in the back. So, the night of the auction, I had James on standby just in case Richard did win. James was going to meet them in the back and take McKenzie away. When you bought her..." He glances at his daughter. "I'm not proud of what I did.

Allowing Phoenix to go through with the ritual, but again, I had a feeling you'd be safer with him than with me."

McKenzie leans forward and places her hand on his knee. "Dad, do you know the hell we've been through because of Alice?"

Marcus' eyes narrow. "What do you mean?"

McKenzie proceeds to tell him about the two times my mother kidnapped her and what happened to her. She leaves out how I forced her to marry me and how horrible I was to her the first few months of us being married.

Marcus' eyes grow bigger the more McKenzie talks. It would be comical if it wasn't so traumatic. When she's done, he leans forward and pulls her into a hug. "I'm so sorry. I had no idea." He leans back and looks between the two of us. "Is that why you missed an auction last year?"

I nod. "Yes. I got her back right before the auction, but she had lost her memories, so I wasn't going to take her to that one. You said you knew she lost her memories."

He nods. "Yes, but I didn't realize it was because she had been kidnapped. Larry didn't tell me that. He told me it was an accident."

McKenzie shrugs, "I didn't tell him I had been. I told him I had an accident." She looks at me and sighs. "I didn't want to talk about it."

Marcus looks between the two of us, regret evident on his face. "I was trying hard to do the right thing. It seems like I wasn't successful."

I put my arm around McKenzie's shoulders and pull her in close to me. "I, for one, am glad you had her come to Brighton. I wish we could have avoided the kidnapping, but I don't regret everything else." McKenzie gives me a small smile and nods in agreement.

Marcus sighs, looking between the two of us. "I did try to approach your father a few years ago, but he didn't want anything to do with me. He was blinded by his love for your mom and he was convinced I was the problem."

"It seems like you're the only man that didn't succumb to her," I say. Kenz rubs her hand up and down the back of my neck.

"Don't beat yourself up. That was your mom. It makes perfect sense," Marcus assures me. "I wasn't sure how you would handle things once you got McKenzie, but I could tell from the calls and letters Kenz and I had that you had feelings for her. So, I was counting on that. I thought you might be interested in buying her, but once you did, I should have kept closer tabs on the two of you. I did go to auctions a couple of times a year, but when I was informed I wasn't allowed at the ones you hosted, I knew you didn't want me there. So, I had my guys keep an eye on the two of you sporadically." He sighs and runs his hand through his hair. "I should have done a better job."

McKenzie and I don't respond. I'm not sure how to respond. I don't agree with how her father handled things, but it doesn't seem like he had bad intentions like my mother did.

"I don't remember the letters you and I shared," McKenzie admits. "I just remembered everything that happened to mom and why I started going to Brighton." She sighs. I know she's frustrated that all her memories haven't come back yet, but I keep assuring her they will. Eventually. I'm hoping I'm right.

Marcus pats her hand. "Hopefully Dr. Pearl can help."

"She says she's going to try hypnosis on her to bring those repressed memories to the surface," I tell him.

"The first session is in a few days. I'm ready," Kenz says. I was nervous when Dr. Pearl talked about this. She said she mentioned it to Dr. Chamberland, but he was against it, so she never mentioned it to me. Now we know why. If Kenz is ready to do it, I'm ready to support her.

"So, what are the plans for future auctions?" Marcus asks.

"We're no longer going to host them at people's residences. The place we went to and handled my mom and Dick is already operational. Victor's partner talked me into allowing them to have them there. We've already purchased the property and construction will begin this week. It should take nine months to a year to get everything completed." It's weird talking to Marcus about this, but he's been doing business a lot longer than I have, so if he can help, I'll accept it.

"Dad, we're not going to be selling drugs at these auctions," McKenzie says quietly. It's the one thing about her father that she hates.

Marcus rubs his hand along his jaw. "I don't do that anymore," he admits, surprising us both. "After what happened to your mother, I stopped. I've actually gone into more legal business. I manage the ports and I keep an eye out for trafficking. That's how I found Anna. I do look the other way if it's not trafficking or drugs and I make those give me a percentage of what they make."

Kenz huffs. "Legal, huh?"

Marcus shrugs, "I said I got into more legal business, not completely legal."

I glance at Kenz. "It's not like we can talk. These auctions aren't exactly legal," I remind her. "Maybe we can merge our businesses," I suggest to Marcus, who chuckles.

"We'll talk."

We stand getting ready to leave, and Kenz gives Marcus a hug. "Dad, you should come have dinner with us. You can see Anna. We'll even invite Larry over."

Marcus hugs her tight. "I'd like that, sweetheart. Tell me when and I'll be there." We walk to my bike and Marcus watches as we put our helmets on. "Take care of my daughter on the back of that bike!" he yells at me and I nod.

"I plan on taking very good care of you on the back of this bike," I murmur into the headset.

"Nix!" Kenz wraps her arms tight around my waist and when I pull out, she cups me over my jeans.

I grunt. "Careful, love, I'll find an alley."

"Promises. Promises," she replies. So, I find an alley and do exactly that.

McKenzie

"You're standing at the edge of a lake. Take one step after another until you're completely submerged." I focus on Dr. Pearl's voice as I imagine what her words say. "You're safe. You can breathe." I suck in a breath, not realizing I wasn't breathing. "Let's go to a day you've already remembered, but perhaps that memory is altered. You're walking down the aisle toward Phoenix."

Walking toward Phoenix, I pretend like this is the wedding I used to dream about in high school. He's my one true love and I'm his. I wish I could tell him. My dad told me to get close to him. Did he mean this close? Does he even know we're getting married?

I don't recognize anyone except Phillip, Clara, and Rex. I wish Anna was here. When I stop in front of Phoenix, the priest doesn't ask who gives me away. Because no one is giving me away.

Phoenix is taking me and there's nothing anyone can do to stop him. I wonder if my father is keeping tabs on me. I miss him. Maybe, one day, when the truth comes out, we can have another wedding and my dad can give me away. Will Phoenix think I deceived him? I didn't know this is what my father had planned. He said he wanted me to get close to Phoenix. I didn't realize he was going to sell me at an auction.

He lifts my veil and cups the back of my neck before bringing his forehead to mine. I suck in a breath and close my eyes, bringing my hands up to cling to his forearms. It's moments like these that make me remember the Phoenix from high school. He's become hard since then. He has a plan but doesn't know anything about my father telling me to get close to him. Is our relationship based on a lie? It feels like it and I hate it.

"I promise I'll make this good for you, Kenz." I open my eyes and stare into his icy gaze. Does he mean the wedding or the marriage? "Both," he answers, reading my mind. I swallow and accept that he will stand behind those words.

"Okay," I whisper. Relief flashes in his eyes and he nods slightly before releasing me, and the priest begins the ceremony. Will he still hate my father when he finds out it was his idea for us to become close?

"We need to adjust her dosage. Phoenix is close to finding her and we can't have her remember," Dr. Chamberland says as he fills his syringe with the drugs they've been giving me.

"We need to kill her," Alice says. I squeeze my eyes shut. This was not part of the plan, but when she threatened to kill Phoenix, I had to do what I could to save him. She's crazy, she would have done it. I feel Alice's presence over me without opening my eyes. "This is your father's fault. If he had just stuck to the plan, but no."

"How long did you poison my mom before she died? She was sick for weeks." I need to know.

"For almost a month. I got tired of waiting so I finished her off that day. I considered poisoning you, too. I should have."

I glare up at her. "How did you get into our house?"

She huffs. "I didn't have to get into your house. I made sure the tea that was being delivered was already poisoned." I have to figure out how to contact my dad and tell him, but I don't know how I'll do that.

William walks in and my eyes widen. I squeeze my legs shut, knowing why he's here. He sneers down at me and rakes his eyes over me with that hungry gleam that makes me nauseous, but Dr. Chamberland walks in front of him and stops him.

"Not today." He brings the needle to my arm and I almost welcome the fog it will bring. "This is a cocktail that will make you forget," Dr. Chamberland says as he sticks the needle in my arm.

I swallow as the drugs course through my veins. Alice walks over and prods my chin with her long pointy fingernail. "This better work."

I'm left in darkness. Complete and total darkness. I wait for them to come back, but they never do. I need to forget. Not just what they did to me, but everything else. What happened to my mom and that my dad asked me to get close to Phoenix. I don't want to think about it anymore. I want to forget everything. So, my mantra begins.

"My name is McKenzie. I'm twenty-three years old. I've been kidnapped. But he will come for me. He always comes for me."

A couple of days later, someone comes in allowing some light, but I can't see their face. They have a mask on. "Do you know who I am?"

"Dr. Chamberland." He doesn't reply. He lifts my arm and sticks the syringe in.

"Don't. Please," I moan as the drugs seep into my bloodstream. He walks out and leaves me in darkness again. My stomach cramps with hunger pangs and I'm so thirsty. Who will come for me? Will Phoenix or my father? I shake my head. I can't remember why I was supposed to get close to Phoenix. Did my father tell me?

Every couple of days, Dr. Chamberland shows up, his face covered and asks me the same questions. Do I know who he is? Do I know who took me? Do I know who I am? Do I know who my husband is? Until one day he comes in and I can't remember who he is.

"What do you remember?" he asks.

"My name is McKenzie. I'm twenty-three years old. I've been kidnapped. But he will come for me. He always comes for me."

"Why do you think you're twenty-three?"

I don't understand the question. "It's the last time I saw my father. He took me to a party." Why did he take me to that party? Had he gone to parties before? I think he did, and I hated it, but it seems like I was ready to go. I just don't remember why.

He doesn't ask anymore questions, but does give me a sip of water. I want more, but he takes the cup away before I can get more. He leaves and I groan. I'm freezing and the chains are rubbing against the raw skin of my wrists and ankles. My body aches. I'm going to die here. They're going to forget I'm here and I'm going to die.

This time, it feels like weeks before someone visits me again. I'm shivering so hard I have no control over my muscles. The person grabs my arm and sticks a needle into it. The drugs warm me up a little.

"Do you know who I am?"

I shake my head. A cup is held to my mouth and I greedily drink the water, some of it pouring out of my mouth and into my hair.

"Do you know who I am?" they ask again.

"No," I croak. I can't remember anything. Why can't I remember?

"My name is McKenzie. I'm twenty-three years old. I've been kidnapped. But he will come for me. He always comes for me." I'm not sure how loud I say the words.

"Who kidnapped you?"

I try to think back. Try to remember when I was kidnapped, where I was kidnapped, but I can't. "I don't know." Tears begin to stream down my face. Why can't I remember?

"Who will come for you?" The tears flow harder.

"No one."

Chapter 41

Phoenix

I told McKenzie I didn't have to be in the room when Dr. Pearl was working with her, but she was insistent. She wanted me in here. Listening to her telling us what happened to her makes me want to kill Dr. Chamberland and my mother all over again.

"McKenzie, it's time to wake up," Dr. Pearl says softly. McKenzie's eyes flutter open and she immediately turns her head to look at me. She begins crying and I'm next to her in an instant. "I'll give you two a minute."

I don't hear Dr. Pearl leave as I gather Kenz in my arms and hold her tight. She wraps her arms tightly around my neck. "I'm sorry. I'm so sorry," she whispers over and over again.

"There's nothing to be sorry for, love." I rub my hands up and down her back.

"I remember feeling so guilty. The day I married you, you thought you were forcing me to marry you. I wanted to marry you. I had fantasies about it in high school. But I felt so guilty because you thought you were making me. I knew you were doing it because of the rules. Deep down, I knew you loved me. Or you wouldn't have gone to those lengths." I sit back so I can look at her. I wipe her tears away with my thumbs, and she laughs. "Shouldn't you be licking them away?"

I chuckle and lean forward, licking one. "Happy?"

"I do like when you lick me," she murmurs and I laugh.

"I like licking you."

She rests her head on my shoulder and gives me a tentative smile. "Are you mad?"

I run my fingers through her hair. "No, love I'm not. You got close to me, yes. But you didn't know why you were doing it. Now we have the bigger picture. We know how you lost your memories and why they were altered. You took a shitty situation and turned it in your favor." I lean forward and kiss her softly. "It looks like this therapy with Dr. Pearl will help you remember everything else over time."

She sighs and rests her head on my shoulder. "I hope so." She runs her fingers through the back of my hair. "I hate not remembering. I hate it."

I'm in my downstairs office looking at the plans for the new property while Kenz is baking. From the smell drifting in, I think it's cupcakes and maybe cinnamon rolls. My phone rings and I pick it up without looking at the name.

"Phoenix," I answer.

"Hey boss," Felix says. "You told me to call you with updates on Shay. She's been talking to Dr. Pearl, working through everything that happened. She says she doesn't want to go back to the fights."

I lean back in my chair. "Alright. That's her choice, and she has every right to decide that."

"That's what I told her, but she was still nervous."

I shrug. "Is that why you're telling me and not her?"

"Yep." He pops the P and I chuckle.

"What does she want to do?" I ask him.

"She wants to go back to school, then open her own beauty shop." He pauses. "I told her she could stay with me until things settle."

"Yeah, that sounds like a plan. Let me know where she enrolls. I'll pay for her school and I'll help her open her shop."

"What? Really?" Felix sounds surprised and I shake my head.

"Yeah, I've told all the girls from day one if they no longer wanted to do that, I would help them do what they wanted," I remind him.

"I know, but..."

"It obviously hasn't stuck. Call a meeting, have everyone be there in two hours." He agrees and we hang up.

Walking into the kitchen, I smirk at the sight of McKenzie leaning over the island with a book in her hand while she waits for the oven timer to go off. I step up behind her and pull her hips into me. She gasps and turns her head over her shoulder to look at me, giving me a knowing smile.

"How did you know I needed you?" she says as she rubs herself against me.

I moan and drop my forehead to the top of her spine. "I was coming to tell you I have to go into the city for a meeting."

Her eyes narrow as she looks at me, but shrugs and turns back to her book. "I thought you said it only took you sixty seconds, but maybe I'm remembering wrong." I growl and pluck the book out of her hand, setting it down on the counter. She giggles as I lift her in my arms and walk into the pantry.

It's the middle of the day, so anyone can walk in on us in the kitchen. She's wearing a sundress, so it's perfect. I yank her panties down and swipe my fingers through her pussy lips. We moan together. I quickly undo my pants and lift her so her back is against the door.

"What were you reading, you naughty woman?" I ask as I sink into her.

Her tight heat wraps around me, and I savor it for a few moments before I begin to leisurely thrust in and out of her. She clings to me as her head lands against the door.

"Since you got pierced, I've been obsessed, so I've read every book I can get my hands on where the male main character is pierced," she admits, and I smirk. I tilt my hips so my piercing rubs against her inner walls and she moans. "Fuck, it feels so good."

"Are you remembering what it felt like before I had it?" I ask her as I lift her dress and stare at where we're connected.

"Yes," she moans, and I don't know if she's answering my question or agreeing to how good it feels. "It's always been good, but—" I pound into her, cutting her off. "Oh god, Nix." Her nails dig into my neck, but I welcome it. I love it when she can't get enough.

She allows me to move her and have complete control. I bring a hand between us and rub my thumb over her clit. She holds tight to me so she doesn't slip as she gives into the feeling. I bite my lip, holding off my orgasm as she rides my dick. She feels so good. If I lose focus, I'll come before she does.

"Nix." She's right there. I feel her getting tighter around me and it takes everything I have to hold off. My balls are drawing up and the tingling in my lower back becomes intense. "Oh, fuck!" she cries out and begins to pulse around me. I groan as I stop myself from holding back, thrusting into her a few more times before coming with her.

Her forehead lands on my shoulder and I plaster one arm against the door and the other goes around her waist as we both try to catch our breath. After a few moments, she leans back and gives me a sultry smile. "I think that was longer than sixty seconds."

I arch an eyebrow at her. "Don't test me, woman," I warn her and she laughs. It causes her to tighten some more around me and I moan. I could go again, but I have to get into the city. I slowly release her and her feet hit the floor. I kiss her long and hard before taking a step back and making myself look presentable again.

She leans down to get her panties, but I grab them before she can. She puts a hand on her hip and arches an eyebrow at me. I kiss her on the forehead. "I'm taking these with me." I put them in my pocket and she shakes her head in amusement. I know she's probably dripping, and the thought makes me feral.

We walk into the kitchen and stop in our tracks at the sight of Phillip, Clara, Rex, and Anna. They're all giving us amused looks. McKenzie's face turns bright red, and she puts her face in her hands.

I wrap my arm around her and pull her into my side completely unashamed as everyone laughs.

"I know what happened to Shay is scary, so I want to apologize to each and every one of you for not taking better measures to make sure each of you is safe. There will be different protocols going forward if you decide to continue doing this. For each shift, you will check in with Felix or one of his guys. If you decide to go home with a client, you'll let us know who the client is, where they live, how long you'll be staying, and you will check in with us when you leave. If we don't hear from you by the time you said you'll be done, we will come find you. You all will be required to have your location turned on your phone so we can track you."

I pause and look at each of the girls. The fighters and all employees are here as well. "If you decide you no longer want to do this after what happened to Shay or if you've been thinking about quitting, I'm letting you know it's okay. The money you make here is yours. I don't take a cut. The only cut I get is from the winnings of the fight. So, if you want to quit, you can."

Everyone is quiet, and I put my hands in my pockets. "That's all I have to say. Are there any questions?"

One of the fighters leans forward. "Will there be stricter policies on who fights? Like background checks?"

I nod. "Yes, McKenzie's father, Marcus, is going to help with that. I'll be introducing you all to him soon." I run my hand over my head. "I thought we had the best, but after what happened with Bill, I realize that isn't true. Marcus has the best."

One of the girls raises her hand. "So, is your father no longer in business with you?"

I shake my head. "No. But he hasn't been a part of this for a while now, so you all won't notice anything different."

The two of them asking questions opens the floor and more people ask questions and some of the girls admit they no longer want to do this. I tell them to stay after and we'll come up with a plan for their future. Whether it's something they want to do on their own or if they want to come work in one of my other businesses until they decide what they want to do.

Overall, it's a great meeting, and for the first time in years, I feel in control. It seems strange to think I wasn't in control, but I had one motive, and that was to find my mother. Now that I know who she really was, I can focus on McKenzie and I. And how I can make our lives better without any outside interference.

Chapter 42

Phoenix

One Year Later

I'm sitting in the chair in our bedroom, waiting for McKenzie to walk out of our closet. Clara and Anna came out a few minutes ago. Anna's hair and makeup was done, and she looked healthier than she did a year ago. She and McKenzie have worked through the shit they went through, both of them seeing Dr. Pearl on a regular basis. All of McKenzie's memories have come back. Some of them have been hard and some of them good. We've worked through it together.

The door cracks slightly. "Are you ready?" she asks, and I chuckle.

"I am." I lean forward, my elbows resting on my knees, and bring my thumb up to my lip as she steps out of the closet. "Fuck me," I whisper.

She twirls and gives me a sultry smile. "Oh, I plan on it." Her raspy voice washes over me and I smirk. She walks toward me and stops in front. "Sit back." I lean back in the chair and she lifts her leg and places her shoe in the middle of my chest.

I smirk at her and lick my lips. She has her heels on, but they're not hooked. They're silver high heels with diamonds. I hook the first, then she places her other shoe against my chest. I hook it; before releasing her, I lean down and kiss the top of her foot right beneath her anklet.

My eyes sweep over her. Her hair hangs over one shoulder, the collar I gave her wrapped around her pretty throat, and the light blue embroidered sheer dress. It's low cut, and the slit reaches all the way up to the top of her thigh.

She sits gingerly in my lap, so I wrap my arm around her waist and adjust her legs so they're on either side of my legs, forcing her to spread hers. She leans her back against my chest and lays her head against my shoulder. "The dress matches your eyes," she whispers as my hands begin to wander over her body.

I rub my thumb over the queen chess piece that was tattooed behind her ear, over her shoulders, her breasts, down her stomach to her thighs. She squirms against me. I told her not to wear any panties tonight. Part of me hopes she didn't listen so I can punish her later. I run my fingers up the inside of her thighs and they meet bare skin.

I kiss the top of her shoulder. "Such a good girl," I whisper. She whines when I rub my index finger and middle finger through her folds. "Should I let you come for listening?" She nods eagerly. I plunge my fingers into her and she cries out. We have to leave in fifteen minutes, but we need to be downstairs in ten. I rub my thumb around her clit and she moans, her lips latching onto the spot just below my ear where the chess piece tattoo I have is.

She rides my fingers as she marks me, moaning and whining in my ear. "Nix," she whimpers as I increase the speed. "I want your dick," she murmurs and I smirk.

"You'll get it when we get to the auction," I promise her just as I apply more pressure to her clit, making her come undone. She cries out as I continue to rub her, making her orgasm last. I pull my fingers out of her and bring them to my mouth. I hum at the sweet taste of her.

"How long do we have?" she asks as she pushes herself off my chest and begins to drop to her knees, but I stop her.

"We don't have time for that." She pouts and I grin at her, dropping a quick kiss on her ruby lips. "We'll have all the time in the world later, love."

McKenzie

Anna sits up front with Rex, and I sit in the back with Phoenix. He hands me my mask and I gaze down at it. "It's so beautiful," I whisper, running my fingers along the diamonds. His is black and silver and reminds me of the Phantom of the Opera mask. He helps put mine on and I help him with his. He's wearing a light blue suit with a white tie.

I requested this color because I knew it would make his eyes more prominent. With his mask on, I know I was right. My stomach swoops like it's the first time seeing him. I lean forward and kiss him. He wraps his hand around my hair and deepens the kiss before we pull away. "You know, you still give me butterflies," I tell him.

He hums against my lips, his mouth tipping into a smile. "Same, love. The butterflies usually make me hard, though." I giggle and playfully smack his chest. He grabs my hand and holds it against his chest. "It beats for you," he whispers for only me to hear.

We've been through so much, and here we are. Happy. I've never been happy like this in my life. I didn't realize it was possible. His father still refuses to speak to him, but I keep hoping maybe one day he'll come around. I never would have thought Nix and my father would become so close. They're in business together now. My dad helps him with the fights and has helped oversee the different properties that want to host auctions.

It's surreal. The man he thought of as his enemy all these years has become like a father to him. We pull up to the new property, our property, he's been working on for the past year, and I'm practically jumping in my seat. This is the first time I'll see it since it has been finished. He's brought me up here a few times, but once the major things started getting done, he told me he wanted to surprise me.

He promised he wouldn't make it look like a museum, and that was all I needed to hear. Rex pulls up into the driveway and I marvel at the trees arching over the gravel as we drive under them. "This is going to be beautiful in the fall," I whisper. Anna and I both have put our windows down so we can get a better look.

There are lights in the trees, but it's still daylight, so it's hard to get the full picture of them. I bet it will look gorgeous tonight when we leave. Unless we're staying the night. Nix never told me. The driveway loops around a huge water fountain. Rex stops in front of the stairs that lead to the entrance. There are two sets of stairs, one on the left, the other on the right.

"We'll have the left staircase closed off, so everyone will have to come up the right. There's also a canopy there so people can stand under it and not get wet if it's raining," Nix points out.

"I'll park and be in soon, sir." The valet are already here setting up, so one of them walks to the SUV and opens the door. Phoenix has already gotten out on his side and walks around to take my arm. Anna chooses to stay with Rex, so it's just Nix and me. We walk up the stairs as I take in every detail.

"It's beautiful, Nix." The house is white. There's two stories, the top story has a wrap-around porch. He sees me eyeing it and smiles.

"People can come out and look at the stars."

I smile at him. "I love it."

When we walk in, my mouth gapes open. It's like we've stepped back outside. It looks like a courtyard. There are circular tables throughout for people to sit at, and to each side there is a buffet table with a bar off to the corner. Straight ahead is a stage.

"That's where the auction will be held. We'll eat, then the auction will happen," Nix explains. I glance up and he chuckles. "You can see the stars here as well, but if it's cloudy or any chance of rain, there is a motorized canopy that will cover the area so we don't get wet."

"I don't even know what to say. It's so different and beautiful." We continue through the courtyard and he shows me where the room is to be watched if people want to be watched. Except for this one, people have to stand outside and look through a window. If the couple in the room want others to join, they can, but only four people can be in a room at a time.

After he shows me everything and we make our way back to the courtyard, I turn to him and clap my hands. "Where's our room?" He told me he had a room made just for us, but he hasn't shown it to me.

He smirks and grabs my hand, leading me back to the front door. "I'll show you that later, wife."

I groan, but follow him. Tonight is going to be fun. It's the first auction we've hosted since the modifications and while all of them have been a lot of fun with the new changes, I know tonight will be different because it's on our territory.

Chapter 43

Phoenix

We greet each guest as they arrive, but I can't keep my eyes off of McKenzie. She's in her element. She's learned everyone's name. The women and men that come to be bought, she asks them questions, making sure they're there willingly. I love that she cares so much. Even though we have vigorous requirements for someone to be considered to be put in the auction, she still wants to make sure they haven't changed their mind.

"I saw you at the last auction," McKenzie greets the woman before us.

The woman smiles and nods. "Yes, I went to see how things worked to decide if I wanted to participate."

She's wearing a silver cuff, so people know she will be up for sale later. Instead of only allowing the buyers to put who they wanted, we also allow those who are selling themselves to put their likes and dislikes. What age they want, their experience, if they're willing to have sex, or if they just want to go on dates and see how things go.

"And you liked it?" McKenzie asks.

The woman nods. I didn't catch her name when she said it. "Yes. I got divorced last year and my ex husband he..."

McKenzie grasps her hand. "You don't have to tell us, Wendy."

I know she said her name for my sake, so I give her a grateful smile. She smirks at me before giving Wendy her full attention.

"I feel like I need to tell someone," Wendy says, taking a deep breath. I make sure I'm giving her my full attention because this is important to her. "He never wanted me. He never touched me. He treated me like a roommate or his mother; it depended on the day. I want to feel sexy."

I tilt my head at her and finally force myself to really look at her. She is pretty. She has curly brown hair that stops at her waist. She's wearing a green dress that hugs her curves and makes her green eyes stand out. I lean down and take her hand, kissing her knuckles.

McKenzie smiles at me, and Wendy's face turns a light shade of pink. "You are sexy. I'm positive you'll find someone here tonight that will make you feel that way before you leave and after."

Wendy gives me a grateful smile. "I hope so."

She walks inside and McKenzie turns to me, then kisses my cheek. "You're so smooth, Mr. Stone."

I wrap my arm around her waist and pull her close to me, my hand sliding to caress her ass before resting on her lower back. "I try, Mrs. Stone."

McKenzie

Everything is so perfect. It's everything I imagined it would be. The auction is perfect. Wendy, who has to be in her late thirties or early forties, gets bought by a man in his twenties. I can tell by her expression she's completely caught off guard, but in a good way. I'm happy for her. Hopefully this man will show her how sexy she is and she'll come out of the experience a completely different person.

Anna watches everything intently, Rex at her side the entire night. She's been out over the past year, but this is the first auction she's attended. I thought she would back out at the last minute, but when she showed me her red dress, I knew she was determined to go and overcome that last obstacle. I'm still confused about her and Rex's relationship. There are moments when I think something is there, but I'm not sure. They'll figure it out, eventually.

When the auction is over, Phoenix grabs my hand with a smile and leads me through the crowd. He leads me inside, through the kitchen, and to the other side of the house that he didn't show me earlier. He looks at me over his shoulder. "No one is allowed past the kitchen. This area back here is ours. So, you can be as loud as you want."

I laugh as anticipation builds in my stomach. He stops in front of a door and pulls a key out of his pocket. Once he unlocks it, he looks at me one more time before opening it. He steps in and I step in after him. My eyes can't take in everything quickly enough. The room is black, gold, and gray, with a few red accents. The bed is in the center with a black and gold comforter.

There's a sex chair on the other side of the bed that's black with gold hooks. I walk over to it and run my fingers along the soft leather. In the corner, there's a gold chair by the window that looks very comfortable. On one side of the wall there's an armoire, so I walk to it and open it. I exhale quickly at the sight of the various floggers, vibrators, and cuffs.

I glance at Phoenix, and he smiles at me. We did these things after I was taken the first time and he's slowly started introducing them again over the past year. I love this side of our relationship. It makes me feel desired. He controls everything, but I know the moment I say my safeword, he'll stop. I've only had to use my safeword once.

There's a pillow next to the chair, so I know what he wants me to do, but first he has to help me get out of these shoes. I walk to him and show him my foot. He chuckles and leans down to help me out of them. Once I'm out, I turn and let him unzip my dress. He helps me out of it, so I'm naked before him.

Turning to face him, I wait. He removes his jacket, then his tie, hanging them up and putting them in the armoire. He returns to me, lifts his fingers and runs them along my collarbone. I swallow as goosebumps break out along my skin and heat settles in my core. He runs his fingers down to my breasts and circles my nipple twice before squeezing it slightly.

I close my eyes and suck in a breath. Wet heat engulfs my nipple when he takes it in his mouth and I moan. "So fucking sweet," he murmurs against my skin before giving my other breast the same amount of attention. "I will never get enough of you." His mouth grazes up my neck, then he's taking my lower lip between his teeth and sucking.

He wraps his arms around me and pulls me in as his tongue thrusts into my mouth and he massages my tongue with his. One hand slides up my spine and grips the back of my head as the other pulls me so tightly against him I can feel his hardness against my stomach.

I cling to him as he fucks my mouth with his tongue. He pulls away slowly and rests his forehead against mine. "Go to your spot, pet."

I swallow and remove my arms from his neck. "Yes, Sir." I walk to the pillow next to the chair and kneel. Placing my toes together and spreading my legs, I place my hands palm up on my knees. I lower my gaze to the ground and wait.

Fabric slides against skin as he undresses. I inhale slowly as I wait, forcing myself to stare at the ground. I want to look at him under my eyelashes and watch him as he slowly undresses. I know he's watching me to see if I look at him. So, I force myself to be a good girl. I'm sure the pillow beneath me is going to have a wet spot if he takes much longer.

He sits in the chair next to the pillow, his leg just in my peripheral vision. I want to close my eyes so I'm not tempted to look at him; instead I lock every muscle in my body so I don't give into temptation.

What would he do to me if I give in? What kind of punishment would he give me?

He runs his hand through my hair, making me jump slightly. "You're being such a good girl tonight," he murmurs, and my insides melt at his praise. "You may look at me," he says, and I do so immediately. He's completely naked. His cock erect, and waiting for attention. "Come and stand in front of me."

I get to my feet and walk to stand in front of him. He widens his legs so I can stand between them. His hand grips his cock and strokes lazily. "What's your safeword?"

"Peanut butter," I respond automatically.

"Good girl." He leans forward and kisses my stomach just next to my navel. He rubs his large hands down my waist and over my hips. "Turn around." I do so immediately. He kisses the top of my ass and massages it. "Put your legs on the outside of mine and sit on my dick."

I swallow, knowing where this is heading. He puts his legs together so I can straddle him. He wraps one hand around my waist as I sit, and the other is around his cock as he guides me. I gasp as I settle on his cock, making me feel full. He spreads his legs, forcing my legs wide.

"How long do you think you can sit here without moving?" he asks as he puts his large hand on my abdomen. He rubs up my stomach to my sternum and pushes me so I lay back against him. I rest my head on his shoulder and he turns his head and licks my tattoo. "Fuck, this still turns me on," he murmurs as I force myself not to move.

He wraps his hand around my throat and squeezes. I suck in a breath and swallow, trying to force myself not to buck. His other hand rubs from my knee, up my thigh, to where we are joined.

"Nix, please."

"Who?" he says as he slaps my pussy.

I groan. "Sir," I correct myself.

"Good girl." He rubs his hand between my pussy lips and my legs begin to shake with the effort to be still. He bucks up into me and I cry out. I can feel his piercing and I want to rub myself against it. "Ride me."

I lean forward and place my hands on his thighs and ride him. Squeezing my eyes shut, I revel in how good he feels inside me. His fingers swirl around my clit and I know I'll come loud and fast. "Sir, you feel so good," I moan. He leans up and places wet kisses along my spine.

"Such a dirty little slut, riding her master's cock. Milk me, pet," he murmurs against my skin and I ride him harder and faster. His fingers swirl around my clit faster. I arch my back and scream as I come undone. My muscles go limp and he helps me off his lap, still hard.

"Sir?" I gesture to him and he shakes his head.

"Not yet, pet." He lifts me in his arms and takes me to the sex chair. He lays me down, my back curving along the back. He sits on the portion where my hips are raised and pulls me so my legs are draped across his and thrusts into me again.

"Oh, god!" I cry out as he mercilessly pounds into me.

"Do you feel my piercing?" he asks and I nod, unable to speak. It's rubbing against my spot, and I know I'll come within a few seconds again. He grabs my clit between his thumb and forefinger, pinching slightly and I come so quick I see stars.

I claw at his arms as he continues to ram into me. "Sir, oh fuck."

"What's your safeword?"

"Peanut butter," I answer immediately.

"Do you need to say it?"

"No." My body is his for the taking. It's been too long since we've had a night like this. Life has been so busy lately and I've missed him. He pulls out of me and I moan. He's still hard, and it's beginning to upset me that he hasn't come yet.

He takes me to the bed and lays me down gently. I grip his face. "Sir?" He holds himself above me as he gazes down at me.

"Yes, pet?" His fingers come up and trace my face.

"Why haven't you come yet?" I ask. I know he sees the insecurity in me because he leans down and kisses me.

"Because I want to make sure you're completely satisfied before I do," he replies. I open my eyes to stare up at him.

"I am," I promise, and his mouth tips up into a smile.

He gets off the bed and walks to the armoire. Grabbing a vibrator, he returns to me. "Do you remember the time we had to have sex in front of the council and I used this on you?" He climbs back onto the bed, turns the vibrator on, and rubs it along my thigh.

I gasp and arch my back slightly. "Yes."

"I couldn't completely lose myself in you that night because I had to make sure you were okay." He lines himself up with me, kneeling before me. He pulls me so I'm practically in his lap, but my back is against the bed. His cock teases my entrance as he slowly enters me. "I've thought about that night so many times over the past several years, and I told myself one day I would reenact it when we weren't being watched." He turns the vibrator on and I suck in a breath.

He rubs the vibrator from my naval down toward where we're joined. He makes short thrusts, rubbing his piercing against my inner walls. I clutch at the blankets beneath me. "I've wondered how many times I could make you come like this." The vibrator reaches my clit and he places it directly on me as he thrusts hard into me.

I come immediately, but he doesn't stop. He continues to thrust in me and hold the vibrator against my clit. One orgasm turns into another and I squeeze my eyes shut. I know I'm being loud, but I can't help it. I want it to stop, but at the same time I don't. He's grunting above me and I know it's taking everything within him not to come.

"Sir!" I cry out. I can't take it much longer. He turns the vibrator off and throws it somewhere as he thrusts into me over and over again, finally coming and collapses on top of me. I wrap my arms and legs around him, cocooning him in my warmth until he finally rolls off me and pulls me into his side.

I know I'm a mess, but I'm too exhausted to care right now. He kisses my shoulder. "Sleep, love." And I do.

Epilogue

Phoenix

One Year Later

McKenzie smiles at me as she walks toward me. She's wearing the same dress I bought her five years ago. Today is our five-year anniversary, and she wanted to commemorate it by renewing our vows. This time her father is walking her down the aisle and she has friends here instead of it being just people I know.

She's like a dream. I can't believe I get to spend the rest of my days with this woman. The first time we did this, I had so many doubts, wondering if I would really be able to keep her. At the time I was determined I would, but I know deep down if she ever told me she wanted to leave, I would have let her. I think.

But now, watching as she steps up beside me, I know this was meant to be. I think back to all those years ago when her memory hadn't returned, and she thought I was married to someone else. She asked me if my wife was my fated mate and I told her yes. I meant it. I still mean it.

We're getting married at the property I built for the auctions. She told me this place was not going to sit dormant and only be used once a year because it was too beautiful for that. So, today marks the day of the first event outside of an auction and starting next month after we return from our honeymoon, we'll begin to have other events here.

It's already booked three years out. And at a few of those, Kenz is making the desserts. So much has changed over the past two years. It's hard to believe this is my life. She smiles up at me as her father hands her over to me. We say our vows. Since this time is different, we chose to write our own.

When it's my turn, I swallow down my nerves and look her in the eye, making sure she sees the emotion of everything I'm trying to say.

"The first day I saw you, I knew you were mine. The day I bought you at the auction made it official. I wasn't going to live without you. I couldn't. I don't regret one single day with you. Every single up and down got us to this point." I place my forehead against hers and grip the back of her neck. "It was worth it. I love you with every fiber of my being. I chose you then. I choose you now. I'll choose you every day for the rest of my life. The rest of eternity."

Her eyes are shining with unshed tears, so I kiss her. I vaguely hear the priest say to kiss the bride and the guests laughing as I wrap her in my arms and kiss her like no one else is there.

McKenzie called me and told me I had to come home. We were on our honeymoon for almost a month and we've been home for about a week, but if she needs me home, everything else can wait. She asked me if I'd stop on the way and grab her some chocolate from the candy shop on River Street. So, I grab the candy and get back as quickly as I can. When I get home, she greets me excitedly, but not as excited as when she sees the chocolate. I try my best not to get jealous.

She takes a big bite and hums. "So good." I cock an eyebrow and wish I had better control of my dick because it gets hard at the noises she's making. She smirks at me like she knows. After she takes a few more bites, she puts it down and turns her attention to me.

"Where is everyone?" I ask as I settle in next to her on the couch in the library. She puts her legs in my lap and I massage her feet and calf muscles. She leans back and groans.

"I asked everyone to leave."

I pause in my ministrations as I study her. "Why?"

She perks up and sits up slightly. "I have something I need to tell you."

I stare at her and wait. My heart begins to pound and I don't know why. I do know whatever she's about to tell me will change my life forever. She sits up and gets on her knees, kneeling beside me on the couch.

She hands me a small box and I glance at it quickly before looking at her. "Open it."

I swallow and open it slowly. It's a long rectangular box. When I open it, I pull my lips between my teeth, staring at it to make sure

I'm seeing what I think I'm seeing. I glance from it to her, then back to it. "What does this mean?" I ask.

"I'm pregnant," she replies breathlessly. For the first time in my life, I think I might cry. I stare at the pregnancy test for a few more moments before I sit back and wrap my arms around her, pulling her into my lap.

She wraps her arms tightly around me as I bury my face in her hair. "Are you sure?" I whisper.

"Yes. I took twenty of those. I have an appointment in a few days."

We hold each other tight as I process this. I wasn't sure if I wanted kids, but after that night, she told me she thought I'd be a good dad. I've thought about it on several occasions. I want the opportunity to prove to myself I could be a better parent than my parents were. But with the auctions and the requirements of the auctions, I didn't think McKenzie would have kids with me and I sure as hell wasn't doing that.

Not with the likelihood of us having a daughter and having to sell her or having to arrange a marriage for her, but with those rules being abolished, it was on the table. I just didn't know if McKenzie really wanted kids. I know what she said, but it could have been her way of trying to encourage me in the moment, and I didn't want to get my hopes up.

"How?" I finally ask. The last I knew, she still had the IUD.

"When I went to the doctor a few months ago, he said it was time to replace my IUD, but I chose to have it removed. I mentioned it to you."

I pull back and finally look at her. "I know you said something about not getting it replaced, but I didn't realize you had actually done it. I forced myself not to be too hopeful."

She grips my face between her hands. "Our lives are going to be different. You're going to be a great father and our children are going to grow up knowing how much their parents love them and how we fought to make the world a better place for them."

"Children?" I ask.

She chuckles. "Of course we have to have more than one. I mean, we're very good at the act that makes them."

I laugh and kiss her. "I love you. So much."

She smiles at me and straddles my lap. "Have you heard that pregnant women get very horny?" she asks as she slowly unbuttons my shirt.

I rub my hands up and down her back. "Is that so?"

She leans forward and begins kissing my neck, sucking my skin between her lips and teeth. "Oh yes, are you up for the challenge?"

I grip the edge of her shirt and pull it off, my lips landing on the tattoo just below her ear. "Always, love. Always."

The End!!

Also by Nicole Abrams

The Society Duet:

He Will Come For Me

I Will Find Her

The Coming Home Series:

Finding Caroline

Losing Ansley

Becoming Bailey

Claiming Becca

Loving Olivia (coming this Fall)

Note From the Author

I hope you all have fallen in love with Phoenix and McKenzie as much as I have. These two introduced me to a world I'm not ready to let go of yet. They were my first venture into dark romance and were so much fun to write. Make sure to join my Facebook group and newsletter to keep up with future releases. You'll see Phoenix and McKenzie again.

XOXO, Nicole

Acknowledgements

To my family! My husband who helped with some of the research of these books and answered SO MANY questions. My son who is always encouraging me and giving me hugs because when I'm tired I look like I need a hug. My mom who is SO ready to read the second part of this book and asked me just about every time I talked to her if I was close to being done writing. I love that you enjoyed the first book so much! And that you support me no matter what. And my sister who is constantly telling me one day I'm going to make it big. I love you all so much and am grateful you support me the way you do.

To Brittany, Mindy, Lakshmi, and Thorunn! The four of you kept me going during the writing process. Thank you for beta reading and for all the times you made me laugh (and sometimes blush) with your comments and feedback. I appreciate your support, guidance, and advice along the way. Thank you for jumping in and supporting me!

To Ashleigh! Thank you for being there for me since day one. You have been my biggest cheerleader every step of the way!

To Scarlett! I'm so thankful for your friendship. Thank you for editing and even bigger thank you for the hilarious comments you leave while editing. Your reactions give me life!

To my VIP team & early readers! You are the reason this book was published sooner. You all wanted answers and you wanted them right away. Your love for *He Will Come For Me* and your excitement for this book filled my heart. All your questions and theories were so fun to behold! Thank you for sharing and reading! I appreciate your support and excitement.

And to the readers! To the ones that have been with me from the beginning, the new, and the ones to come. I appreciate each and everyone of you so much. If you loved *He Will Come For Me* and *I Will Find Her* (and even if you didn't), please consider leaving a review on Amazon. They help so much! Thank you for following along on this journey with me.

Printed in Great Britain
by Amazon